THE DEFENDER

BOSTON HAWKS HOCKEY
BOOK 5

GINA AZZI

THREE CITIES PUBLISHING LLC

TRIGGER WARNING:

This book contains sensitive subject matters dealing with loss and grief including the loss of a baby and loss of a spouse.

PROLOGUE

JAMES

Two Months Earlier

My shoulders stiffen the moment I enter Taps. I glance around at the patrons, at Pete behind the bar, at the laughing groups of friends and knowing glances between couples.

Panda hits me on the back. "You good?"

"Yeah, man." I force a grin. Because I'm supposed to be good by now, right?

I follow some of my teammates and their significant others to the bar, but I walk slowly, hang back a bit. Noah has his arm wrapped around his pregnant girlfriend, Indy. Easton's muttering something into Claire's ear.

It wasn't that long ago that I was *that* guy. The one in the happy, committed, healthy relationship. The guy who was expecting twins and then, a first-time dad. The guy that liked to swing by Taps with the team for a drink before heading home to my woman, my family, my goddamn everything.

I look down, sucking in an inhale to ease the tightening of my throat. It's been over a year since Layla passed and still, it's hard to visit any place I once went with her. Which means, it's hard to go anywhere. It's even more excruciating to be at the house, in the *space* she made into a home. If my kids, Milly and Mason, weren't so attached to the place, I would have sold it the week after Layla died.

"You want a beer or shot?" Yaeger clasps my shoulder.

I clear my throat. "Whatever you guys are getting into."

"Line 'em up!" Panda calls out, smacking the top of the bar. "Patron. You new?"

I squint as a bartender I've never seen before comes into focus. She introduces herself to Panda as Bella, and the name fits because, God, she's gorgeous. Gorgeous in a way that even strangers on the street would take note of. Her long brown hair is pulled back into a ponytail but some strands have escaped. Her eyes are a startling shade of blue, a contrast against her dark hair and tanned skin.

She indulges whatever lame ass lines Panda spits with a laugh that hits me square in the stomach.

I look away quickly, shame rolling through me. How dare I check her out? How dare I appreciate the curves of her body and the sweetness of her laughter when I once had Layla? But God, is this ever going to end?

The constant anguish? The debilitating second-guessing? The acute loss that I still feel, no matter how I try to cope? Once upon a time, I had my happily-ever-after. I had a loving and giving wife. We built a home and filled it with the loud wails and peals of laughter from two beautiful, silly babies. I was fortunate enough to turn my passion, hockey, into my career. Men like me, men who already had it all, don't get second chances at that type of happiness.

Bella's melodic laughter pulls my attention back to the bar where she's filling up a line of shot glasses with chilled tequila. She talks quickly, joking and smiling, but when she looks up, her gaze slams into mine. I suck in an inhale, recognizing the shadows in her eyes. Pain. Longing. Emptiness.

She holds my gaze for a beat before looking away, her cheeks coloring.

But I continue to watch her because dammit, I *see* her. I see *it.* I have a deep understanding of the void in her eyes because for too damn long, I've worn it. Recognized it in my own reflection.

Bartender Bella wears a cloak of concealment. Everyone who sees her, chats her up, would never suspect that she's not good, not happy. I mean, she's smiling, right? But underneath, there's something. I catch it in the shadow that passes through her eyes when her gaze lingers on Indy's swollen belly. I spot it in the slow exhale she releases when she punches in Panda's order and thinks no one's watching.

Maybe it's the hint of loss that draws me to her. Two similar hurts in a sea of merriment. I accept the shot of Patron. I throw it back, hissing when it collides with my throat. I slip onto a barstool and watch the gorgeous bartender with lonely eyes and a too big smile.

When she turns to me, she falters for one blink. A jolt of surprise, a flicker of worry, a moment. In that moment, something shifts. My world, a cocoon of hurt and loss and grief, opens the tiniest bit. For the first time in over a year, it allows me to smile at a stranger and open myself back up, knowing that I'll never find what I once had. Knowing that I don't deserve to find what I once had, because I already had the best. But also knowing that right now, maybe I deserve just a little bit more than what I've been drowning in.

"Can I get you a beer?" she asks, her fingers curling around the top ledge of the bar. Her fingernails, a deep purple, tap restlessly.

Her nervousness settles me some and I nod. "I'll take an IPA. Whatever you have on tap. I'm James, by the way."

She turns to look at me over her shoulder as she grabs a pint glass. "Bella."

"Good to meet you."

She fills the pint and places it down in front of me. "I've filled in for Selina a few times and these guys always roll through"—she gestures to my Hawks teammates—"but I don't think I've ever seen you here before."

I shrug, picking up my beer and taking a sip. "I don't come out much."

She quirks an eyebrow, partly in question, partly in disbelief. "No?"

"Nope."

She leans forward and her scent, a light floral perfume I'm relieved I've never smelled before, wafts over me. She smiles, biting the corner of her lip. "What changed your mind tonight?"

Is she flirting with me? Is this what flirting is? Whatever the hell this exchange is, I'd be lying if I said I didn't like it. No, I like it too much. The way the blue in her eyes brightens, the scent of her perfume, how her new position pushes her firm breasts forward.

"It seemed like the right time to finally let these guys drag me out." I gesture to Panda and Yaeger, ignoring the delighted expression on Panda's face.

My words cause her expression to shift for the tiniest of moments before she offers a throaty laugh. "Well I'm glad you decided to come. It's nice to meet you too."

She smiles again, more open this time. I feel it wash over me like sunshine, dragging out a smile of my own when I've done nothing but glare for months.

Another guy on the team, Sims, pulls me into conversation that leads to a game of darts. But I keep glancing over at Bella, making sure she's okay as she navigates a full bar with a bunch of rowdy athletes.

Between her presence and the guys ribbing, I drink more than I'm used to. When last call sounds out, a ripple of panic darts down my spine. Milly and Mason are sleeping at my sister-in-law's tonight. They attended the team BBQ with me this afternoon and then I dropped them at Maia's for a slumber party. But I haven't checked in once.

Guilt replaces my worry as I pull out my phone and shoot off a message.

JAMES

Hey, sorry I didn't check in. How are the kids?

MAIA

Hi! Don't be ridiculous. I'm relieved you're not interrupting our movie and sugar marathon with questions.

I ignore her good-natured joking and focus on the more important part of her message.

JAMES

The kids are still awake?

MAIA

No, worry wart. They're sleeping. They are wonderful and we had a great time. Now go hang with your team and HAVE FUN. She'd want you to live your life.

A lump clogs my throat at Maia's words. It hurts because deep down, I know Layla would want me to live my life. But how can I live half a life now that I've already experienced a full one? Maybe I'm resigned to living the bare minimum that life has to offer.

"Hey man." Sims bumps my shoulder. "You good?" He glances at me before turning to look over his shoulder where a redhead plays with the ends of her hair, clearly waiting for him.

I chuckle, appreciating how the guys always look out for me. But I don't want to cockblock Sims so I nod. "I'm good, Sims. Get out of here. Use protection."

He snickers and walks toward the redhead, slinging an arm over her shoulder as he leads her out.

I turn back to my phone.

JAMES

I'll pick the kids up tomorrow morning.

MAIA

I promised them waffles so just message in the morning. No rush, JR. Really.

JAMES

Thanks.

I slip my phone back in my pocket and head to the bathroom. When I reenter the main bar area, I'm surprised that it's nearly cleared out.

"Hey." I stop next to the ledge.

Bella turns toward me, a bar cloth in her hand as she wipes down the well bottles. "Hey."

"Can I settle up?"

She shakes her head. "Panda took care of the team bill."

I mutter a swear. It's customary for one of the guys to pick up the tab but since I haven't come out in ages, I was hoping that tonight, that guy would be me. I dig into my wallet and pull out a hundred-dollar bill, sliding it across the bar.

Bella shakes her head. "Put your money away, James. You want to do something nice for me?"

What? My mouth drops open before snapping closed. Where is she going with—

Bella laughs. "Relax." She tips her head toward a barstool. "I was going to ask if you wanted to hang for a few, have a beer, and then walk me to my car. Pete usually does but he had to leave early." She shrugs, dropping a vodka bottle back into the well and picking up a rum. "Besides, it looks like you could use an ear."

I plop down on the barstool and snort. "Am I that obvious?"

She tilts her head. "You do a pretty good job concealing it."

"It?"

"The hurt."

"Ahh," I agree. "If we're going to have a heart-to-heart, then I'll need something stronger than a beer. I'll take a whiskey. Neat."

She grins, as if my words please her. She pours two tumblers of whiskey and taps hers against mine before taking a pull. "Bad breakup?" she guesses.

I shake my head. "My wife died."

Her face falls, stricken. But instead of feeling awful, the way I always do, a part of me is relieved to admit the truth. To have that part of this conversation already over with.

"I'm so sorry, James," Bella whispers.

I dip my head. "Thank you. Layla passed about a year and a half ago. In March." I look back up, offering a small smile. "And it broke me."

She nods, her eyes wide and empathetic. There isn't an ounce of pity in them, just compassion and a sliver of understanding.

"This is not the same thing, at all," she emphasizes. "But I got divorced almost two years ago and that..." She trails off and a sarcastic laugh twists her mouth. "Well, that fucked me up pretty good."

At the hurt in her expression, at the hardness in her tone, I can tell she's still battling that demon, searching for closure. And man, closure in situations like ours is fickle. It's hard to make your peace when the other person isn't around to help you find it.

"I'm sorry, Bella."

"Yeah," she agrees, refilling my whiskey glass. She leans

forward again and I try my damnedest not to let my gaze dip to her breasts. "How are you coping?"

I take a large gulp of whiskey, my head buzzing. "I'm not," I admit on a chortle.

She tips back her glass and smacks her lips. "Me neither."

I watch her for several minutes, the silence between us comfortable, natural, as she closes out her register. When she's done, a bar rag flung over her shoulder, she rolls her lower back across the ledge of the bar and faces me. Her posture is casual, arms crossed over her chest, feet crossed at her ankles. Her expression is unreadable. But her eyes burn, deep blue filled with longing and loneliness that I relate to.

The music playing on the speakers changes to the next song. Brad Paisley's "Whiskey Lullaby" floods the space and I shake my head as she bites her bottom lip.

"Pretty depressing, huh?" she chuckles, pushing to her full height.

I laugh with her, reaching over to press the stop button on her Spotify playlist. The music stops and a new sound, a silence pregnant with unchartered territory, rushes in.

"Does it ever get easier? Better?" she murmurs, her voice threaded with yearning. For what? Her ex? The life they once shared? The elusive sliver of peace?

"I don't know," I admit. "So far, for me, there hasn't been one easy day. Just moments, sometimes stretches of minutes, where I feel like I can breathe."

Her eyes meet mine and hold. She swipes her tongue over her bottom lip and I can't look away. I grip the underside of the bar ledge, simultaneously wanting to bolt for the door and never move from this spot.

My hands want to reach out to touch her. To feel her soft skin, her smoothness. My body wants hers. But my mind, fuck, my mind is racing. *This is wrong. It's too soon. It's too much.*

Still, I can't move. The silence of the bar rings in my

eardrums, pulses in my temples. Bella's pain mixes with mine, swelling into something both dangerous and comforting between us.

I breathe in an inhale and hold it in my lungs.

It feels like I'm on the edge of a precipice. The next decision I make is going to redefine my present, shake up my future.

"Bella," I murmur.

Whatever she hears in my voice has a sad smile tugging at the corners of her mouth. "It's okay. Walk me to my car?"

I nod, standing from the barstool. I wait for her to round the bar and we walk out of Taps together. I pause for her to lock up. When we enter the parking lot, my fingers naturally settle in the small of her back. The heat of her skin seeps through the thin material of her tank top and unable to stop myself, I press my entire palm to the center of her back.

She slows and glances up at me, her eyes uncertain in the moonlight.

"Come with me?" I whisper.

She stops walking and turns to face me. Her hands settle on my hips and even though they *should* feel wrong, they don't. They feel right, wanted, *needed*. "Are you sure?"

I nod and clear my throat. I feel like a dick for what I'm about to propose but, "There's a hotel a few blocks over."

Understanding passes through her expression and instead of the anger I expect, relief flares in her eyes. "Yes. I'll drive."

I slide my hand to meet hers, stopping shy of her fingers and grasping her wrist instead. We walk to her car.

"Just so you know, I don't ever, I mean, I don't do this type of thing," she clarifies, clearing her throat.

I smile as she stops beside a red Mercedes Benz. "I know. I don't either."

She unlocks the car doors and we slip inside. I lean back against the seat and turn to look out the window.

Is this okay? Is this allowed?

You're an adult, James. You're allowed to enjoy the company of a woman.

What would Layla think? Will my kids hate me if I date?

Why are you thinking about dating? This is a one-night thing.

But what if it could be more than that? Bella is the only woman in the past year I've even noticed, let alone connected with.

It's too soon. It's been long enough.

Bella eases her car in front of the hotel and passes her keys to the valet. She keeps her back straight as she rounds the car and I reach for her hand again, tugging her against my side as we step up to reception and secure a hotel room.

We take the elevator in silence and as we draw closer to the room, I keep waiting for panic to rush through me. I keep waiting for her to turn around and bolt. But neither of those things happen.

In fact, when I close the room door behind us and turn toward Bella, I feel a flare of that peace I'm always searching for. To date, I've only ever found it on the ice. But at my age, even hockey will soon come to an end. Then what will I do?

My pulse slows, my head clears, and her presence fills me with desire.

My hands grip her hips as she pulls her shirt over her head. She tugs out her hair tie and a waterfall of dark curls roll over her shoulders.

My throat dries, my body humming with awareness and want and a flicker of shame I snuff out. Not tonight. Tonight, I'm choosing peace. Tonight, I'm choosing Bella over my demons.

Her bra is red and sexy, her curves delicious, her skin so goddamn silky.

I slide my hands up and down the sides of her body as her fingers deftly undo the row of buttons on my shirt. She pushes it off my shoulders and pops the button on my jeans.

I cup her chin, angling her face so I can peer into her eyes. "You sure about this, Bella?"

"I'm sure, James. Please, make me feel something good."

I nod, understanding exactly what she means. We're both too broken to be whole but maybe, just maybe, we can be whole together for this night.

I drop my mouth to hers and when our lips touch, I revel in her soft sigh. I kiss her fiercely, months of dormant need unleashing in an instant. Her lips part under mine and my tongue dips into her mouth, exploring. She tastes like whiskey and summertime, like shooting stars and lost dreams. There's something exquisitely tragic in her kiss and I'm drawn to it, to her, in a way I never imagined I would be again. I slow our connection for two heartbeats, savoring the taste of her mouth, the feel of her touch, the naked desire in her moan.

But that sound, her want, snaps something inside of me and my own need takes over. Our bodies come together fast and desperately. There's no time for tenderness, there's no more room for generosity and compassion. We lose ourselves completely, filling each other up with want.

When we're spent, a sweet sorrow envelops us. Bella curls up against my chest and I wrap my arms around her. Right before I doze off, I wonder if I've arrived at a turning point.

Can I date Bella? Can we grab a coffee or even breakfast tomorrow?

But when I wake in the morning, she's gone. Vanished with the sunrise. Just another ghost to haunt my thoughts.

CHAPTER 1

JAMES

I swipe my fingers across my forehead, trying to keep my voice level, fighting against the swell of frustration that fills my throat at my sister-in-law's words.

"Make sure she's a registered first responder. And, you want to hire someone who has a degree in education or psychology or even—"

"Maia, I got it," I say as calmly as I can, glancing at the screen of the phone. We've been having this conversation for seventeen minutes and thirty-four seconds. "Look, the nanny is going to be here any minute so..."

"Right, okay. Well, good luck, JR. Not that you need it but—"

"'Bye, Maia." I hang up, glancing out the front window to make sure a car hasn't pulled into the driveway. I do a final sweep of the living room, making sure there are no stray crayons or LEGO pieces from when I picked up this morning.

Yanking on the back of my neck, I blow out a sigh and begin to pace back and forth in front of the television. Am I really going to trust a stranger to live in my house? To stay with the twins when I'm traveling with the team?

I glance out the window again before checking my watch.

She still has ten minutes to show up before she's late. Punctuality is important, right?

God, why am I so nervous about this? Deep down, I know Maia is right. I need to hire a nanny. My parents passed years ago, and with no other family to lean on, my in-laws stepped up in every way imaginable to provide a support system for the twins and me. Since last season, Maia has been the real MVP, taking Milly and Mason for sleepovers or staying at my house for extended amounts of time. But it's not fair for her to continually juggle pseudo-parenting with a demanding career and an overly understanding fiancé.

Besides, Clark, a professional baseball player I met a few years ago at a fundraiser for youth outreach programs in Boston, highly recommended Isabella. He said he'd rather homeschool his kids just so they could keep her. But now that his youngest started boarding school, they don't need a live-in nanny.

Isn't that fortunate for me? That someone so qualified, with excellent references, magically became available just when I was starting to panic that I didn't line up childcare for the twins like I should have months ago, when Maia first mentioned it?

I blow out another exhale as a flashy, red Mercedes pulls into my driveway.

I turn away from the window, my nerves pinging around. I shouldn't judge the woman by her car but why couldn't she drive a sensible, navy sedan or something? I fill a glass of water and take a deep sip, trying to relax.

This is so far out of my wheelhouse. I don't know the first thing about hiring childcare. We never had to formally arrange it before because Layla was always with the kids. Even after she got sick, her sister or mom would step in when needed. But now Zainab relocated to Delaware, where Layla's brother and his wife recently had a baby and Maia can't juggle my demanding hockey schedule. Nor should she have to.

I can do this. I can hire a nanny for my kids.

I wipe my palms along the thighs of my jeans.

Shit, why the hell does this seem more stressful than playing in a Finals game?

The doorbell rings and I stride forward. It's just a conversation. I'll be friendly but professional, warm but direct. I got this.

I pull the door open and the gorgeous brunette on the front porch looks up.

Startled blue eyes stare back at me, her mouth dropping open.

"Bella?" I spit out, my nerves from a second ago evaporating as a rush of surprise, quickly followed by a surge of anger, washes through me.

"James?" She squints, as if she can't believe it's really me. Which makes no sense because she would certainly know my name, right? I mean, Clark would have told her who she's interviewing with.

She clears her throat, her eyes darting over my shoulder.

Right. "Come in." I step back.

She crosses the threshold of my home, her floral perfume hitting me like a reminder I don't want to remember. She glances around the living room and I briefly wonder what she sees when she looks at my home.

Professional athlete? Doting dad? Devasted widower?

I shake my head, letting my annoyance take hold once more. A couple months ago, she ghosted me. Just disappeared with the sunrise. I lift my hand to my chest and press, as if that will help alleviate the embarrassing memory of waking up alone. Talk about a hit to the ego.

She turns and looks at me, hitching her purse higher on her shoulder. "Clark kept calling you Ryan. I didn't..." She pauses to wet her lips. "I didn't put it together. How are you?"

I chuckle, the sound derisive. "Do you want a coffee?" I ask instead, remembering my manners. Isabella Andrews is one of the most sought-after nannies in the Boston Professional Athlete circles. As uncertain as I feel in this moment, I know better than to completely blow her off.

Her eyebrows pull together before smoothing back out. "Sure."

I turn on my heel and assume she's following me into the kitchen. When I pop a coffee pod into the Keurig and turn, she's already seated at the kitchen island.

"How do you take your coffee?" I ask, my voice too polite. Forced.

"Just two sugars please."

For an awkward stretch of seconds, the only sound is the sputtering coffee machine and our breathing. We both take a beat to collect our thoughts and figure out how to navigate this mess.

I can't hire the woman I slept with, can I?

Shame burns through me, so intense it borders on painful.

Bella is the only woman I've been intimate with since Layla passed and now...*she's* going to live here? Watch my kids? Play fucking house?

I laugh again. The sound is harsh and Bella winces.

"Look," she says, "I know this is uncomfortable. If my being here is too much for you, or this is going to be too difficult to manage"—she gestures between us—"I can just go."

I narrow my eyes. "I thought you needed this job."

Her gaze narrows right back and her toughness impresses me. "I do."

I nod and set the coffee mug in front of her. "Why'd you leave?"

She rears back, her eyes blown with surprise. "Seriously?"

"Seriously." I lean back against the kitchen counter and cross my arms over my chest.

She blushes and dips her head. When she meets my gaze again, there's an apology in her eyes. "I was embarrassed."

"Embarrassed?" I repeat, not buying it for a second. Embarrassed is what I was the following morning, when the bed was missing a warm body.

She nods, tossing an arm in my direction. "You're a nice guy, James. And that night…" She pauses, as if searching for the right words. "It wasn't a good night for me. I was lonely, searching for something. I pushed you into—"

"You didn't," I mutter, clearing my throat.

"I didn't want to witness your regret," she admits, her voice so low I need to strain to hear it.

I study her, noting the earnestness in her expression, the heat in her cheeks. At her sincerity, some of my anger fades and I nod once, curtly. "I can do this if you can." I motion between us.

"Be professional?" She lifts an eyebrow.

I nod.

"I can too," she says decisively, picking up her mug and taking a sip. She sets it back down with a thud.

"That night, that won't ever happen again," I say, cringing at how blunt I am. But I need her to know that I need a nanny, not a woman of the house. "I need a caregiver for my kids. Your references are excellent and unparalleled and if I'm being honest, I'm in a bit of a time crunch."

She licks her lips and I catch the movement, averting my gaze a second later. *She's about to become your damn employee.* "I understand," she agrees, her voice cracking. "I'm familiar with the shifting routines of families in the professional sports industry. I'm flexible and able to adjust my schedule as necessary."

I frown, narrowing my eyes at her. Is she that hard up for cash? First bartending, now this? Who in their right mind wouldn't want the freedom to plan out their own calendar? To always be tied down to the whims of another family?

"You'll have to move in here for the season. From mid-September to mid-June."

"That's fine." Her tone is even. She possesses the level-headedness that I've been searching for but for a moment, her willingness to agree with everything I say pisses me off.

"When Milly and Mason have a sleepover at their aunt's, you'll have the night off. I'll try to make sure you always have one to two days off a week but it will vary, depending on my schedule."

"Okay."

"Do you have any questions?" I lift my eyebrows, wondering what the hell kind of interview this is. It's too easy.

"When can I meet them?"

"My kids?"

She nods. "To connect, make sure we're a good fit."

I glance at the time. "They'll be home in fifteen minutes. If you want to stick around, you can meet them then."

"That'd be great."

I huff out a sigh, not sure why the hell I'm annoyed, but I am. The woman sitting in front of me, Isabella Andrews, is nothing like the woman I met at Taps. She's too agreeable, too closed off, too…polite instead of friendly. She's treating me the same way she treated the other patrons at the bar. But that night, with me, she was *different*. She was real.

Isn't this what you wanted? Professionalism? Christ, I'm giving myself emotional whiplash.

"Let's talk compensation," I blurt out, not caring how tactless it is.

She sits up straighter in her chair and raises an eyebrow.

I yank the back of my neck and run through the salary, health insurance, and benefits package I'm willing to offer.

Just as I'm wrapping up my spiel, the front door bangs open and Mason's voice fills the air.

"Dad! We're home!"

Immediately, Bella's expression changes. Gone is the pinch between her brows and the tightness in her lips. Instead, she looks positively radiant as she smiles and slips off the barstool, turning to meet my kids.

They skid to a stop right before the threshold to the kitchen when they spot Bella.

"Are you our new nanny?" Milly asks, curling her fingers into her palms and scratching the way she does when she's uncertain. She started doing it when Layla got sick and since her mom passed, it's gotten worse.

"I think so." Bella chances a glance in my direction before squatting down to the twins eye level. "I'm Bella," she holds out a hand.

Mason takes it and shakes seriously, his eyes contemplative. "Mason."

"Nice to meet you, Mason. And you are?" Bella turns to Milly.

"Milly," my daughter replies shyly.

"Milly," Bella repeats, a strange expression crossing her face. For a beat, she almost looks stricken but in the next breath, she grins. "That's a beautiful name."

"Thank you." Milly curtsies and Bella and I laugh.

She glances at me over her shoulder, her eyes a deep blue, and colored with a shade of hope. Some of the anger I felt toward her, mostly because I was so damn embarrassed, melts away.

"Well, I'm happy to meet you guys. If it's okay with your dad, maybe we can go play for a little bit? You can show me your favorite toys and tell me about your hobbies before supper?"

Mason nods eagerly, a smile splitting his face. Milly's a bit more hesitant but I can read the curiosity in her eyes.

"Can we, Dad?" Mase asks.

"First, show Bella her room and bathroom. Then you can show her the playroom," I agree, clearing the emotion from my throat. Seeing Bella with the kids, a woman showing them kindness when they've already experienced so much loss, affects me a hell of a lot more than I thought it would.

Bella follows the twins out of the kitchen and toward the stairs. Right before she clears the door, she turns and catches my eye. "That night, it's in the past now. Let's just move forward."

My jaw clenches at how blasé she sounds, as if that night was nothing more than a one-night stand. *Which it was.* Then, why the hell did it feel like more than that? Instead, I say, "We're professionals. My kids come first."

"Absolutely."

Then she's out of sight but the feel of her still lingers in the house, even hours after she leaves.

That night, when I collapse into bed, I close my eyes and blow out a sigh.

Am I doing the right thing? Making the right decision? Or is this a bad idea?

I fall asleep worrying about the twins, the future, and the woman who's taking up space in my mind even though she has no right to be there.

"HEY," Austin's face comes into view above the bar I'm benching. He spots me as I continue my reps.

When I'm finished, he eases the bar back onto the rack and I sit up, wiping a towel over the back of my neck. "What's up, Aus?"

"Nothing much. Just checking in with the guys. Seeing

where everyone's head is at since we're about to start the season."

"My head's good," I lie, not wanting to give away just how confused I've been since Bella re-entered my life.

She was a ghost I put to bed. Sure, the days following our hookup threw me for a loop but I recovered. I got past it. I even got past the dumb idea that I was in any shape to think about moving forward, dating again.

Now, the ghost has come back to life. With Bella living in my house, caring for my kids, I can't *not* think about her. I can't will myself to have amnesia regarding that night. That shit is messing with me big time.

I grip the collar of my tank top and rub it against my chin, glancing at a paper with my next set of exercises.

"You sure?" Austin asks, lowering his voice.

I glance up at my team captain, noting the concern in his gaze, the compassion in his expression. After Layla passed, Austin went above and beyond to make sure I felt supported by the team. And I did. It's just, I was dealing with a grief that none of my teammates had ever experienced. Grief isn't something you can truly understand unless you've experienced loss as well.

It's not something that magically disappears or heals with time. It comes in waves and by Austin's expression, I know he thinks I'm twisted up over something related to Layla.

I blow out a sigh. The last thing I want to do is have my captain, my team, question my commitment to this season. My head and heart are in the right place after a shaky start to last season. I *need* hockey. The ice is the only place where I feel whole, where I don't feel like I'm constantly failing Layla or the twins, where I can breathe again. Wanting Austin to understand that I'm ready for our season opener, I tell him the truth. "Remember that bartender from Taps? The one who was filling in for Selina a couple months ago?"

Surprise flashes through Austin's eyes. "The brunette?"

"Yeah."

"I remember. Chloe thought she was really nice."

"She was. Is," I amend.

Austin sits down next to me on the bench and leans forward, resting his elbows on his knees as he waits for me to continue. It's as if he knows that whatever's coming is going to be a big, earth-shattering revelation. In my life, it is.

"That night, we, I uh…" I trail off, uncertainty blazing through me. How the hell do I admit that I slept with someone? Will he think I betrayed Layla? How do I—

"I got it."

I chuckle, the sound forced and nervous. "She's the new nanny."

"What?" Austin's head snaps up, his eyes wide with shock. "The girl Clark recommended?"

I nod.

"Shit," Austin murmurs, scraping a hand over his face. "Is it too late to find someone else?"

"I'd say it's damn near impossible to find anyone with her qualifications and referrals. She has a master's degree in children's psychology and has worked for three different athlete families. She gets the lifestyle."

Austin whistles low.

"She moves in next week," I add. "And my kids, especially Milly, damn near adore her already. She's been coming to the house every afternoon to spend time with them after school. All I hear is their nonstop chattering and laughter."

"How do you feel about it? About her?" Austin asks slowly.

I shake my head. "I don't know, man. It's messed up, isn't it? The woman I, you know, and now she's living in my house, taking care of my kids. It's just…it's fucking with my head."

"How could it not?" Austin wonders, making me feel

marginally better about being so twisted up over Bella. "Do you trust her? I mean, with Milly and Mason?"

"Yeah," I reply automatically, surprised by how much I already trust Bella to properly look out for my kids. "It's everything else that's confusing. As much as I don't want to remember that night..."

"You're still thinking about her. Like that."

I look at Austin and nod slowly, feeling like dirt. "I told her we'd keep things strictly professional. That I need a nanny and nothing more but...I trust her. More than with Milly and Mason. I trust *her*." Now that I know why Bella left the morning after we hooked up, I've been running that night through my mind on a loop. I recall the thrum of excitement, of anticipation, without bitterness. I remember the hope she filled me with after I had wallowed in despair for so long.

The fact that I've already softened toward her, in such a short amount of time, none of it spent just the two of us, worries me. Pretending I don't care about her, about what she thinks, is a lie, but I don't *want* to care, and that's complicating things.

Austin sighs, fixing me with a serious look. "I know you, James. And I know that whatever went down between you and Bella was big. But you can't overthink this. Right now, you've got reliable childcare and an upcoming hockey season. Focus on that. Yes, it's confusing that you guys have a history, but don't make it more complicated than it has to be."

I nod, knowing that Austin is trying to help me clarify my thoughts. He wants me in the right frame of mind for our season opener and twisted up over Bella Andrews isn't it. I stand from the bench and clasp his shoulder. "Thanks, Austin. I need to finish these exercises and get home in time for dinner. I swear, I'm good for the season. If anything, I need hockey now more than ever."

Austin stares at me for a beat, his eyes narrowed before nodding. "If you want to talk about anything, hit me up."

I shoot him a smile. "Will do. Thanks, Cap."

CHAPTER 2
BELLA

"You're sure about this?" my friend Selina asks me for the third time as I close the trunk of my car.

"I'm sure," I laugh, spinning to face her. I gesture toward her townhouse. "Aren't you happy to have me out of your hair and have your space back?"

She pulls me into a hug. "You know you're always welcome here."

"Thank you for taking me in," I say sincerely. Since my contract ended with the Clark family three weeks ago, I've been sleeping in Selina's spare bedroom. She's one of my oldest friends and one of the only people who truly stood by my side as I dealt with loss after loss the past three years. Placing my hands on her shoulders, I pull back and smile. "Milly and Mason are…they're good for my soul."

Selina raises an eyebrow, unconvinced. "And their father?"

I blush but laugh it off. "He's not awful."

She snorts. "Not awful my ass. You said he was the best you—"

I clamp my hand over her mouth before she can finish that statement. Shaking my head, I say, "We're not going there,

Lina. What's in the past is in the past and—" I stop at her widened eyes, knowing she's calling me out on my own bullshit. I sigh. "Look, I'm trying. I'm trying to move past everything that happened."

"No, you're not. You're running, babe. Even your therapist—"

"There's no need to bring Dr. Carlisle into this."

"—thinks so. You've been on the move since you and Jerry split. You haven't given yourself any time or grace to deal with the loss of—"

I tap my palm over her mouth again, my eyes pleading with her to stop talking. She sighs and drops her chin in acknowledgement. I remove my hand and shuffle back a step. "Can you just be happy for me? James Ryan is a great dad, his kids are amazing, and nannying for them will be good for me. I can feel it."

Selina sighs but doesn't offer any more comments. "Okay," she says reluctantly, pulling me in for one more hug. "But if you need to come back, my guest room is yours."

"I don't deserve you, Lina."

"You deserve a hell of a lot more than you let yourself have, Bells."

I pull away and flash a smile, not wanting to think about her words. They bring up too many painful memories of the past and today, I'm not going there. Today, I'm taking a step into the future. "I'll call you tonight?"

She nods. "Happy moving day and congrats on the new job."

"Thank you." I slip into the driver's seat and honk once before backing out of her driveway.

The moment I turn the corner, my smile slips and I relax into the plush seat. What am I thinking? How can I live in the house of the guy I ghosted over the summer? But how can I not when his kids and I share such a natural connection?

The moment I met Milly and Mason, I understood the

depth of their loss. Maybe it's because I studied children's psychology and education or maybe it's because I've experienced loss of my own. Whatever the reason, I felt kindred spirits in Milly and Mason and truly believe that my supporting their family through this transition will be beneficial for them.

But will it be beneficial for me?

One glance at James and all those thoughts and feelings from summer came rushing back. The slice of magic I found with him that night has been at the forefront of my mind from the moment he pulled open his front door.

I recall that night with perfect clarity. How his whiskey-colored eyes held mine and he stared directly into my soul. What's more? He didn't flinch at the ugly he saw there.

I felt his understanding sweep through me like a tornado. The depth of his compassion left me reeling. Even though my attraction to him—deep brown eyes, dark, neatly styled hair, and an irresistible cleft in his chin—was immediate, it was his demeanor that drew me in. The way he dipped his head when he asked a question, as if he was unsure if he should ask. I liked how he leaned closer to me when I spoke and how he seemed to perceive more than he let on.

James Ryan is the only man since my divorce who looked at me like I wasn't broken beyond repair, like there was still hope for me to find a semblance of happiness. I ran straight toward him, desperate to soak up more of his kindness and compassion.

Now, I'm going to live with that man, the one who's been occupying my thoughts and dreams. I pull into his driveway and turn off my car, sitting for an extra minute to build up my courage to face him.

I need a fresh start. Couldn't this be it?

I shake out my hands and blow out one more exhale before opening the car door just as the front door to the house swings open and two little munchkins fly down the porch steps.

"Bella!" Milly shrieks.

"You're here!" Mason hollers.

"Happy move-in day!" They clap in unison.

Some of my anxiety leaks away as I squat down for their hugs. "I'm so excited to move in," I tell them truthfully. "Will you guys help me unpack?"

"Of course we will," Mason says, walking to my trunk. "Pop it open."

I laugh, pressing the key fob to open the trunk.

As Mason and Milly reach inside, looking through some of my belongings, James steps onto the porch and I freeze.

Why does he have to look so good? Broody? His dark eyes blaze with emotions I can't pinpoint. His hair is styled but he's dressed simply, in gray sweat shorts, a white tank, and sandals. His biceps pop when he moves toward me, a predator concealing just how dangerous he truly is.

To a heart like mine, fragile and warped, the attentions of a man like James, empathetic and deep, have the ability to level me when I still haven't found my footing.

"Hey," he greets me, his voice rumbly and low. It's sexy and manly and definitely not what I should be thinking about as his kids tug my suitcase from the trunk.

"Hi." I lift a hand in an awkward wave.

"Guys, hang on a sec." He moves to my trunk and easily lifts the two suitcases and one duffle bag I packed. He glances at me. "Is this it?"

"That's it."

He frowns, peering into the back seat of my car as if suspecting I have more packed baggage hidden there. I don't. All the packed baggage is stuffed down my throat, clogging my chest and expanding in my stomach. I work a swallow and close the car door and trunk.

"Come on, let's get you settled," James says as he lifts

both of my suitcases, the strap of my duffle bag pulling taut across his chest.

Milly and Mason each take one of my hands and lead me into their house. It's sweet, the way they're so excited for me to move in. It's the extra encouragement I need to smile at James as he places my luggage down in my new room.

"Thank you." I place a hand on the back of the desk chair. The room is all white, simple and airy, with a crispness that I like.

James nods, shooing his kids out of the room. When he reaches the threshold, he pauses, and turns back to me. "If you need anything, just holler."

"I'll be okay," I say.

He nods, his eyes intense as they hold mine. "I hope so, Bella." He closes the bedroom door behind him, leaving me to wonder about his cryptic words and the meaning behind them.

"HOW ARE YOU SETTLING IN?" Dr. Carlisle asks during our weekly therapy session held via Zoom.

I tilt my head as I weigh my words. "It's only been four days."

"And?"

I smirk at him. I've been speaking with Dr. Carlisle at least once a week for three years now. The man sees through my bullshit without blinking. "I'm settling in fine. The Ryans are a great family. Milly and Mason are both in school during the day. And James, the father, is busy. His schedule is filled with team meetings, workouts, practices, you know the drill."

"This is the same James from the summer?"

I roll my eyes, wishing I didn't fill Dr. C in on my summer hookup. "It is."

"Ah."

"What's that mean?"

He shrugs, his eyes amused. "I just find it interesting that you don't have more to say about him, considering you're now living together."

"We're not living together. I'm in his employ."

"All right." He steeples his fingers in front of his mouth. "So, it's been a seamless transition."

I sigh, knowing I can't lie to Dr. Carlisle. Not if I want to keep making progress. And I am, even though I occasionally stumble. "I wouldn't say seamless."

"Are you running?"

"Every morning," I admit. "At least ten miles."

He nods but the space around his eyes tightens and I know my response worries him. "Eating?"

"Yes," I say truthfully.

"And the time you're left on your own?"

"I'm filling it as best as I can. Learning the family's schedules and supporting their housekeeper, Justine. Helping the twins with their homework."

"Sleeping?"

"Not great. But—"

"You never sleep well."

"Exactly."

Dr. Carlisle tsks. "That doesn't make it okay, Bella."

"I know. But I am trying."

His expression is skeptical but he doesn't press and I don't volunteer any more information. "Any more thoughts on re-enrolling in your PhD program?" He changes tactics neatly.

I raise my eyebrows, only half joking when I mutter, "Have you been talking to Colton behind my back?"

Dr. C smiles. "Your brother doesn't want to see you give up on something you worked so hard for."

"I know that. But I still don't feel ready. I still don't feel like I'm able to make that commitment."

"Why not?"

I shrug.

"Bella," Dr. Carlisle says, his voice gentle.

"It's a lot of hours, a lot of work. It's not the kind of career you can have without sacrifice."

"A lot of careers require sacrifice."

I work a swallow past the lump growing in my throat. He's going to make me say it; of course he is. "I still want a family, Dr. C. I've given up on a lot of my dreams but I haven't given up on that."

"Nor should you," he replies immediately, easing the sting of tears behind my eyelids. His expression softens as he stares at my face through the screen. "We're out of time for tonight, Bella. Tomorrow, try to sleep in a little later."

I snort, shaking my head.

"Run nine miles instead of ten. Try journaling for fifteen minutes instead," he tries again.

I bite my lower lip. "We'll see."

"You've made a great deal of progress, Bella. I'm proud of the strides you've made. This week, try to channel your restlessness into something other than running. Okay?"

"Okay," I agree, promising myself that I'll make an honest attempt.

"Talk to you next week. If you need anything before then—"

"I'll reach out," I say, relieved I haven't had to do that in over a year. "Thanks, Dr. C."

"Have a good night." He disconnects our call and I log out of Zoom.

Walking over to my bed, I flop back and stare at the ceiling. James doesn't leave for his season opener for two more weeks and I'm already desperate for him to be gone.

He's more of a distraction than I anticipated which is

comical considering he's barely here. When our paths do cross, my awareness of him heightens and my skin tingles. He meets my eyes with barely concealed longing, his mouth parting as if he wants to say something. Except he never does. We toe the line between us cautiously, but I know it's only a matter of time before one of us dips a toe on the other side.

Whenever my eyes connect with his, a rush of desire or a beat of attraction flares through me. Then, I recall his words to me about how that night, our night, will never occur again. That's the only reminder I need to ensure our interactions are professional, polite, and centered on his kids. Just the way they should be.

Still, it takes me twelve days and another session with Dr. Carlisle until I'm able to reduce my morning runs to eight miles. Old habits and adrenaline spikes die hard. In order to keep my thoughts centered on the present, and *not* on James Ryan, I need to keep my body moving and my mind engaged. That way, I'm too exhausted to think at bedtime. Much too tired to remember. And entirely too drained to dream.

BY THE TIME October begins and James is ready to leave town for his season opener, an away game in Chicago, I'm ready to have space from his presence. In fact, I need a break from all the complicated feelings he conjures up inside of me.

The way his fingers brush mine when he passes me a mug of coffee in the morning. The curiosity that blazes in his eyes when he sees me in workout clothes and sneakers. The extra-long side glances, the shaky exhales, the questioning expression on his face even though he never voices his questions, unnerve me. It's like I'm teetering on the edge of my chair, waiting for James Ryan to decide if I lean back into the plush cushion or fall on my ass.

My first test in my new role comes the night before James's departure.

"I can't find my stuffy!" Milly wails from her bedroom. Her cries, nearly hysterical, have escalated beyond the normal range of frustration and sound downright panicked.

I race toward her bedroom and nearly collide with James in the hallway outside her door.

His hands dart out, clasping my waist to steady me. His eyes flash, a warning with an edge of nerves, before he pulls back and flies in his daughter's bedroom. "Milly? What's wrong? Are you okay?"

I follow close behind, my heart sinking when I note the tears streaming down Milly's face, the way her fingernails dig into her palms.

"I-I-I can't f-find my s-stuffy," she sobs, collapsing into James's arms.

He scoops her up effortlessly, cradling her against his chest. Something about their embrace, the concern held in the tightness of his jaw, the helplessness in her voice, scrapes at me.

"Is it your hippo stuffy?" I ask softly.

Milly nods. "M-mama g-gave her to me. I s-sleep with h-her every night."

"She must help you have sweet dreams," I say gently.

Milly nods. James catches my eyes over his daughter's head. His expression is unreadable but he doesn't say anything. Perhaps he's waiting to see how I handle this situation. Or perhaps he's relieved he doesn't have to.

Luckily, I spotted Milly's stuffed hippo hanging on the bathtub ledge earlier. I dash to grab it and when I re-enter the room, Mason is sitting on his sister's bed, his expression twisted.

"This her?" I ask, holding out the hippo.

"Mellie!" Milly cries, jumping from her father's lap to snatch Mellie up.

"She just needed to take a bath. Too much playing in the mud," I explain, wrinkling my nose.

Milly smiles and Mason's expression smooths out.

Milly hugs her hippo tight and kisses the top of her head. "Thanks for finding her, Bella."

"My pleasure, Ms. Milly. Would you guys like me to read a chapter of one of your books before sleep?"

They both nod, blurting out their requests at the same time.

"It's my turn. You went last night," Mason reminds Milly.

I grin. "How about we read two chapters tonight? One from *Matilda*"—I glance at Milly—"and one from *How to Train Your Dragon*"—I look to Mason.

They agree eagerly, scurrying to grab their books.

James stands from Milly's bed, stretching his long legs. His eyes haven't left my face and when I meet his gaze, I'm unsure what to make of the turmoil in his eyes.

"Is that okay?" I ask, wondering if he's annoyed I'm letting the kids stay up to read a second chapter.

"That's fine," he murmurs, rolling his lips together. He steps closer and it's the closest we've been since that night. The scent of his cologne, masculine and spicy, washes over me.

Part of me wants to reach out, place my hands on his hips, and feel the strength of his body move under my palms. Another part of me wants to shuffle back and add distance between us.

I don't do either. Instead, I remain motionless, waiting for him to make a move. Or not.

He surprises me by touching my arm, his finger swiping from my elbow to my wrist before dropping back to his side.

"You're really going to be okay with me gone," he says, a note of surprise in his tone.

I bite back my smile. "We really are. So are you."

He nods, looking unconvinced. James clears his throat, gratitude flooding his expression. "Thank you, Bella. For being here. For doing…all of this." He gestures wide, encompassing Milly's bedroom.

"You're welcome," I whisper back. "Now go pack. I'll tuck them in and when you come home, bring a win."

He smiles, the corners of his lips turning up in that same smirk that's equal parts surprise and genuine. James kisses the twins and wishes them good night before stepping into the hallway.

Milly, Mason, and I pile into Milly's bed and I open *Matilda* to chapter four.

The kids snuggle in deep as I read and I revel in the moment, wondering if I'll ever snuggle kids of my own. Wondering if I even deserve to anymore.

CHAPTER 3
JAMES

She enters the kitchen just before midnight and jumps when she spots me sitting at the kitchen island, drinking a tea.

"Couldn't sleep?" I ask, raising the tea to my lips.

Bella shakes her head and reaches into the cabinet for a mug.

"The kettle's still hot," I offer, watching as she moves around my kitchen with ease.

She already knows where everything is. She already knows what the hell she's doing with Milly and Mason even though it took me months to adapt to their schedules, schoolwork, and extracurriculars after Layla passed.

As much as I didn't want to admit that I needed help, Bella has already proved how valuable she is to my family in just over two weeks.

With a mug of tea in hand, she scoots onto a barstool. Her signature floral scent washes over me, making my stomach knot as desire I've tried to ignore rushes forward. My eyes flit over her frame, noting the slope of her neck, the beauty mark next to her elbow, the swell of her breasts. I blink and take another sip of tea.

Bella tempts me without even trying. Living with her for the past two weeks has been a delicious kind of torture, one I both crave and loathe. It's why I've tried to keep busy and stay out of the house. I've taken on extra workouts, watched game reels at The Meadow, and even swung by Panda's place to play freaking video games. Anything to avoid my house, my safe haven, Bella Andrews and her tantalizing scent and sweet voice.

We sit in silence for several seconds before I feel compelled to break it. "Your being here is strange. You're letting me leave tomorrow morning with a clear head."

She smiles softly, blowing on her tea. "Yeah, well, that's the goal, right?"

I chuckle, nodding in agreement. I turn my body toward hers, my forearm brushing against her bare upper arm. Her inhale causes the knot in my stomach to pull taut. Even the slightest whisper of attraction between us blazes into a scream of want when we're too close. Like we are now.

Does she feel it too? The tightness in the air, like a darkening summer sky, painted with thunderclouds, offering both a promise and a warning?

Bella smiles but shadows mar the delicate skin beneath her eyes. My awareness heightens as I realize how exhausted she is, my concern spiking. Is this too much for her? Are my expectations too high? Although I've been careful to keep my distance, it hasn't escaped my notice that she goes to sleep late and wakes up early to run. Where does she find the energy to keep going? "Why can't you sleep?"

She shrugs, glancing at me from the corner of her eye. It's the most personal question I've asked her since she's moved in and my curiosity, no, my concern, edges the needle from professional to...friendly.

"My mind races at night. Too many thoughts, too much quiet," she offers and I nod, understanding exactly what she means.

It isn't the first time I've wondered what the hell went down with her ex for her to be this beaten up several years after a divorce. She and her ex don't share any children. They don't seem to share a business or property or anything that would legally bind them together.

Did he hurt her? Did he scare her? Is she not over him?

The questions hover on the tip of my tongue and I take a large gulp of tea, burning the roof of my mouth. I hiss and Bella's eyes dart to mine.

"You okay?"

I nod, swearing under my breath. "Does tea usually help?" I ask instead, playing it safe.

She chuckles and shakes her head. "No, but I'm a sucker for self-help rituals."

I grin. "That psychology degree, huh?"

"Something like that," she agrees. "What about you? Why can't you sleep?"

"I can never sleep the night before the season starts. In the past, Layla would stay up with me and we'd watch *The Mighty Ducks* and eat caramel popcorn." I angle my body toward hers. "I'm not ready to watch the movie or eat the popcorn but I still can't sleep."

"Tradition."

"Exactly."

"I liked *The Mighty Ducks*."

I laugh and it releases some of the tension in my shoulders, increases the easygoing vibe between Bella and me. "It's a classic but I can't get either Milly or Mason into it."

"Ahh, kids these days," she jokes.

"They're partial to DC superheroes and Super Monsters."

"Wait 'til Fortnite kicks in," she warns and I groan.

"I don't get this about kids today. I mean, I know mine are still on the young side but Evans, on my team, was telling me how his oldest would rather meet up with his friends through

Fortnite than at the park. Or you know, at one of their houses."

Bella laughs and shrugs. "It's a different generation. A lot of in-person socializing has shifted to virtual. Look at online dating."

I groan again. "Panda tried to make me a profile on some of those sites."

This confession sparks her curiosity and her eyes twinkle. "Please tell me more."

I swat at her and her laughter bubbles over. Instead of removing my hand, I let my fingers hover over her arm, gliding down her smooth skin. Her eyes track the movement and her expression grows serious. When my fingers reach the crook of her elbow, I squeeze once and force myself to remove my hand even though I remember, with perfect clarity, how her skin felt beneath my touch that night. Like silk. "He tried to make me into some hockey legend."

"You are pretty legendary," she murmurs, causing my chest to swell with pride instead of unease.

"Care to elaborate on that?" I flirt back but Bella shakes her head.

"No way. Did you get any matches?"

I shrug before nodding. "But it wasn't anyone I was interested in."

"Why not?" Her tone is conversational but her eyes spark with curiosity and something…more.

I roll my lips together, wondering how honest I should be. The air between us snaps again and I'm suddenly very aware of the darker blue, nearly navy, rings around her irises. Her chest rises a tiny bit faster, her lips part. Unable to look away, I admit, "I met a woman this summer and…I still can't stop thinking about her."

Bella draws in a shaky inhale, a flicker of hope in those eyes I want to drown in. Partly because I want her and partly because I hate myself for admitting it out loud.

"You said—" she starts but I cut her off.

"I know what I said." I drop my head and rake a hand over my hair. "It's only been two weeks and as much as I'm trying to keep my distance—"

"You've been doing that on purpose?"

I chuckle, tipping my chin in acknowledgement.

"James," Bella whispers and my name on her lips in that tone… I look up. Her eyes are nearly midnight now, the navy ring expanding inward. "I don't know how to do this. I don't know what lines I shouldn't cross and when to back up. You're, well, you confuse me."

My laughter is nervous this time. "I know. I confuse myself."

The corner of Bella's mouth tips up and she takes a sip of her tea, her eyes holding mine over the rim.

"I'm attracted to you, Bella, even though I don't want to be. Not because I'm not interested or intrigued by you but because it would be…easier if I wasn't," I admit the full truth, laying it all out on the kitchen island. I'm in my mid-thirties, a widower, and a single dad. My days of playing guessing games with the opposite sex are long gone.

Bella's hand settles on top of mine. "I'm attracted to you too. And I wish I wasn't because the things I feel for you, things from that night, your mixed signals since I moved in, well, it's a lot for me. And most days, I struggle to handle the bare minimum."

I flip my palm over and clutch at her fingers. "I under-stand that. And if you want to talk—"

She shakes her head and I sigh.

"I'm breaking all my own rules. I know that. But, for honesty's sake, I still think about that night too. I think about *you*. And I'm not sure what to do about it."

"Do we have to do anything about it? Or could we just…"

"Take things one day at a time?" I offer.

She chuckles but nods. "Yeah. I need this job and—"

"And I need your help. I don't want to jeopardize anything with you caring for the twins. They've bonded with you and you're already important to them."

"I'd never bail on Milly and Mason," she declares, affronted that I'd suggest otherwise.

"So, can we be…friends?" I ask hopefully. "I don't know if I can avoid my house for the entire season."

This time Bella's laughter is genuine. "I can do friendship. Just know that I'm also checking out your ass."

I snicker, squeezing her fingers again. I feel better now that we've addressed the tension between us. Even though I'm not going to act on it, it's a relief to know that the attraction is mutual. It's nice to know she's thinking about me too. "I'm checking out yours too. Especially when you wear those Lululemon leggings."

Bella rolls her eyes but her cheeks are flushed, her expression happy. "All right then."

"Okay," I agree, feeling like a weight has lifted from around my shoulders. I like seeing Bella at ease and smiling. "So, you'll have no problem in my absence?"

"None whatsoever," she quips, but then her expression grows serious. "I know it's hard for you to go tomorrow. The first time is always the hardest because this is new"—she gestures between us—"and you haven't known me that long. But James, trust me when I tell you that I will care for Milly and Mason as if they are my own. I've been doing this for years and have many experiences and resources at my disposal. Don't worry about us."

I heave out a sigh. "I know. Logically I know all of that. This just feels…"

"Different."

"Harder."

"Yeah," she breathes out, her eyes scanning my face. Two bottomless pools of blue fill with understanding and reassurances I desperately reach for.

"You'll call me if you need anything."

"You'll be the first call after 911," she says and I rear back, taking a full breath before I realize she's messing with me.

Bella laughs, that deep, melodic sound and I swear, shaking my head at her before joining in.

"That was mean." I point at her.

"That was necessary," she counters, her eyes flashing with amusement. "Trust me. I got this, Jer."

Huh? "Jer?" I question.

In an instant, the vibe in the room changes. All our playful banter and flirty joking disappears as an unsettling energy sweeps through the kitchen. Bella pales, looking visibly shaken. She works a swallow and sputters out, "JR."

At the nickname, one only Layla and her family used, I tense up. "You said Jer," I repeat, my tone harder than it was a moment ago. The easygoing vibe between us evaporates.

She shakes her head and slips off her barstool. Rounding to my side, she places a hand on my shoulder. It's shaking. "I promise everything will be fine. I'll keep you updated on the twins and you can call me as much as you want. It's all going to be okay."

"Okay," I murmur, trying to read from her expression what the hell just happened. Why would she call me Jer?

She slips her hand from my shoulder, places her mug in the kitchen sink, and pads back toward her bedroom, muttering "good night" over her shoulder.

I watch her walk away, waiting to see if she'll turn around, confide in me, give me *more*. She doesn't.

It isn't until I hear her bedroom door close that I realize she never answered my question. Is Jer her ex-husband?

I shake my head, knowing I shouldn't get caught up in Bella's personal drama. Not when I'm already overstepping. Not when my thoughts, my feelings, are already twisted up over her. Not when I have a game to think about and the twins to consider.

Instead, I stay up for another hour wondering all the ways Jer hurt Bella. All the scenarios that could have left her shaking and reeling the way she was when she slipped out of the kitchen.

I CHECK Chicago's center into the boards and gain possession of the puck, flipping it to Easton to move up the ice. As I resume my defensive position, a sense of calm washes over me.

This is where I'm meant to be. It feels better than I could have imagined to be back on the ice, surrounded by my team, plunged into a world I know and love.

East scores and we take the lead. I flip my chin at Yaeger who pumps his fist in the air. He's starting for his first NHL game and I love seeing the uninhibited joy and pride that washes over his face.

If there's one thing I've learned in the last three years since Layla was first diagnosed, it's to appreciate the small things. Simple joys are the most important ones. The moments I used to take for granted hit differently now.

I skate backwards and drop into position for the face-off. Then I tune out the noise in my head, push down the lingering hurt in my chest, and give this game, my team, all of my focus. We win 5-3 and it's a natural high I cling to. In fact, I ride it until the following day, when I'm walking back into my house.

Milly and Mason rush to greet me, throwing their arms around my legs and clamoring for my attention. I drop my bag, wrap them up in a hug, breathe in the scent of home, mixed with something delicious wafting from the kitchen, and count my blessings.

For the past year, I've focused so much on what I lost. On what I'll never have again. Instead, I need to be appreciative for what I do have, for all of the good in my life. My healthy children. An exciting career I love. The finances to acquire the support my family needs to thrive.

With Milly and Mason tucked into my sides, I step into the kitchen and stop short at the sight of Bella stirring a pot of sauce at the stove. Her hair is curled at the ends, hanging to the center of her back. She's rocking tight, skinny jeans that hug her curves and highlight her lean legs. A spot of sauce stains her shirt but she doesn't seem to notice, or maybe she just doesn't care.

She looks up when I enter, her blue eyes sparkling, and grins. "Welcome home, hot shot. That was some game."

I smile back and I'm surprised that it comes easily. Other than text messages that strictly discussed Milly and Mason, we haven't spoken since she walked out of the kitchen the night before I flew out.

But whatever awkwardness existed then is gone. Instead, I revel in the brightness she exudes. I like seeing her here, in my kitchen. I like knowing she's caring for my kids. I had no idea how much peace of mind her presence in my home would bring. It gives me the freedom to go all in on the game, to show up the way I used to for my team. It feels good to be back and I owe more of it than I realized to the unsung hero before me.

"Thanks, Bella. Did you guys watch?" I glance at Mason. Since it was the first game of the season, I gave my permission for the twins to stay up past their bedtime to tune in.

"Of course we watched, Dad." He wraps his arms around my waist and squeezes. "Uncle East scored three goals!"

"He was so fast," Milly agrees.

"Hey! Your dad stopped the puck a bunch of times too. Saved a tough shot on goal," I remind them, knowing that my position as defenseman doesn't hold the same appeal as a winger.

"You were great, Daddy," Milly says in an appeasing tone that makes me chuckle.

I glance back to Bella, who is now straining a pot of spaghetti. Did she do this for me? A thrill shoots up my spine. "You didn't have to cook. Justine usually leaves some meals to heat up."

"She did," Bella explains, ladling sauce on top of the spaghetti. "But we wanted to surprise you."

"Wait 'til you try this sauce!" Milly squeals, exchanging a look with Mason. "We got to add all the spices."

"And the basil leaves," Mason adds.

"We're going to plant some in the garden," Milly tells me, leading me to the set table.

"Where?" I ask, my eyes roving over the place settings. Folded napkins, the blue plates from Crate and Barrel that Layla bought on a whim because she liked the color, glasses filled with lemon water. Grated cheese. Red pepper flakes. Extra basil. A bowl piled with meatballs. I haven't seen the table prepared like this in a long time and seeing it now fills me with a strange sense of nostalgia. Longing mixed with gratitude.

Wait. There are only three settings. I frown, turning and nearly colliding with Bella. My hands clasp her elbows to keep her steady.

She releases a nervous laugh and reaches around me to place the bowl with spaghetti in the center of the table. "Thanks, James. That was close."

"You aren't eating with us?" I ask, wondering if I pushed too hard the night before I left. But then, why would she cook us this meal? Her eyes meet mine and I don't see hesitation in them, just…uncertainty.

She shakes her head and tips her head toward my seat.

"Not tonight. You guys should have a family dinner. Enjoy being together."

Her consideration of Milly and Mason, of their needs, is touching. But what about her? I touch her wrist and her eyes snap back to mine. Bottomless, blue and clear, they're the kind of eyes a man could get lost in. It scares me that some days, I want to.

Her lips curl in a soft smile as she gazes at my kids. *"Buon appetito!"* She brings her fingers to her mouth and kisses them with a loud smack, the way the guy in our local pizzeria does.

Milly giggles and Mason emulates her.

I grin at the twins. It's nice to see them relaxed and goofing off again. Since Bella moved in, some of the sorrow that's hung over our home like a thundercloud has eased. Little rays of sunlight are peeking through now and this time, I don't take them for granted.

"Sit and eat. Stay with us, Bella," I say, pulling out a chair. "Please."

She falters for a moment, surprise washing over her face.

"Told ya," Mason announces, scurrying to the cabinet to pull out another plate.

Milly gets a fork and napkin.

"Are you sure?" Bella asks, lowering her voice.

I pat the seat of her chair, knowing that this invitation is deeper than common decency. I insist anyway. "Very."

She nods, an unreadable expression on her face. But she sits on the chair and thanks the twins as they arrange her place setting.

I pile all the plates with spaghetti and meatballs, the scent of garlic and basil washing over me. Clearly, Bella is also one hell of a cook.

Milly raises her glass. "I have a toast," she announces seriously.

I bite my lip to keep from laughing. Bella turns her attention to Milly, raising her glass.

"To Bella," my daughter says formally, "Thanks for teaching us to make sauce."

"And for cleaning our fish tank," Mason adds.

I choke on my laughter but Bella beams. "Anytime, guys."

"Cheers!" the twins say in unison.

We all clink glasses and dig into our meal.

"So, what happened while I was gone?" I ask, my fork hovering over the plate. Man, this spaghetti is delicious.

"We watched a new movie on Disney Plus," Milly says, looking pointedly at her brother.

"It was superheroes!" Mason gushes, pumping a fist in the air.

"It was really good," Bella says, a note of surprise in her tone.

"And Bella taught us how to play Rummikub," Mason adds.

"We gambled!" Milly exclaims, her hands fluttering with excitement.

I snort back my laughter as Bella blushes. "With Oreos," she explains.

"I won," Mase declares as Milly sticks out her tongue.

"And we finished our books," Milly tacks on.

"*Matilda* and *How to Train Your Dragon*?" Now it's my turn to sound surprised because I didn't expect them to finish their books for another week.

"Bella had us read for thirty minutes each night," Mason explains.

"To make up for the cookie gambling." Bella smirks and I smile.

"Sounds like you guys had a great few days," I say, finally taking my bite of spaghetti. I chew it thoughtfully, a strange warmth spreading through my chest. The twins were really fine without me. More than that, they seemed to thrive during their first stay with Bella.

"It was a blast," Mason says, confirming my thoughts.

I catch Bella's eyes, enjoying the brightness that sparks in their depths. "Thank you," I murmur so only she can hear.

She tilts her head in my direction, her expression softening. Then, she spears a second meatball and adds it to my plate.

In a way, this meal feels like a homecoming. Sitting around the table and listening to Milly and Mason fill me in on school, watching Bella add a second helping to Mason's plate, laughing along with a silly story that happened on the playground, clarifies something important in my mind, shifting my perspective.

For months, I've been lost in a cloud of grief. Right now, I can see a hint of the blue sky again, flickers of better days on the horizon.

I catch Bella's eye and smile. She grins back.

A pang hits me in the chest and while I should turn away, I don't. Instead, I lean into it. Into this moment. Into my family's new norm.

CHAPTER 4
BELLA

"Ahh!" I shriek, jumping back and pulling an ear pod from my ear. The loud music I was jamming out to stops abruptly.

James laughs, closing the refrigerator door. "Sorry, I didn't mean to scare you."

"I didn't think anyone was home," I explain, dropping my ear pods on the counter. Even though I ran this morning, it wasn't enough to shake the agony that wraps itself around my bones and sinks its teeth into my limbs as autumn passes. It's the season I hate more than any other even though it used to be my favorite. As a result, I've increased my sessions with Dr. Carlisle to two a week, just to get me through the next few weeks.

"My car is getting an oil change," he explains.

I pull open the refrigerator to fill up a glass of water and James reaches around me, swiping a carton of eggs. When I turn, I'm surprised he hasn't stepped back, but remains planted in front of me. I almost lose my balance but James's hand darts out, grasping my forearm.

He frowns as he takes in my appearance. My shirt is sticking to my skin with sweat, my hair falling out around my face below my Boston Hawks baseball cap. I pushed hard today, clocking twelve miles in my second run before my legs turned to jelly and my lungs protested.

"Didn't you already run this morning?" James asks, his eyes narrowed. Since we came clean about our mutual attraction, we've been doing a delicate dance. One where we come together and separate again, over and over. It's both complicated and thrilling.

Some days, we're buddy-buddy, other days, we're formal and polite. And every now and then, we're shaky inhales and bedroom eyes. To date, neither one of us has made a move but I'm always acutely aware of James when we're the only two people in a room.

But his question, personal and probing, causes me to clamp my mouth shut. I didn't realize he tracked my early morning runs. Today, my eight-mile sunrise workout didn't cut it. My thoughts wouldn't slow and after I dropped the twins at school, I couldn't quiet the noise in my head.

"What are you doing here?" I blurt out instead, not wanting to discuss my running.

He lifts an eyebrow, his eyes flashing with amusement, momentarily distracted from his questioning. For a second, he looks more like the guy I met in Taps instead of the solemn and sexy single-dad I've come to view him as. "You mean, in my house?"

I roll my eyes. "Okay, smartass."

His mouth drops open in mock horror.

I chuckle, enjoying this playful side of him more than I should. Over the past few weeks, we've settled into an easy routine. For the most part, our conversations have circled around Milly and Mason. Still, this version of him, amused, joking, and a teeny bit flirty, is my favorite. "I just meant I thought you were at practice."

"I was. It ended early." He moves to grab a frying pan. "Yaeger dropped me off."

I frown. "Are you hungry?"

"I was just going to make an omelette."

"Oh, I can do that for you," I offer, cringing after I do because this is the type of shit I always did for Jerry. The cooking, cleaning, and pretty much doting on him even though I worked just as many hours, if not more, outside the home.

James shakes his head. "No worries. I got it. Are you hungry?" He glances at me. "You must be starving after pushing yourself that hard…"

He lets his sentence trail off but I don't offer any more information. Because I can't seem to form words as I stare at the kind, observant, thoughtful guy before me. I recall exactly two instances when Jerry made me food. Both occurred after our loss, the one that cut me off at the knees, and I think he only cooked at his mother's prodding. Even then, he grumbled about doing it, as if I was being dramatic by preferring sleep to food at the lowest point of my existence.

"That's a yes," James decides. "Go grab a shower and then we'll eat lunch."

"To-together," I stutter, wondering if he means anything *more* than just…lunch.

"Is my company really that awful?"

"No, of course not." I shake my head, blushing. "I just—"

"Go put on some dry clothes, Bella." He glances pointedly at my chest, where my white shirt is practically see-through, giving a glimpse of my colorful sports bra.

"I'll be right back."

"Okay."

I scurry out of the kitchen and back to my room, needing a moment to collect myself. This is James Ryan, a man I've already admitted makes me feel…things. Why am I blushing and bumbling my words?

I blow out a breath and shed my sweaty workout clothes. I take a quick shower and pull on a pair of leggings and a simple, olive green tee. I glance at myself in the mirror, wincing at my wet hair. I pull out my blow dryer and dry it quickly, scrunching it for some body and volume. When I'm done, I assess my reflection.

Considering I pulled myself together in fifteen minutes, it's not awful. I mean, I'm not going to win any beauty awards but…is that what I'm even going for?

James has already seen me in my pajamas. In my robe. Naked.

I cringe at that reminder. My boss, James Ryan, has seen me completely naked. In intimate positions and sexy poses.

Why am I more nervous about eating lunch with him than I am about my former striptease?

Because you like him. A lot. Even more than you let on.

The words whisper through my mind like a spring breeze.

I flush. Of course I do. I mean, how the hell could I *not*?

James Ryan is a hot, sexy, confident dad who understands the bowels of despair and has been lost to the throes of grief. He's the only man who's looked at me and seen past the facade I shield myself in. In one night, James managed to make me feel more than I have in years and then, I ran away.

Even after our paths crossed again, he's been kind and considerate toward me. More than that, he's been curious and concerned. He's admitted his attraction, his feelings, his worries about our delicate situation. He's been upfront from the start and eating lunch together doesn't change anything. It's just lunch.

This isn't a date. This is James being friendly. Considerate. His kindness makes me like him even more.

I walk down the stairs and enter the kitchen just as James places two plates on the kitchen island.

"Smells good," I comment, trying to keep my voice light. Casual.

"Thanks." He gestures to the plates with a spatula. "I can really only do breakfast."

"I love breakfast for dinner. Or lunch." I take a seat on a barstool.

"Same," he agrees, rounding the island and sliding onto the stool next to mine. "Layla used to hate it. Said it wasn't a real meal but every other Friday when I didn't have a game, we'd do breakfast for dinner. Pancakes, waffles, eggs, the whole thing. The twins loved it."

"I bet." I cut into my omelette and spear a bite with my fork. "I used to make breakfast for supper the first Wednesday of the month. It was this weird rollover from college." I take my bite and moan. "This is delicious."

James's eyes glimmer. "Glad you like it."

I nod. "I can't remember the last time someone made me something to eat," I admit.

James's eyebrows dip for a moment. "Did your ex-husband, was he, did he ever cook?"

I snort and shake my head. "No way. Jerry wasn't really into doing anything...domestic," I say, not wanting to admit that Jerry, while a hard worker and provider, was very firmly planted in the gender role he thought men should occupy. The partner who goes out and brings home the bacon. The fact that I too earned bacon was lost on him, even when I sometimes earned more.

"Jerry, huh," James says, eating a bite of his omelette.

I flush, recalling the night over a week ago when I slipped and called him Jer. It just popped out, a random thought in my mind that I voiced aloud.

My shoulders rise as I duck my head. "Yep."

I wait for James to comment on that night or dig for some Jerry dirt. Instead, he surprises me by saying, "You were right."

"About?" I ask, enjoying more of my omelette.

"We were all okay." He smiles.

I smile back. "See? How was Chicago?"

He wipes his mouth with a napkin and leans back in his

stool. "You know, it was really great. I forgot…" He pauses and shakes his head, as if recalling memories. "I forgot how it feels to go all in. To focus everything I have on the game, leave it all on the ice. For the past few years, all of my thoughts, even when I was playing, would creep back to home. Was Layla feeling okay? Were the twins letting her rest? And then, after she passed, were the twins driving their aunt Maia nuts? Were they sleeping through the night?" He glances at me, tilting his head. His eyes are lighter today, more gold flecks than usual. "Of course, I was nervous leaving the twins. It was the first time they've ever stayed with someone who wasn't family and I…I didn't know what to expect. But after I spoke with them before the game, something clicked."

I stare at him, waiting for him to continue. I like that he's sharing his thoughts with me. I like that he's confiding in me about *him* and not just his kids.

"I felt…calm. A lot of the anxiety and thoughts that circle on a loop just eased. I skated onto the ice and was able to block everything out the way I used to. I think it's because I knew, really *knew*, that the twins were in good hands and happy. So for that, Bella Andrews, I thank you."

I smile so big from his praise that my cheeks sting. It's been a long time since someone other than Selina or Colton paid me a real compliment. "You're welcome."

"You really like what you do, huh?"

"I love it. I love working with children, being with them. Their perspective on life, their outlook, it's refreshing. I wish more people could be as open, as adaptable and accepting, as kids."

"Yeah. They sure are resilient."

"Yeah," I agree, my stomach looping into a knot. Resiliency is something I've lacked in recent years. But I'm trying to push through it, right? The loss and the hurt and the gnawing failure that's eaten most of the good in my life?

I'm here, aren't I? Doing a job I love, supporting a family I relate to?

"You okay?" James's voice is low, pulling me from my thoughts.

I turn toward him and whatever he reads in my expression prompts him to reach out. His hand lands on my knee, comforting.

"You are too," he says, as if knowing I need to hear the words. As if he recognizes that I'm searching for assurances. "Resilient."

I let out a sigh and smile. Before he can remove his hand, I place mine on top and line our fingers up. Lacing mine with his, I squeeze once. "Thank you, James. I didn't realize how much I missed family until you invited me to spend time with yours."

His expression softens and tenderness sweeps through his eyes. "We're going to be okay, you and I."

"I think so too." I'm finally in a place where I can say that and mean it.

"YOU SEEM DISTRACTED," Dr. Carlisle comments on our session that night.

"Just tired," I say.

Dr. C lifts an eyebrow.

"He made me lunch today. Nothing fancy, just an omelette. But it was...nice."

"James?"

I nod, my cheeks heating.

"You're fond of him."

"I like his family." I bite my bottom lip at how defensive I sound.

If Dr. C is put out, he doesn't show it. "You're fond of the family then."

"Of course."

He waits, steepling his fingers the way he does when he wants me to make a connection without his having to prompt it. After a moment of silence, Dr. Carlisle sighs. "Are you fond of them because they're a nice family trying to move on from a tragedy? Or are you fond of them because they are a family you can see yourself belonging to?"

My throat dries at his words. It's no secret, especially not between Dr. Carlisle and me, about how anchorless I've felt since my divorce. Most days, I feel like a ship aimlessly sailing across the world, belonging to no place, having no destination in mind. "I want a family, you know I do."

"I do. But you have a family. Your—"

"My parents have their own lives, as they should. My brother will most likely marry and have children of his own one day. It's not the same thing."

"It's not," Dr. C agrees, confusing me further.

I shrug. "What do you want me to say?"

"Whatever you feel like sharing with me."

I huff out a sigh. "I like the Ryans. Milly and Mason… they're wonderful. I like James. I'm comfortable with them. I, I fit in with them."

"I understand that. Given your history with James, I just want to dig a little further. You seem different with the Ryans than you have with other families. Is it because you can see yourself as part of their family? Is there a romantic element—"

"No," I say firmly, even as James's and my flirtation comes to mind.

Dr. Carlisle lifts his eyebrows and I swear.

"I don't know," I admit, cringing with embarrassment. I'd be lying if I said I don't feel more for James than I have for other employers. I also feel more for Milly and Mason than I have for other charges. I mother them more, am more tender and empathetic toward their feelings, than with my previous charges who hadn't suffered such debilitating loss.

"Do you still want a family one day? A family of your own?" Dr. Carlisle asks, his tone gentle.

I nod, dashing a traitor tear away with the backs of my knuckles. I swear this good doctor has seen me cry more than anyone else. "You know I do."

"Yes. What I'm trying to understand is, how do you see that family? Could you join a family, like the Ryans? Or do you still want to marry, become pregnant, and create a family in a more traditional way? Are you open to adoption, even as a single parent? For over a year, we've talked a great deal about family, but what does that family look like to you?"

I pause, my mouth opening and closing several times before I admit, "I don't know."

Dr. C smiles. "That's okay. It's just…food for thought."

I snort, drying my eyes.

"Let's talk again on Thursday," he suggests, tilting his head as he studies me. "I know this is a difficult time of the year for you. I know I'm asking a lot of tough questions. You're doing great. Try to get some sleep, Bella."

"Thanks, Dr. C," I say before disconnecting the call.

For months now, I've been feeling the agonizing ache of being alone. For years, my understanding of family was rooted in a traditional outlook. But Dr. C raises a valid point. How do I envision a family? Given everything that I've been through, the traditional understanding may no longer apply. It's not the only option available for consideration.

Food for thought. I snicker at Dr. C's words but he's right. It's an idea, a series of questions, I think about over the next two weeks as things shift into place in the Ryan home.

I embrace my new life with open arms, feeling some of the hurt I've carried around for far too long ease. Milly and Mason inject my days with a lightness that's restorative. My last family, the Clarks, were wonderful. But their children were older and my last charge, Brayden, was already mentally checked into the new adventure boarding school promised.

Being surrounded by younger kids again, kids who see the world with wonder and awe and want to spend time with me, has made a big difference in my overall outlook.

Plus, there's James. When he's not traveling with the team, he's home. Hanging in the kitchen while I heat up Justine's meals, going all in on an epic game of Monopoly, or even joining the kids and me when we visit the New England Aquarium on a Saturday morning. Even though our flirty banter remains consistent, we're both cautious about rocking the boat.

I think at the forefront of our minds, we're both hesitant to do anything that could affect our arrangement, that could affect Milly and Mason. But James was truthful about offering his friendship and as we all adjust to our new normal, my walls start to come down.

I spend evenings playing Monopoly or Rummikub with the twins. They read me bedtime stories before sleep, helping to quiet my mind. On weekend mornings, I blast my favorite country or pop hits and we jump on my bed, hairbrushes clenched tightly in our hands as microphones.

Things with James shift too. Dinners are infused with laughter and lively conversation. Morning coffees are sipped between an exchange of newspaper headlines. Holiday plans, Thanksgiving and Christmas break, are discussed and the future begins to look hopeful.

I find myself smiling more, laughing deeper, talking passionately with the full use of my hands. My eagerness to meet each day increases. My morning runs allow for more reflection, with less of an emphasis on exhausting myself. I look forward to the moments when we're like a *family*, the four of us doing something fun and spontaneous together. It's a little bit reckless, leaning into someone else's family with so much heart, but it also fills me with hope. In the recesses of my mind, Dr. C's words float around, reminding me that families look different for everyone.

Maybe one day, I'll truly belong to a family like the Ryans. Maybe, I'll even have children of my own, who look at me with wide eyes and crooked smiles, like Milly and Mason do. Maybe one day, I won't be alone.

CHAPTER 5
JAMES

My heart rate thrums in my temples as I corner the player controlling the puck. For several seconds, it's just the two of us. The noise of the fans, the chill of the arena, our teammates hollering instructions, fades away.

I laser in on the puck, my body quick and reflexive as I block his attempt at scoring. After decades of training, years of building muscle memory, I've settled in as a leading defenseman. The past year, I lost some of my focus, but right now, it comes barreling back.

This guy won't get a shot off all game if I have anything to say about it. I block his attempt, regain control of the puck, and surge up the ice. Spotting Austin in the corner of my eye, I pass him the puck and watch as he navigates down the ice for a goal.

Yaeger hits me in the back. "Nice job, Ryan."

I nod, biting back my smile.

Shit, that felt good. It felt better than good.

I used to be a dependable player that always put the game first. The past few years have messed with my head, messed with my game, and shaken my confidence in my ability to ever be that player again. But now, it's all coming back.

I settle into position for the face-off which Austin secures. Once Easton has the puck, he scores again, putting us in a comfortable lead over Tampa. We win the game 6-3 and the whole team is in a damn good mood as we skate off the ice and head to the locker room.

The usual chaos unfolds as players shower and change, give interviews and goof off. But I take a moment to soak it all in. I'm thirty-six years old. My days on the ice are almost done and I want to savor the moments like this, the seconds where I feel whole again, as long as I can. Because I know what it's like to be on the other side. Drowning in grief, leveled by heartbreak, spending day after day after day just scraping to keep my head above water and suck in enough oxygen for the next hit.

"Good game, James!" Noah hits me on the back as I reach my locker.

"Thanks, Scotch. You too. How's the little one?" I ask.

He smiles, his face lighting up in the proud glow of new fatherhood. "Emmaline is incredible. I swear, man, she's a little genius like her mama. She's already sleeping through the night."

I grin back. "That's incredible, dude. And I'm sure she's perfect. But you know what they say, right?"

"What?"

"If the first one is a good sleeper, the second one is a—"

"Pure hell raiser," Evans, one of our second-line offensive players who has four kids declares. "It just keeps going downhill."

Evans and I laugh while Noah narrows his eyes skeptically.

"Trust me," Evans continues, "I didn't believe it at first either. But wait, the more you have, the more buried you are under diapers, sippy cups, and a serious lack of sleep." He glances at me. "And you had two at once."

"Yeah," I agree. "Layla and I didn't sleep for a solid year

but, once we were past that initial phase, we never went back." After the twins, a boy and a girl, we never even discussed having more children. I think we were both relieved by the time we made it to potty training that the thought of starting over seemed too exhausting.

"Smart man." Evans grips my shoulder.

"Nah, let's not ruin this for Scotch. He's still new to the club," I say.

"Enjoy it while it lasts," Evans snickers, turning around as Coach calls his name.

I glance at Noah. "Seriously, man, I'm really happy for you and Indy. Emmaline is beautiful."

"Thanks." Noah smiles. "Hey, did you hear, Torsten and Rielle are expecting?"

"What?" I shake my head. "Man, that's incredible news."

"Right? Big Daddy is gonna be—"

"A Daddy," we say in unison.

"Yeah, Torsten knocked her up on their honeymoon," Austin adds.

I shake my head. "Greece must have been incredible." I pull open my locker, frowning as my cell phone lights up. I pick it up, realizing I've missed another call.

"I'm hopping in the shower. See you on the plane." Noah smacks my back.

"Yeah," I agree, my concern heightening as I unlock the screen to see three, no, four missed calls from Bella. What the hell happened? My panic blazes and I relocate to a corner of the locker room that isn't as crowded to call her back.

Dread unfurls in my veins as a sick feeling washes through my stomach. Suddenly, my desire to count my blessings sounds like bullshit to my own ears. Of course it was too good to be true. Something is wrong; I can feel it.

My heart hammers and my palms grow cold as the phone rings, leaving me feeling like I'm suspended in air.

Then, "Hello?"

"Bella, what's wrong?" I blurt out.

"Oh James, I'm so glad you called."

"Are the kids okay? Are you all right?" I slam one palm against the wall for support as a wave of weakness hits me in the knees.

"It's Mason. He's okay. He's just, we're at the hospital."

My vision blurs and every imaginable worst-case scenario flickers through my mind, ending with *Mason has cancer.* Fuck, no he doesn't, he's fine. I try to rationalize with myself but I can't help the fear that memories of Layla trigger whenever I hear the word *hospital.*

"What is it? What's wrong?" I whisper, clenching the phone.

"He had a little fever earlier today but I gave him Advil and then he seemed fine."

I nod, remembering the text she sent when she gave him Advil.

"But then it came back and it was really high. A hundred and four."

I close my eyes and drop my forehead to my hand.

"He was shaking and his speech started to slur. I think he was hallucinating. I couldn't get his fever down so I asked Justine to come and stay with Milly. We came right to the ER and we've been here for three hours. That's why I kept calling."

"Have they seen him yet? How's he doing?" My voice is gruff.

"His fever hasn't broke yet. He's alternating between chills and sweating. I just spoke to the doctor before I tried you again. They think it's viral and he should be fine in a few days. In the meantime, they want to keep him overnight to monitor him. He's getting fluids through an IV to stay hydrated. He doesn't want to eat or drink anything. But he's okay, James. Really." Bella delivers all of this in a calm voice. I can tell from her tone that Mason is fine. If he wasn't, she would be hysterical, right?

I don't know. Would she?

She's not his mother. She wouldn't be hysterical. Not like me. I doubt she's sitting there trying not to vomit, fighting against the overpowering sense of fear.

But I know she cares about my son and is relaying all the information she has. Still, I hate that she's there and I'm not. I glance around the locker room again, noting that a few of the guys are shooting nervous glances in my direction.

"I won't be home for a few more hours," I mutter, pissed off that I'm not going to be with my son when he needs me the most. When I need to hold him in my arms and tell him he's going to be okay.

Everything is going to be okay, right? It has to be.

"I know. If you're okay with Justine staying with Milly, she offered to spend the night. We called Maia but she's—"

"In New Orleans," I say, remembering she had a bachelorette party this weekend.

"Yeah."

"If Justine doesn't mind, that would be good. I'll call her on the way to the airport."

"Okay."

"Bella," I hesitate.

"Yes?"

"He's really okay, right? You're sure?" I know it's unfair to ask her that but Jesus, I need to be with my son. I need the reassurance that he's fine. Layla always knew what to do when the twins were babies and would spike a fever. She would rock them in a chair by the window, singing sweet lullabies in English or Arabic, while staring at their flushed cheeks and fluttering eyelashes.

I'm not good at this. I don't know what to do with the panic blazing through me. Logically, I know he's fine but being so far away, when my son needs me, fills me with irrational worry.

"He's okay, James. I promise I'm doing everything I can to keep him comfortable. I'll be with him the whole time, right by his side," she says and I can hear the sincerity in her tone.

"Okay," I whisper. "Just, give him a kiss for me. Tell him I'm on my way."

"We'll be here." She rattles off the hospital and room number and we end our call.

I blow out a deep breath.

"Everything okay?" Easton asks, his eyebrows dipped in concern.

"Mason's sick. He's, he's in the hospital," I stutter, emotion clogging my throat.

"Shit," East mutters. "Is he okay?"

I shrug.

"Maia with him?"

"Bella, his nanny."

"The bartender," East says, probably recalling that night at Taps.

"Yeah."

"So, he's in good hands."

"Yeah," I repeat.

"Come on, we're heading out soon. Go take a shower and get your stuff together. He'll be all right, James," East says.

"Yeah," I mutter, heading in the direction of the showers.

I go through the motions as the team prepares to fly back to Boston, but my head is buzzing the whole time.

Should I have taken more time off? Should I retire? Find a job in the city with zero travel? Would it have made a difference if I was there and not here? Would Mase be in the hospital if I was taking care of him instead of a virtual stranger?

By the time the plane lands in Boston, my body is coiled in tension and my nerves are shot. I power on my phone and dial Bella the moment the wheels touch down but she doesn't answer. What the hell?

I call two more times but both go unanswered. Panic swells in my chest and I feel hopped up on adrenaline, ready to snap. I jump in a taxi straight from the airport, forgoing the team bus back to the arena where my SUV is parked.

When I arrive at the hospital, I book it straight up to Mason's room and collide with Bella.

"Why the hell aren't you answering your phone?" I demand, gripping her upper arms and staring into her face. In the next moment, my eyes dart to the bed and my heart sinks that it's empty. "Where is Mason? Where's my son?"

Bella stares back, her eyes wide with shock. She looks exhausted, with half-moon purple stamps beneath her eyes. Her mouth opens and closes several times but no words come out.

I lose my patience and snap, "Bella! My son. Where is he? What the hell happened? Say something."

CHAPTER 6

BELLA

I feel suspended between my past and present as I stare back into James's dark brown eyes. They're nearly the color of midnight, shaded with worry and blazing with panic. But for a glimpse, they're not brown at all. No, they're the deep blue of Jerry's eyes.

It's his voice that I hear ringing in my ears. *What the hell happened? Say something!*

We were in this exact hospital, two floors up, still in the delivery room, when I received the news about my baby. Jerry was demanding answers, desperate for facts, the same way James is now.

"Bella, I need to see Mason. I need my son," James repeats, his eyebrows furrowing as I continue to gape.

I need my son. Hadn't I said the exact same thing to Jerry that night? *I need my son.* Except Miles was gone and I never had the chance to meet him. Not really. I gave birth to a stillborn baby boy that had my nose and Jerry's chin and we never even heard him cry.

Around me, everything spins. Sounds are muffled, colors blur into each other. I know I need to tell James about Mason. About how he had a seizure and was rushed into another room. About the tests the doctors are running. But I can barely breathe as my past pulls me backward and my concern for Mason rips me wide open.

I suck in an inhale and it's like breaking the surface of the ocean after waiting too long to come up for air. James's voice rattles my brain and the scurrying of nurses in the hallway resumes. My hands visibly shake as I wrap them around James's forearms. His hands still grip my upper arms, squeezing.

"He had a seizure," I manage to say.

"Fuck!" James erupts, releasing me and turning away. "Fuck. Where is he?" He turns back sharply, his eyes wild and unfocused. "Bella! I'm dying here. I know he's not your kid, but please, tell me what you know," he demands.

I know he's not your kid.

He's right, of course. Mason isn't my son. But from the second he sank into my embrace, his body burning with fever, his words incoherent, all I could think about was Miles.

I shrink into myself at the anger in James's voice. It magnifies moments and memories I've tried so hard to forget. Jerry's anger, the way he snapped at me. His disappointment. The way he looked at me like I failed him. *Like I failed Miles.*

A sob bubbles up from my throat and I smack a hand over my mouth.

James looks truly stricken.

I close my eyes and force myself to say the words. "He had a seizure. They took him to another room to run some tests. The doctor should be here any—"

"Mr. Ryan?" Dr. Leeds enters the room.

James turns toward the doctor as I press back against the wall. I wish it would swallow me up, make me invisible, and take me away from this wretched place where my greatest sorrow lies.

Dr. Leeds speaks with James but I can't hear the words. I can't hear anything except the frantic beating of my heart, the anger in Jerry's tone, the sounds of my wailing when I learned the truth.

No heartbeat. Stillborn.

"Bella." James touches my arm.

I blink slowly as Jerry disappears and James comes back into focus. He frowns at me, his mouth thinning. "You can leave. I've got it from here."

I nod but his words rip scabs off my still healing wounds. I failed Mason. I failed Miles. I failed Jerry and James and myself. Again.

"Milly'll want to see you," James adds in a low voice.

But I know he doesn't mean it. He just wants me out of here. Gone. Because I brought his son to the hospital, swore he was okay, and then watched as his little body shook in a series of convulsions and his eyes rolled back in his head.

"You can go now," he says again.

I shake off his touch and gather my belongings. "You'll call when—"

"Yeah," James says, sitting down in a chair and pulling out his phone. His gaze darts up to mine for a flicker before he starts tapping on his phone. "I'll check in with you in a bit."

"Okay." My voice is small and thin. Fragile. Like those shavings of wood, reeds, that I used to need for my saxophone. I always thought I'd have a child who flourished in music. The way my dad did.

When I don't move, James raises his head again and lifts his eyebrows.

Right. I'm dismissed. I avert my gaze and leave the hospital room with my head down, my shoulders rounded, and the feeling of failure heavy in my chest.

The whole way home, I can't shake the old inadequacies that surfaced tonight. James snapped at me the same way Jerry used to. The feel of the hospital, all loss and grief, rolled through me the way it did three years ago. But worse than that is the way my heart broke all over again.

Whatever progress I've made the past few years, the past few months, evaporates in an instant. I send Dr. Carlisle a message.

I was fooling myself in thinking I'd ever belong to a family again. My family is ruined. Gone. And I'm the only one to blame.

MASON RETURNS from the hospital two days later. He's a little paler, a little weaker, but his spirits are high. His fever broke nearly as quickly as it had spiked and with his febrile virus and seizure behind him, the doctor released him.

Physically, Mason is fine. But the emotional and mental anguish the Ryan family suffered as a result makes it clear they are still gripped by grief from Layla's passing.

"I'm off." James gives a nod on his way to the front door, his hockey bag slung over his shoulder.

"Have a good game." I lift a hand in farewell, glancing surreptitiously at Milly and Mason.

Both kids stare after their father, waiting for him to kiss them goodbye or tell a silly joke the way he usually does. But the door closes firmly behind him and I catch the confusion on Mason's face, the disappointment in Milly's eyes.

Knowing firsthand just how much a health scare, any scare, can eat up all the progress a person has made in the wake of tragedy, my heart goes out to James. But the twins are my priority and their father's checked-out mental state and clouded-over eyes frustrate me. On top of that, his shortness with me, his snapping at me, aches more than I'd like to admit.

"Come on, guys. Want to go to the park? We can shoot hoops before supper," I say with more enthusiasm than I feel.

Mason yawns and Milly gives me a look of disbelief. Right, that was way too ambitious. Mason is still recovering. Aren't we all?

"Or," I stall, wracking my brain for a bright idea. Luckily, one springs to mind and I snap my fingers. "I got it! Let's make s'mores."

At this, both kids perk up. "S'mores?" Milly asks, letting the question dangle.

"Yes, ma'am. You've got a firepit, right?"

"Out back," Mason confirms.

"And we have all the ingredients," I hurry on.

"We do?" Mason asks.

I roll my eyes. "As if I'd not be prepared for s'mores. Don't insult me, Mase."

Milly snickers. I move to the kitchen and gather up the necessary ingredients. "Now you guys bundle up warm and I'll get the fire going. And then, dessert before supper."

The twins grin, their eyes twinkling. A surge of excitement runs through me as well. Not that this is walking on the wild side but it's definitely breaking the rules I try to stick to. "Sometimes, rules are meant to be broken," I continue. "Tonight, we're going to throw caution to the wind and have some fun."

"Okay!" Milly cries out, racing to the front closet for her winter gear. Mason follows, shooting me a grateful grin.

Once the fire is going and the twins are bundled up, we trek outside and sit around the firepit. I pass out sticks and we place marshmallows on the ends, leaning over the fire. The flames flicker and dance, casting the twins' faces in rosy glows and shadows.

"This is fun," Mason says after a beat.

"And it's a school night," Milly adds.

They look at each other and laugh, their faces giving away the innocence of their ages, the delight they're experiencing.

"You sure Dad won't mind?" Milly asks after a moment.

Even though I'm not sure how James will react, I know that I'll deal with him if he's angry. Something tells me he won't be. Right now, the twins need something fun, something to distract their concerns away from their father's worried expressions and stretches of silence. "Nah, he'll be okay," I say gently. Removing the marshmallow, I press it between two graham crackers, already coated with chocolate. Then, I pass the s'more to Mason and make one out of his marshmallow for Milly. When we all have a s'more, we tap them over the fire in cheers and take a big bite.

"Oh my God," I groan, the melty marshmallow fluff sticking to my lip. "This is good."

"So good," Milly adds.

"Remember that time we went camping?" Mason asks his sister.

She nods, her face beaming. "Mommy stepped through a log."

"Fire ants!" Mason exclaims, his laughter bubbling up. "It was the worst," he says to me.

"Mommy's leg was burning."

"And she had little red dots everywhere," Milly says, demonstrating by poking all over her leg.

I wrinkle my nose. "Oh man, that sounds brutal. Did you guys keep camping?"

Mason nods. "Oh yeah, Daddy fixed Mommy up and we made a campfire."

"And s'mores," Milly adds.

"We told scary, spooky stories," Mason recalls.

"Daddy's was the scariest," Milly tells me. "It had a dragon in it."

I grin. "That sounds like a fun trip."

The twins nod again, old memories filtering through their eyes as they stare at the campfire.

"Did you ever go camping?" Mason asks me.

I shake my head, not telling him I'd rather get a root canal than go camping. "I'm more of a city girl."

"I like shopping, too," Milly says, as if that sums it up.

I laugh and nod. "What's your favorite camping memory?"

"Stargazing," Milly says without hesitation.

"See there?" Mason points to the sky, dragging his finger in a line. "That's the Big Dipper."

I squint and look up, trying to follow his movements. Slowly, the shape he's tracing appears and I exclaim, "I see it!"

"Pretty cool, huh?" Milly asks me, popping another marshmallow on the end of her stick.

"Super cool," I agree, listening as Mason points out additional constellations.

Sitting under the stars, eating s'mores with Milly and Mason makes my chest ache. While I revel in the time I share with them, their happy expressions and wistful memories dip my personal loss in heartache.

As November 8 nears, so does the restlessness coursing through my limbs. I push myself to run every morning before the sun rises until my body edges on total collapse. While Milly and Mason ease a lot of my pain, they also cause me to confront it head-on.

On the morning that Miles would have turned three, I wake up earlier than usual, a dull throb in my temples, an itchiness in my palms, a restless energy that won't subside.

I step out into the chill of a Boston autumn morning and run too many miles to count. Slowly, the sun peeks through the clouds and the neighborhood stretches awake, but in my mind, there's only room for darkness. I'm back before the twins wake, preparing their breakfast when James enters the kitchen.

He glances at me warily, as if surprised to find me in his home, his kitchen. Things have been strained since Mason's hospital stay and while I tried in the immediate aftermath to make things right, I gave up when I was met with silence and indifference.

Today, of all days, I don't have it in me to put myself out there. Not when my heart feels so tender, my emotions so raw and close to the surface. Today, I feel like one of the burnt orange leaves curling in the street—fragile, thin, and dying inside.

I butter Mason's toast and don't even look up when James clears his throat.

"Good morning, Bella," he says, stepping around me to pour a cup of coffee.

"Morning," I manage to reply, snapping the lid back on the butter.

He fixes his coffee and I hear the spoon clink against the side of the mug. I feel his gaze on my back, settled right between my shoulder blades.

A heavy sigh falls from his mouth. I cut Milly's toast into four squares.

"How are you doing?" James's voice is gruff, still layered with sleep.

"Fine. You?" My voice is controlled, direct. My fingers tremble and I feel brittle, weak enough to shatter right here. Swells of grief rise in my chest and I glance at the clock.

How is it only 7:38 a.m.? How am I supposed to endure this day? Survive it?

But I have. I've already done it several times. All I've learned is the people who say time heals all wounds are liars. Because how the hell can a mother ever move on from *this* type of devastation?

"What are your plans today?" James asks, shifting closer.

I feel the heat of his body at my back, not quite touching, but near enough that I could sink into his warmth if I let myself. I don't. The last thing I need right now is kindness. Because kindness will shatter me and I don't want to shatter before 9 a.m. when I have a job to do. When I have a memory to honor.

"Going to run some errands," I say noncommittally, mentally running through the list of items I need to buy. "I told the twins we'd do a craft this afternoon."

"A craft," he murmurs, neither a statement nor a question.

I don't say anything else. Instead, I give a jerky nod and leave the kitchen to wake the twins up for school. Right before I exit, I turn to look at James.

He's staring directly at me. His eyes are turbulent, churning with emotions that I both recognize and despise. Heartache, loneliness, grief…pity? His expression is severe, his lips thin. I can tell he wants to make things right between us but today isn't the day for that.

I sever our connection by taking the stairs, calling out for Milly and Mason as I go.

I focus on the routine, on the things I have to do. I force myself to move forward, to put one foot in front of the other. I smile when Milly wishes me good morning; I help Mason style his hair. But the entire time, breathing feels like having a knife plunged in my chest. Every single thing about today hurts.

The text messages from my family, the calls I ignore from Colton and Selina, checking in on me.

The lack of a message from Jerry acknowledging the loss of our son.

On days like today, even the best of intentions, the thoughtfulness of loved ones, the comfort my parents and big brother offer, burns me from the inside out. Kindness aches just as deeply as indifference.

Milly squeezes me extra tight before she bounds down the

steps for breakfast. Three years ago, her mom was diagnosed with cancer the same week that I lost Miles. Maybe she remembers that time, maybe she feels the hopelessness in the impending winter.

Or maybe she saw my face and sensed that I needed a hug.

Whatever the reason, I decide that the three of us will make memory wreaths today. To honor. To remember. To accept. And maybe, to begin to heal.

CHAPTER 7
JAMES

"How are the twins holding up?" Austin asks as I slam the door to my locker closed.

Practice today was brutal but I welcomed the intensity. I even welcomed the hits. Ever since Mason was hospitalized, my head has been all over the place. It's like I was plunged back into the darkest days of Layla's illness.

Now, with the anniversary of her cancer diagnosis just days away, I feel the same helplessness grip my throat. This time of year is always hard for me but this year, I think it's affecting the twins too. I know I haven't been there for them the way I need to be, the way I *want* to be. It's another failure that's difficult to swallow.

I look up at my captain, wondering how he manages to keep it together all the time. Leading a team isn't easy, and Austin always offers insight and support.

"They're doing all right. If anything, it's me. I need to be there for them more."

"It's a tough week," Austin says thoughtfully.

"Yeah," I agree. It's more than tough. It's fucking crippling. Every year at this time, I feel like I got TKOed. Then again during the week Layla passed, the week of her birthday, the week of our anniversary… Will life ever not feel like a fucking struggle? If I didn't have the twins, I don't know how I would manage any of it.

"How are things with Bella working out?" Austin asks.

"She's…great," I say truthfully, not voicing how I need to do better by her too. An image of her from the hospital flickers through my mind. She was in agony. Her eyes were burning, her mouth open. She looked like she was on fire from the inside out, a slow torture that I felt in my bones. "I, uh, I snapped at her at the hospital when I went to see Mase. Things are a little…strained at the moment."

Understanding streaks across Austin's face and he swears softly. "Don't be so hard on yourself, James. You were worried about Mason."

"Yeah," I agree, scratching my cheek. "Still, it was shitty of me. She treats my kids like her own and I was unfair."

"Did you tell her that?"

I shake my head and Austin lifts an eyebrow.

"I need to apologize," I say finally.

"Yeah, man. You should talk to her. When you were in the moment, you were probably overwhelmed and worried about Mase. People say things they don't mean when they're—"

"Scared," I murmur.

Austin nods, clasping my shoulder. "But if you like Bella as much as you say, and she's great with the twins, then you need to talk to her."

"I need to do a hell of a lot more than that." Austin gives me a look and I snort, shaking my head. "Not like that, man. I just mean, I need to do right by her. She's made the transition, the school year, this season, easy. Twins adore her. I…she's good for me, too."

"That's great, man. Don't be so hard on yourself, James. You're doing a hell of a job raising those kids and adjusting to this new reality."

I nod, touched by his words. Even though Austin

believes them and means it as a compliment, the only thing that runs through my mind are my shortcomings. The way I haven't given the twins the attention they need over the past week. The way I cut Bella down instead of building her up.

"I'm gonna head out. See you tomorrow?" I shoulder my bag.

"Yep," Austin agrees, watching me curiously. "Have a good night."

"You too," I say, knowing that my night will be anything but good. It will be another sleepless night where I recount all the ways I'm failing my children, Bella, and Layla's memory.

By the time I arrive home, I'm in a piss-poor mood. But when I step into the warmth of the house, hear the twins' laughter, it recedes a bit. Then, I stop short. Because three wreaths are laid out on the dining table. I can tell which ones the twins made and which one Bella created, mainly because Bella's is neater, and also the most cryptic.

Milly's is made of scraps of fabric I recognize from her baby clothes and buttons. Buttons that Layla collected from concerts when she was a teenager and at some point, let Milly play with.

Mason's wreath is threaded with gold, Layla's favorite color. It contains patches that Layla used to sew onto the back of his denim jacket.

Seeing the pieces of our past, of our family, causes tears to well in my eyes. I clear my throat and look away. My gaze lands on the third wreath.

Did Bella make a wreath just to help my kids cope with the loss of their mom? To help them make sense of the month that changed our family forever.

I frown, squinting at the light cream, pale yellow, and soft green ribbons woven throughout the wooden sticks holding the shape of her wreath.

There's something inherently innocent about it. Something

sweet and simple. Still, the sight causes the swell in my throat to thicken and I turn away, making my way into the kitchen.

When I enter, Bella, Milly, and Mason stop speaking and look up at me. They're seated at the kitchen table, eating chicken, mashed potatoes, and corn on the cob.

"Hey guys," I say, lifting my hand toward the dining room. "Those are really beautiful wreaths you made."

Milly smiles as Bella jumps from her chair to grab another plate. I touch her wrist. "I got it."

She doesn't smile or say hello. Instead, Bella dips her head in acknowledgement and retakes her seat. Something in my chest sinks at her dismissal, even though I deserve it.

"They're memory wreaths," Mason explains as I sit down at the table with a plate and cutlery setting. "We made them for Mom."

"They're really special," I say, meaning it.

"Bella made hers for her baby," Milly adds.

I hear Bella's audible inhale and feel it like a jab to my chest.

Bella's baby. Memory wreath.

My stomach twists painfully as I put two and two together. My gaze snaps up but Bella keeps her eyes trained on her plate. Her head is down, her hair slipping forward, over her shoulders, in a protective shield.

"She had a baby boy," Milly continues, oblivious to how much pain Bella is suffering at the moment.

"He died like Mom," Mason adds, his words soft but direct.

I place my fork down, my appetite gone.

Bella looks up slowly and her expression guts me. Pain swims in her eyes, a shimmering blue slick with tears. She rolls her lips together and sucks them between her teeth trying not to cry.

Her hurt steamrolls me. I recognize the grief she's buried under. I acknowledge that while I've been suffering, thinking the universe owed me a great debt for taking my wife away, Bella's been drowning in her own agony. But still, she showed up for my kids on the days I couldn't and suddenly, I feel like a piece of shit for not seeing her pain as clearly as she recognized mine.

Milly and Mason chatter on for the rest of dinner. I ask them questions about school and their friends which they answer happily. Bella barely says a word and I draw my kids' attention away from her so she can keep it together as long as possible.

When dinner is over, I put a movie on in the den for the twins to watch.

"Let me," I tell Bella, taking a plate from her hand.

She lets go of the dish, murmurs thank you, and turns on her heel.

But I can't let her go like this. I can't let one more second go by without her knowing how much I value her. How grateful I am that she's the woman caring for my kids when I can't. How much I care about her, want her, even though it could ruin everything.

"Bella," I murmur, my voice thick. Emotion clogs my throat. The air in the kitchen is dense, like a gathering thundercloud, laden with the expectation of a summer storm.

She turns slowly, a heaviness to her gait that is part exhaustion, part wariness. I step forward, pulling her into an embrace that envelops her completely. Her body stiffens for a moment, surprise in her gasp, but I don't give her a chance to second-guess my sincerity.

I tug her against my chest, wrap her in my arms, and cradle her. Running my mouth over the top of her head, I kiss her hair and murmur, "I'm so sorry. I had no idea. But God, Bella, I am so fucking sorry for your loss."

She breaks apart slowly, like air seeping from a balloon, deflating, instead of a glass shattering against a wall. First, her shoulders tremble, then, they shake as her tears turn into cries that give way to sobs. I hold her as tight as I can, trying to keep the pieces of her together.

"Shh, I got you, Bella," I whisper. "You're okay. You're okay, baby." The term of endearment bursts in the air but given the weight of the moment, it's quickly absorbed.

I don't know how long we stand in an embrace in the kitchen but when Bella's sobs quiet, she pulls away and hides her face in her hands.

"God, I'm so sorry," she says, finally looking up. The tip of her nose is red.

"Don't apologize for anything." I push her hair away from her face. "It's me who should be apologizing. I was wrong to snap at you that night. I was worried and I—"

"I know. It's okay."

"No, Bella, please. Look at me."

Slowly, she drags her gaze back to mine, running a hand across her tear-stained cheeks. Her eyelids are puffy and her lips are swollen. Still, she looks beautiful, radiant in a heart-breaking way.

"It's not okay. You have been keeping my family together for weeks. You have been incredible with the twins and with me." I work a swallow. "I couldn't have done everything without you and I want you to know how much your being here means to me."

"Thank you," she whispers, her shoulders dropping a bit as tension leaks from her body. "Thanks, James."

"Don't thank me, Bella. What I owe you…" I shake my head. "Why didn't you tell me about your son? Not even that night when I, I shared so much about Layla."

She clears her throat. "It hurts too much," she explains, her words strangled. "He would have been three today and it hurts just as badly as it did the day I lost him."

My heart breaks at her words. My soul twists at the suffering in her eyes. I pull her back into my arms and kiss her forehead. Then I walk her into the living room and usher her onto the couch. Hurrying back into the kitchen, I pour two glasses of wine and leave them on the kitchen counter.

"Give me five minutes, Bella. Just wait, okay?" I pop my head into the living room.

She watches me warily but nods.

I round up the twins and get them ready for bed. Once they're tucked in with books to read, I return to the living room and hand Bella a glass of wine.

Then, I sit next to her. "Tell me about him. If you want, I mean. But I'd love to learn about your son."

Tears well in her eyes, one slipping over to land on her cheek as she takes a long sip of wine. She places the glass down on the coffee table and wrings her hands together. "His name was Miles."

"Miles," I repeat. "It's a good name."

"It's my father's name. I went into labor on his birthday and told him if it was a boy, I'd name him Miles. I never thought Miles would die." She presses the heels of her hands against her eyes. "My baby died on his namesake's birthday. How awful is that? I think my dad hates today almost as much as me."

I shift closer. "I can't imagine."

"No one can."

I reach over and take her hand in mine, threading our fingers together. "If you want to talk about Miles, about any of it, I'd love to listen. I'm here for you. Always. You and me…we're more than this thing we're dancing around."

She snorts, shaking her head.

I squeeze her hand. "I promised you friendship, Bella. And I meant that. I meant that and more. Let me help you, baby. Talk to me. Trust me."

She drops her hands slowly, her eyes meeting mine. They swim with hesitation, as if she doesn't know if she can trust my words. "Really?" Her voice cracks.

I squeeze her hand gently. "Really." I shift closer, until our thighs press together.

She inhales shakily, her eyes darting up to mine. "We tried to conceive for two years. The day I learned I was pregnant was the happiest of my life. I've never seen Jerry look so happy."

My stomach twists at the mention of her ex. Knowing how much their divorce wrecked her, I can imagine how this tragedy devastated their marriage. But I hate to think that in the aftermath, he couldn't hold her together the way she needed. I hate that she's had no one in her corner for so long, and suddenly, I'm resentful toward this guy I don't even know for not being enough for her. Resentful and relieved that he's no longer in the picture. The realization messes with my mind and I shut it down, wrapping my arm around Bella's shoulders as she continues.

"We didn't know if we'd have more kids so we wanted to keep the sex a surprise. I bought everything in creams and whites. Soft yellows and greens. It took me months to decorate the most perfect nursery. But I loved every second of it. When I went into labor, we knew it was early. But still, I wasn't worried. I was nearly thirty-four weeks. I called my parents on the way to the hospital and I was nervous but excited. I wasn't freaking out or...scared. Not the way I should have been.

Everything happened quickly after that. I was rushed into a delivery room. The doctor performed an emergency C-section, a team of doctors rushed in. Everyone swarming around. Jerry's hand in mine went limp and I remember asking to see my baby. You had a son, someone said. A boy! I smiled at Jerry who looked stricken and that's when I knew. Why wasn't he crying? Why weren't they placing him against my chest for skin to skin?" Tears slip onto her cheeks and roll slowly to her chin, before dropping to her shirt. "It was the worst moment of my life on what I thought was going to be the best day. They let me hold him afterwards. He was so small, so fragile." She shakes her head, her tears coming harder now. "That day broke me. I wasn't the same afterwards. Neither was Jerry. And no matter how hard we tried, we couldn't get back what we once had. Maybe we didn't even want to anymore..." She pauses, swiping her tongue over her bottom lip. "Today guts me every single year."

I hold her firmly against my side, turning my head to kiss the top of hers. "You're one of the strongest women I've ever met."

"I don't feel strong."

"You're also one of the most giving," I continue. "To surround yourself with children, to lose yourself in their lives the way you do. That's more than just strong, Bella. That's brave. Courageous."

"Maybe," she says slowly, looking up at me. Her eyes still leak tears, her cheeks streaked, but she looks beautiful. Real. "But I don't want to be brave, James. I want to be whole. I want a family. I want to be a mother."

Her words, *that* confession, make my soul ache. I look at her and see all the parts she buried, all the pieces she doesn't believe in anymore. We sit together for a long time. Our conversation ebbs and flows, our broken dreams and spoiled plans spilling out through words, knowing glances, comforting touches. It's after midnight when I walk Bella up the stairs to her bedroom.

For the first time since I helped her move in, I cross the threshold and pull back her duvet cover. She slips between the sheets and I tuck her in. She watches me, her face lined in exhaustion.

"Sleep, baby," I whisper, brushing her hair away from her face. "It's time to sleep."

Her eyes flutter closed and I wait, running my fingers through her hair, until her breathing evens out and sleep claims her.

Then, I head to my own room but sleep doesn't come easily for me. Bella's heartache twists my gut and offers a fresh perspective.

I'm not the only person in the world suffering from loss. I'm not the only one swimming in grief. On the days that I've shut down, she's stepped up.

Now, I need to step up for her.

CHAPTER 8
BELLA

"Morning, Bella," James greets me easily the next morning when I come in from my run.

I pushed myself today, the emotional hangover of yesterday leaving me restless when it should have left me drained. Even now, after ten miles that felt like two, I can't stop the pounding in my mind, the tremble in my hands. I have a session with Dr. Carlisle before lunch and it can't come soon enough.

James pours me a mug of coffee and fixes it just the way I like—two sugars, no milk—before placing it down in front of me. He's rocking a black tank top that show off his biceps and grey sweats.

I try not to check him out too hard but...I'm only human. There aren't many dads who look like James Ryan and if his bod could be the new dad bod standard, well...

"How was your run?" he asks, leaning over the island while I pick up the coffee mug and take a sip.

The strong taste centers me and diffuses some of the emotional overload I suffer from following any anniversary dates. "Not bad."

"Liar."

I snort. "Thanks for listening last night." I meet his eyes, letting him read how much his sincerity meant to me. James stayed up late while I sobbed and shared all about sweet Miles.

I don't know if it's because he understands the heart-wrenching depth of a loss like mine but confiding in James was a hell of a lot easier than talking to my parents, or Colton, or Selina. The words flowed from my mouth, torrents of rambling I couldn't stop if I wanted to. And I didn't want to. Not last night when I almost wished Jerry would call me just so I could remember Miles with someone who loves him as deeply as I do.

But Jerry didn't call. James stepped up to the plate, pulled me into his arms, and listened for more hours than he needed to.

What's more is I wanted him to. I needed the time, attention, and concern, from someone who would truly understand. I needed *him*. Last night shifted something between us and I smile, because I don't want to go back. I like having James Ryan in my corner; I like having a man in my life that I can count on. Confide in.

He studies me for a beat, his expression soft. "I'll listen anytime, Bella. I mean that. I'm always here for you, okay?"

I nod, taking another gulp of coffee. The strange thing is, I believe him. Of course I can call up Colton or Selina and they'd listen. But not the way James tuned in to my feelings, to the anguish that twists my soul, to the deep ache that lives inside of me and never truly vanishes.

"I will too," I murmur back, giving him a serious look.

He smiles and reaches out, his big hand covering my cheek. It's comforting, the steady weight of him, the knowing that someone will keep me tethered to reality when I feel like I'm drowning in the past. "I know."

I turn into his touch, pressing a kiss against his palm, and the kitchen shrinks. The space presses in on me, along with a lack of oxygen. James feels it too because a desperation sweeps his eyes, turning them black.

My mouth parts as his thumb brushes over my cheekbone, his fingers wrapping around my neck. His eyes drop to my lips, lingering for a beat too long, a beat I want to lose myself in.

I don't want professional anymore. I don't want friendly and neutral and platonic. I want James Ryan. All of him. The messy, the complicated, the solemn. Since living under his roof, my flicker of attraction has fanned into a flame of desire. One that is curious, excited, and hopeful.

Suddenly, I want nothing more than for James to close the space between us and kiss me. I want him to taste my lips with the same intensity that he listened to my hurts. I want him to drag his mouth along the curve of my jaw and I want to slide my hands under his shirt and press my palm against his heart.

"Daddy!" Milly shrieks, bolting down the stairs.

James pulls away immediately and my spine snaps ramrod straight. Even though we weren't doing anything wrong, I feel my cheeks burn and drop my head to sip my coffee.

Milly scurries into the kitchen, talking a million miles a minute about a squirrel she saw outside her bedroom window. James grins at her and picks her up in a hug. He plops her down on the kitchen island and pours her a smoothie.

"Drink this and wake your brother up. I'm taking you to school today."

"You are?" Milly and I ask at the same time.

"I am," he repeats, kissing Milly on the forehead before helping her back to the floor. She runs back in the direction she came, bellowing for her brother.

"You don't have to—" I start but James cuts me off.

"Take a shower. Get dressed. After I drop off the kids, let's go get breakfast."

My eyebrows nearly fly off my face. Did he just read my thoughts?

James laughs at my reaction. "C'mon, let's mix things up today."

I bite my bottom lip, studying his expression. Am I reading too much into this? My heart races as I grip the handle of my mug. "Don't you have practice?"

He smiles at me, the little notch in his chin flaring. "Not until this afternoon. I already got a workout in in the basement. You had a shit day followed by a rough night, don't deny it."

I shrug, not bothering to refute him since I know he'll see through me. It's the worst club to belong to—the grieving family member—but once you're in it, you see a lot more than club outsiders could possibly notice.

"Let me take you to breakfast. I never got to properly apologize for acting like a dick at the hospital."

"You were worried about Mason."

"True, but I never should have taken it out on you," he says softly. "I'm sorry, Bella."

I look up, my mouth falling open for an entirely different reason. The fact that James can acknowledge when he's wrong and apologize for it blows my mind. Years of marriage to Jerry taught me not to expect much in terms of making past wrongs right. But—"Thank you, James."

"So, breakfast?" he asks hopefully, lifting an eyebrow.

"I'd love that," I say, smiling back. We hold each other's gaze for a moment, the shadows shifting into something hopeful, ringed in promise.

"Good."

Milly and Mason stumble down the stairs.

"A herd of elephants," James mutters under his breath,

pouring Mason a smoothie. "Go on." He tips his head toward the stairs. "Go take some time for yourself."

"Have a great day at school, guys," I tell the twins as I pass them.

Mason frowns and Milly reaches for my arm. I stop and smile down at them but both of their expressions are wary.

"Are you sick?" Milly asks.

"What?" I laugh, shaking my head. "No, silly. Why?"

Mason's frown eases but Milly still watches me intently.

"Why aren't you taking us today?" she asks.

"Because I wanted to do the honors," James slips in smoothly, redirecting their attention. "And I begged and pleaded with Bella to let me be on carpool duty today. You know what?"

"What?" Mason asks.

"She made me arm wrestle her for it!"

Milly smacks a hand over her mouth, stifling her laugh.

Mason glances at me. "Dad won?"

I grin at their playfulness. "No way, dude. I won." I flex an arm. "Can't you tell? Your daddy can't beat this!" I make another pose and the twins burst into giggles.

James snickers, winking at me.

"Since your dad is such a sore sport I told him he could take you anyway." I pause at the doorway and turn back to point at them. "But only today, you hear?"

They both nod and climb up onto the barstools, peppering their father with questions.

I turn back to the stairs and make my way toward my bedroom. I step into the shower, the hot water easing some of the tension I carry in my shoulders and neck.

This isn't a date, right?

No, of course not. It's just two people with a shared loss connecting.

Friends who flirt grabbing a midweek bite. It's casual.

But I'd be lying if I said I didn't spend extra time blowing out my hair. Or adding a swipe of lipstick and mascara when I'm usually makeup free. And I did try on two, ahem, three different shirts before settling on a white, long-sleeve shirt, with a deep V-neck. I pair it with tight, ripped black skinny jeans and sexy, over-the-knee, black boots.

Studying myself in the mirror, I admit I'm balancing that casual/dressy vibe pretty spectacularly. I laugh, my gaze flicking up to my face. My eyes don't look as haunted as they usually do. I almost look…excited.

WHEN JAMES REENTERS the house after dropping the twins at school, I'm already waiting in the living room. His eyes widen and the corners of his mouth tip up in appreciation.

"You clean up well, Andrews." His tone is teasing but his expression heats and I revel in the compliment.

I lift my chin at him, taking in his ripped jeans and a light gray Henley under his open coat. I swear, dads didn't dress like this when I was younger. If they did, I would have totally been into older men. "You do too, Ryan."

James holds out his hand and I hesitate for an instant before taking it. He grips my hand lightly, swinging our arms as he helps me into my coat and leads me out of the house. When he turns to lock up, he drops my hand and I curl it into a ball.

Is he just being friendly? Or is this more than that? Did we already cross the line between friends and something more? Or are we hovering at the edge, about to cross over?

It's been so long since I've done this, I don't know what signs I'm supposed to look for. Am I reading this right?

"You okay?" James asks me, appearing totally normal while I'm kind of freaking out inside.

"Yep." I smile too brightly.

James gives me a look before unlocking the doors on his SUV. We slip inside the car and he eases it out of the driveway.

"How do you feel about Meg's Diner?" he asks.

"Oh, I love their waffles." I settle back against the seat, some of my nerves dissipating now that I know we're headed to the casual, corner diner I frequent.

"Yeah, so does Mase." James glances at me. "I want you to know that it's okay to take time for yourself. Now that we're past the initial transition, we'll work something out so you have more time off."

"Ah." I wave a hand, a flare of panic blazing in my chest. I don't want time off. Time alone means thoughts and what-ifs and more reflection on my failures. Time off means more sessions with Dr. Carlisle.

"I couldn't have survived the past two months without you."

"You would have figured it out, James."

"It wouldn't have been nearly as painless as you've made everything."

"It's fine. It's my job."

"No." He shakes his head, taking a left turn. "You go above and beyond your job. Don't think I don't notice."

"Is that why you're taking me for waffles?" I ask, trying to lighten the mood and get a read on him as he pulls into the parking lot.

"Nope," he says again, parking. He turns to face me fully, his eyes serious. "I'm taking you for waffles because I've done a shit job looking after you."

"It's not your job to look after me," I murmur, my voice almost a whisper.

James holds my gaze. I feel the crackle of electricity

between us, more intense now than it was in the house. He reaches out slowly, his hand wrapping around my wrist. "What if I want to? I know I said friends but…I think of you a hell of a lot more than I should."

"Wh-what?" I stutter, my heart rate suddenly jumping into my eardrums. Did I hear him correctly?

James wooshes out a heavy exhale. "I like being with you, Bella. You make me laugh even when I don't feel like it. I thought having you nanny for my kids would be awkward after everything that went down between us."

I flush, closing my eyes for a beat as I recall sneaking out of that hotel room.

"Look at me, please." He squeezes my wrist.

I force my eyes open and my breath freezes in my throat as I get a good look at his expression. Warm brown eyes, mouth pressed in a line. James is serious, straightforward. He doesn't play bullshit mind games or say one thing and do another. What you see is what you get and suddenly, I'm so grateful for that, I could cry.

"I think of you when I'm not with you. I trust you with my children. I feel better knowing that you're looking after them. But last night…fuck, Bella. Seeing you sad wrecked me and I realized, who the hell is looking after you?"

"You're not supposed to take that on," I remind him.

"But I can't not worry about you. After Mason got sick"— he winces, recalling the awful stretch of days where time seemed to stop and we scurried around each other like strangers—"I know I was an idiot. But the whole time I was putting space between us, I was thinking about you. What you were doing. How you were feeling. I don't know how to do this, Bella." He glances at where he's holding my wrist. "I don't know how to be with a woman anymore. Not after so many years and not after so much…loss."

"I don't know how to do this either," I admit.

"But do you want to?" he asks, his eyes flipping back to mine. Melted chocolate and hot cocoa and heat.

I swipe my tongue over my dry lips and James zeroes in on the movement. Slowly, I nod. "I left that night because I got scared."

He frowns. "Scared?"

"Yeah." I let out a small laugh. "I was way out of my league with you. I was embarrassed too, knowing you'd wake up in the morning and regret it. Wish I was…someone else. I'm damaged goods."

"I could never regret being with you. You're perfect," he refutes, a flare of anger in his eyes. "Don't say that about yourself, Bella. The ones with the damaged hearts are the ones that life happened to. You'd be hell-bent to meet someone worth connecting with nowadays who wasn't a little bit tarnished by life's heartaches."

"I know."

"So you really weren't just ghosting me because of the sex?" he asks.

My mouth drops open. "Is that what you think?" I snort, shaking my head. "Jesus, James. In one night, you flipped my world upside down. I had no idea sex could be that…intense. And then, with a stranger no less. You really thought I left because—"

"It wasn't good," he finishes my thought.

I groan, pushing my head back into the headrest. "That couldn't be further from the truth."

"Neither is you beating yourself up so badly," he replies, reaching over to place a hand on my leg.

I glance down, liking the weight of his hand on my thigh. "So this…" I glance out the window toward Meg's Diner.

"This is me wanting you to know that I'm here for you. That I'm thinking about you. As *more than* friends but always friends first. That I'm willing to do whatever you want and if you don't want to do anything, that's fine too. But I'll still be looking out, Bella. I can't *not* worry about you."

I smile slowly, feeling his words warm places that have been frozen for too long. "Okay."

"Okay," he agrees, flipping off the ignition. "Waffles?"

"Yes, please," I say, exiting the SUV.

We walk toward Meg's and James holds the door open for me.

We're seated at a corner booth and when the server comes by, we order Belgian waffles and strong coffee.

It's the best non-date I've ever been on and my favorite Tuesday of all time.

CHAPTER 9
JAMES

I slide across the ice, my gaze wandering up to the team's family and friends' booth. I can't stop the grin that splits my face when I see Bella sitting up there, laughing at whatever Mason is saying. Milly waves to me and I kiss my fingers before extending them toward her. She does the same back.

It's something Layla and I used to do before the puck drop at home games. My body relaxes some now that Milly has picked up her mom's tradition. Maia brought the kids to a handful of my home games last season but the loss of their mom was still too fresh. They would fall into long periods of silence after each game that I stopped asking if they wanted to come.

Mason surprised me yesterday when he asked if he and Milly could bring Bella to a game. "I think she'd like it, Dad," he said seriously.

I grinned at my little heartbreaker and agreed. I love how much the twins care for Bella. The three of them have their own relationship and while I thought I'd feel left out, instead, I'm often relieved that Milly and Mason have connected so strongly with Bella.

That's why now, when I look up, three of my favorite

people are rocking my number and dancing in their seats. Indy, Claire, and Chloe are also in the booth and I know Bella and the twins are in good hands. Mase waves and I wink, smirking at Bella, before taking my position.

"It's good to have them back," Noah says to me over his shoulder.

"Yeah," I agree, my gaze darting back to the booth for one more look. This time, my attention is snagged by Bella. She left her dark hair loose and it tumbles down her jersey and around her shoulders. Her eyes looks brighter, bolder, fringed by long lashes.

A bolt of excitement shoots through me. I like that she's here. I want her to watch me play. It's ridiculous really but I suddenly feel like a college kid again, wanting to impress the girl I was crushing on with my moves on the ice. I should already know it's my moves off the ice that count but that old, competitive mindset, with the need to show off for a woman, flares to life.

I shift into my stance moments before the puck drops. My mind clears, my body tightens, and my play takes over. I focus all of my energy, all of my drive, on the game.

It's necessary because Vancouver comes to play. The game is intense, just bordering on nasty, with a couple hard hits and under-the-belt roughness.

In the third period, all hell breaks out when one of the Eagles' players, Jace Edwards, skates by chirping off, "You gonna put a ring on it or just knock her up, Scotch? Don't you think your daughter deserves more?"

Shit. Noah's expression changes in an instant and I understand it immediately. Jace is talking shit about his woman, about the mother of his child, and there's no way Noah is going to let that slide. Plus, fuck Jace for bringing Emmaline into it.

My limbs lock down and anger blazes through me. Talking shit is one thing but you don't involve a man's family.

Ever. So when Noah pulls back his arm and lets a jab fly, I jump into the mix. I grapple with their center until he's got a bloody nose and I can feel the side of my jaw swelling up.

"Shit," East mutters amid the ref's whistles. He pulls me back by the neck of my jersey, shaking his head. "Let me see your face."

I spit out a wad of blood before I catch Noah's eye. Even though Scotch looks fucking murderous, when he sees my expression, he grins. I smirk back. Then we both start laughing and Easton swears again.

"Scotch! Ryan!" Coach Phillips bellows from the bench.

I skate over and try to school my expression. Damn, I shouldn't be laughing. But it felt good to step up for my teammate, for his family. It was the right thing to do in the moment and it's exactly the kind of reaction I would have had if someone said shit about Layla. Or Bella.

Bella! What the hell will she think of my fighting?

Layla used to call me a hothead when we first met but a lot of my reactionary tendencies wore off the longer we were together, especially after we had the twins.

The twins. My stomach sinks and I turn to look in the stands. I'm prepared to meet their horrified or disappointed expressions. Instead, Mason's fist pumping and Milly's bouncing in her seat. She flashes me a thumbs-up. At that, Bella laughs and I smile and we have a quick conversation through our eyes.

Nice hit, hers say.

Thanks. Glad you're not pissed.

Nah, he deserved it.

"Ryan!" Coach snaps again. I turn back to the team, take my scolding in stride, and get back on the ice.

"I fucking hate Edwards," Scotch mutters to me. "Thanks, man."

"Got your back, Scotch," I reply. "Now let's finish this."

The team goes all in for the final period and Noah scores a

buzzer beater, securing our win of 3-2. He flips Edwards off and by the shit-eating grin on his face, I know the win must feel even better.

The team slaps his back in congratulations and we head to the locker room to celebrate. I always hate playing the Eagles. They're notorious for shit talking and last season, Noah got into it with Edwards too.

"Coming to Taps?" Sims asks, as I leave the shower.

"Nah, man. Going home to my family."

"I saw the kids in the booth. What're they gonna think of their old man fighting?"

I snort. "You always protect your team," I tell him. It's something I explained early on to Milly and Mason. While Layla tried to instill them with the good sense to do the right thing, to use their words instead of their fists, I tacked on that sometimes, fists are necessary. That you always protect your own—family, friends, teammates. No matter what.

I mean, I definitely don't *want* my kids to see me fighting. I don't want them to think I'm a hothead either. But I do want them to know the importance of sticking up for the people you care about.

Sims nods slowly, thinking that over. "Good game, Ryan."

"You too, kid." I close my locker and shoulder my bag. "See you tomorrow."

"Have a good one."

I wave to the guys and say my farewells before heading out of the locker room. My grin splits my face the second I spot Bella and the twins.

"Daddy!" my kids shout, racing toward me. Bella hangs back, offering up a shy smile that I return.

My arms wrap around my little rascals who pepper me with questions, mostly about my fight with the Eagles player.

"You busted him good, Dad. His nose bled," Mase says seriously.

Bella frowns over his head but I chuckle, seeing the same disapproving look that Layla used to give.

I drop my bag and squat down in front of my kids. "You should never start a fight," I tell them seriously. "But if one of your people, your friends, your family members, each other"—I gesture between them—"is in trouble and a fight breaks out then—"

"You finish it," my kids say in unison.

"Yep," I agree, grinning at Bella's eye roll. "Just don't let Bella catch you." I stand up.

Bella swats at me and I laugh, catching her hand and pulling her toward me. "You're not going to congratulate me on not getting my ass handed to me? You know, I could have been that Eagles' player's dad," I joke.

She rolls her eyes again but this time, it's playful. She bites back her smile but her eyes blaze with amusement. After weeks of witnessing her hurt, it's pretty damn nice to see merriment in her gaze.

"Some dad, encouraging his kids to fight," she mutters.

I laugh, tossing an arm around her shoulders and steering my little family toward the parking lot. I note the curious way Claire glances at me and the interest in Indy's eyes as I pass them. I tip my chin in their direction and they both wave hello.

For a second, a flare of unease rolls through me. Will they know Bella and I are a thing? Is it too soon? Will they judge it? But then I spot Chloe and the sincere happiness in her expression, the warmth in her hello, eases some of my worry.

Of course my teammates, and their women, will be happy for me. Bella and I aren't doing anything wrong. We're friends. We're more than friends. We're...us. I don't need to label it. I don't need to explain it. I just need to be here for it. For her.

I pull her closer into my side and she shoots me a glance. I smile at her. "Thanks for coming tonight."

"You played one hell of a game," she admits and I laugh.

"HERE." Bella tosses me a bag of frozen peas after tucking the twins into bed.

I lift an eyebrow. "Seriously?"

"Put it on your jaw. Maybe it'll help the swelling."

"He didn't hit that hard."

She snorts and shakes her head. "Please? Do it for me. I hate seeing the bruise." She wrinkles her nose.

My mouth drops open. "Bella Andrews, is that concern I detect in your voice? And here I thought you were disapproving of my parenting style."

"You shouldn't tell the kids to fight," she retorts, plopping down next to me on the couch and kicking her feet up on the coffee table.

"I didn't. I told them to finish it," I explain, holding the peas to my face. Not that I'd admit it but it feels good against my hot skin.

"Same difference. But I get it," she adds after a minute. "You're a team. What did that guy say to Scotch anyway?"

I fill her in on the details, loving how her expression morphs from skeptical to outrage. "He mentioned his daughter? Emmaline?"

I nod. "See, I had to get involved."

"Yes, you did," she agrees, crossing her arms and huffing out a huge breath.

I chuckle. "You're cute when you're heated, Bella."

She looks up quickly, her lips parting.

I know she's thrown by me calling her cute. To be honest, for a second, so am I. But it's the truth. She's adorable, petite and tiny, getting all worked up on behalf of one of my friends.

Her cheeks blush a delicious shade of pink and her eyes widen, shimmering when they're usually clouded over. Bright and open when I'm used to seeing hurt and emptiness.

A thrill rocks through me. I could look away. I could scoot over on the couch. I *should* let her take the lead and set the tone for whatever comes next. Instead, I raise my hand to cup the side of her face. "You're not *just* cute. You're beautiful, Bella."

She runs her tongue across her bottom lip. For a moment, I wonder if she's holding her breath. "James."

"Did you have fun tonight?"

She nods. "I liked watching you play," she admits, leaning the tiniest bit into my touch.

But I feel it and hope flares in my chest. I latch onto that and turn toward her fully. "I liked having you there."

Her hand comes up and wraps around my wrist. I'm not sure whether she means to remove my hand or anchor it but for a breath, we both sit still, neither daring to move a muscle.

"What are we doing?" she whispers.

"I want to kiss you, Bella," I admit the truth. The truth that's been poking at me for weeks. A truth I've tried to deny, tried to overlook, but I don't want to anymore. Instead, I want to taste her lips, run my fingers along the lines of her face, and relive a bit of our night together.

Her inhale is sharp but she doesn't pull away and I take that as a good sign. Her eyes are blown, desire, need, and worry flaring in their depths. "If we do this...it could get messy." Her eyes trail from my eyes to my lips.

She's right. We're about to play with fire. How could we not get burned? But—

"Messy is nothing compared to what we've been through," I mutter back, closing the space between our mouths.

She watches me for a moment before her eyes flutter closed and she lifts her chin the tiniest bit to meet my kiss.

Awareness rushes through me as my mouth hovers a millimeter away from hers. This isn't a drunken night filled with painful memories. This is a step forward, together. My skin tingles and my heart hammers. Am I ready for this? So slow it's almost painful, my lips meet hers. I kiss her slowly. Sweetly. Once. Twice, her bottom lip. Three times.

And then, the sweet morphs into a heat that consumes me.

My hands hold the sides of her face. Her arms snake around my neck and back, pulling me closer. She shifts into my frame until our limbs twist together. I tilt my head and angle hers, deepening our connection, as our mouths meet in an explosion of fireworks.

My eardrums ring and a flush of heat, of desire so potent my hands shake, rushes through me. Wild, uninhibited, desperately, like I'll never get enough.

I want Bella Andrews with a ferocity I've never experienced. Not just her body. Not just tonight. But all of her. Even the broken parts she tries to hide.

It feels like the past two months have been one long stretch of foreplay, culminating in this grand finale. Our coming together.

Our tongues duel. Bella moves up on her knees, swinging a leg over my lap and straddling me. I groan as she lowers herself, grinding against my rock-hard length. My hands drop to her waist, squeezing and kneading her skin.

She moans, pressing her breasts into my chest as I kiss her long and hard.

"Daddy!" Milly shrieks.

We both break apart, panting. Bella's eyes are hazy, clouded over with a sheen of lust. I'm sure mine look the same.

"Bella!" Milly hollers again.

"Shit," I mutter, knowing from her voice that she's had a nightmare. "I'm right here, Milly," I holler, gently placing Bella next to me on the couch. Uncertainty flares in her eyes and I shake my head. "I'll be right back, Bella. But don't do that."

"Do what?" She frowns.

"Second-guess this. It's for real," I tell her before jogging up the stairs to calm Milly.

After I settle my daughter, I return to an empty living room. For a second, a swell of disbelief, followed by anger, rushes through me. Did she try to ghost me again, in my own home? But then I hear Bella humming in the kitchen.

I enter and relax when I see her pouring two mugs of tea.

She looks up and smiles. "It's not exactly hot and heavy but…tea?"

I dip my head. "Please." I sit at the kitchen island. "I've never met anyone like you, Bella Andrews."

"Back at ya, James Ryan." She places a mug in front of me.

I take a sip, wincing when it burns my tongue.

"James?"

"Hm?" I look up.

"What do we do now?"

"What do you mean?"

"Well, you kissed me…"

"I plan to do it again," I tell her the truth.

Amusement laced with excitement flares across her face. She dips her head for a moment, biting her bottom lip, and I can tell she's trying to school her expression. Her sweetness makes me smile. I move my mug over, waiting for her to say something.

"That right?" she says finally and I laugh.

"Bella, we're doing it all backwards. We slept together, live together, and now had our first real kiss."

She laughs with me. "True. But, if I'm being honest, doing things in the right order didn't exactly work out for me." She smiles but it fades and she looks down, toying with the handle of her mug. She raises her head, her voice hesitant. "What do you think this is?"

I look at her for a long beat, noting the way her hands fidget, the way she can't meet my eyes. She's scared of taking this next step and I don't blame her, I'm scared too. Still, excitement thrums through my veins and for a moment, I embrace the recklessness that courses through me. Maybe I don't want to know what comes next. Maybe I like the anticipation, the adventure, of *not* knowing. "Real," I say finally. "Whatever happens or doesn't, this is real, Bella."

She grins at my answer. Reaching over, she laces our fingers together and squeezes. "For me too, James."

"Good." I smile back before a thought zips through my mind. In the past, I wouldn't voice it but now, I'm too old, experienced too much, to not be upfront. "But please don't ever ghost me again, Bella. If you're unsure of something or worried, just… talk to me." I try to keep my voice light but I know from her expression that she hears the truth, the need for honesty, in my tone.

She leans forward and brushes a kiss over my lips. "Okay."

"Okay."

CHAPTER 10
BELLA

For an independent woman in my thirties, with a career caring for children, I shouldn't be sneaking around with the boss. But I so am. And it is so hot.

I fancy myself a heroine in a historical romance as things with James heat up from sweet flirtation and witty banter to stolen glances, desperate touches, and kisses that make my heart race.

Since both James and I are hesitant to confide our budding relationship status to the twins, finding time to be together proves difficult. But after a week of James traveling for hockey, of sneaking kisses that turn steamy *real* fast, I'm desperate for some extra alone time with my guy.

Luckily, Maia offers to take the twins for a sleepover on Friday night.

"I'm dropping them off," he tells me, wagging his eyebrows.

"Now?" I check my watch. "It's only 4 p.m."

"Hey, Maia said to drop them whenever." He holds up a hand and I snort.

"I'm sure she didn't mean directly from school."

He shrugs and bellows up the stairs for the twins to

change out of their school clothes and pack a bag for a slumber party at their favorite aunt's house. Their elated shrieks makes me feel a little less guilty that James and I are desperate to shlep them off and have some alone time.

"We're really going out?" I ask, making sure James isn't having cold feet about being seen out together. In public. Where anyone can snap a photo and the social media trolls can pick apart that he's dating his nanny. Or worse, that he didn't wait enough time before falling into a relationship.

Sigh. Thinking of all the ways our new thing could be misconstrued—and ruined before it even has a chance to blossom—fills me with unease. I'm about to suggest that we just stay in and order takeout when James wraps his arm around my waist and tugs me flush against him. His hand rests above the swell of my ass as he looks down, studying me.

"We're going out, Bella. I'm going to take the kids so you can do…whatever it is girls do to get ready—"

I chuckle.

"And have time to yourself before a date. A real date with a sexy hockey player who's pretty taken with this badass chick—"

"Chick?"

He kisses the tip of my nose and smacks my ass. "Go take a shower. I'll pick you up at 6 p.m."

I tilt my head back and laugh, loving the way his eyes lighten at the sound.

"I'll be ready," I promise.

He nods, his gaze growing serious. "See you in a bit, babe."

"Get out of here." I shoo him toward the front door as the twins race down the stairs.

"'Bye, Bells!" Mason zooms past me. Milly smiles and waves over her shoulder.

"See you guys tomorrow," I call after them as they bolt through the front door and out to the car.

"Two hours." James points at me.

I blow him a playful kiss and he leaves.

Once the car pulls out of the driveway, I squeal. I haven't had a real date in years. Too many of them to count. Excitement rushes through me as I take the stairs and dial Selina.

"Hello?" she answers.

"I'm going on a date."

"Oh my God. Seriously?" she screeches.

"Yes!"

"With your boss?"

"Don't say it like that."

"But it is like that," she retorts. "Well, maybe not, since you boned him—"

"Ew."

"Before you worked for him. Okay, I'm on board."

"Gee, thanks."

"What are you wearing?" She changes topics to the more important matter at hand.

"That's why I'm calling you, Lina. I haven't done this in years."

"Gotten dressed?"

"Gone out," I clarify.

I can hear her smile through the line. "I got you, Bells. I was just messing with you. I'm happy you're going out with James."

"Thanks."

"You deserve this. It's been too damn long since you've gotten any."

I groan, lifting my hand to my forehead. Why the hell did I call Selina? Because she gives better fashion advice than Colton. Barely.

"I was starting to worry that your vagina had shriveled up

and died," she continues. "That's sad for a thirty-two-year-old. You need tonight. You need hot dad dick."

I cough, holding the phone away from my ear and squinting at it as if that will help clarify why Lina has no filter. Still, she's my oldest friend and I love her for always having my back.

"Okay." I clear my throat. "An outfit?"

"Right." She switches gears, her voice growing serious. "Wear that black long-sleeve dress with the cutout in the back."

"I haven't worn that in ages! It barely covers my ass."

"All the more reason to wear it. I know you have black tights on hand. Pair that with

your camel cashmere coat, the one with the thick sash. Oh, and definitely gold jewelry."

I mentally breathe a sigh of relief that I have all the things. "Got it. Okay, thanks."

"Where's he taking you?"

"I don't know. Out to dinner somewhere."

Selina whistles. "This is pretty serious, Bells. For him to take you out in the city, where anyone can take a pic and blow up what you've guys got going on…that's big."

"Right?" I agree, voicing my concern aloud. "Do you think it's too soon?"

"No way," she answers immediately. "There's no rulebook for things like this."

"But there's a lot of judgement when—"

"People are always going to judge. And talk. And voice their opinions to anyone who will listen. But, be honest, whose opinions really matter to you?"

"My parents and Colton. You. James."

"Okay. Do you think any of the above are going to have anything to say about you and the hockey hunk dating?"

"No."

"Exactly. So what are you really worried about?" Selina asks.

"I just don't want him to get slammed with a bunch of negative press. He's still working through Layla's death and things are so good between us right now. I guess I just don't want to rock the boat."

Selina's quiet for a moment. "Boats are meant to be rocked."

I roll my eyes.

"No, but seriously? It will never be a good time. No matter when you and James get together, someone will have something to say. That's just the way it is. Do you think he's having the same concerns?"

I think about the past week and all the ways James showed up for me. "No."

"Then don't worry about it, Bells. You deserve this. You've been through a lot and you finally have a good guy, no, a great guy, who understands all the grief and loss you've experienced. More than that, he respects the hell out of you for it. Are you really willing to pull back on that because strangers are gonna gossip?"

"No," I say decisively. The thought of not exploring what's between James and me is a hell of a lot more stressful than the idea of being gossip fodder for a week or two. "You sound like Dr. C," I add, recalling how he brought up similar questions during yesterday's session.

She cheers at this. "I'm going to start charging you."

I laugh.

"I'm happy for you, Bells! Now go shower and get dressed. You've got a hot date with a hockey heartthrob."

This time, I smile for real. "Okay. Thanks, Lina."

"Anytime, babe. Call me tomorrow and tell me all about it. Especially the sex and—"

"Good night, Selina."

She chuckles. "Night, Bells."

After I hang up, I take a quick shower. When I realize the time, I race through drying my hair, keeping it casual enough to let the natural wave come through. Then, I apply my makeup, sticking to nudes and peaches for a natural, dewy look that makes me look great but doesn't scream trying-too-hard. I'm just zipping up my boots when the doorbell rings.

I grin, already liking the start of our date. I grab my purse and head downstairs, taking a deep breath before pulling the front door open.

My ability to breathe fails me. Too dramatic? Probably.

But for a woman who hasn't had a man look at her like she's everything he's ever wanted in more than three years, the intensity in James's eyes hits me like a lightning bolt.

I'm not sure where he changed but the man who left an hour ago rocking sweats and a hoodie is gone. In his place is a sexy, smoldering man in dark wash jeans, a black trench coat, with a hint of his white collared shirt peeking through. A slight stubble coats his jawline and his eyes flicker with heat, all amber and honey.

I'm so taken aback by his appearance—the sexy and the smolder—and the fact that he rang his own doorbell to notice the flowers in his hand until he holds them out. My chest feels melty at the thought he's put into this evening.

"Thank you." I grin, taking the flowers and inhaling. "These are beautiful."

"You're beautiful, Bella," he says solemnly. It's not a line. It's not cheesy. It's his truth and I bask in it, feeling prettier than I have in a long time.

I step back and make room for him to enter. "You didn't have to ring the bell."

"Of course I did. It's our first date."

I smile, biting my lip. "Let me put these in water," I say, raising the bouquet of flowers.

James follows me into his kitchen, not the least bit surprised that I know where the vase is. I fill it, drop in the flowers, and place it in the center of the dining table. He watches me the entire time, his eyes drinking me in like his favorite whiskey. With appreciation, with gratitude, with *need*.

"You ready for dinner?" he asks, holding out his hand.

"Early bird special," I joke, glancing at the clock.

He chuckles. "Got a whole night planned."

I soften toward him, truly touched by his thoughtfulness. I take his hand and thread our fingers together. "Dinner sounds perfect."

"Good." He leads me toward the door.

"Where are we headed?"

"Carter's."

"The steakhouse?" My eyes widen, my heart lurching.

He nods.

It's definitely fancy for a first date. Carter's is one of the best, most exclusive steakhouses in Boston. It's actually where Jerry proposed to me and for a second, that image fills my mind.

"What? Don't tell me you recently became a vegetarian?" James jokes, his voice light, his expression serious.

I shake my head, forcing a smile. "It's not that."

His hand drops away from the doorknob and he turns me, until my back is pressed against the door and he's standing in front of me. His hands plant against the door on either side of my body and he dips forward, his words a whisper. "Then what it is, Bella?"

I swallow, my heart rate increasing, my body naturally moving toward James's, to close the space between us. "It's just, it's where Jerry proposed," I admit. "But I don't want you to feel weird or uncomfortable about it," I blurt out, internally cringing for being so open and ruining the nice dinner James planned.

Tenderness sweeps his expression even though his eyes harden for a beat. He clears his throat and shakes his head, the tip of his nose nearly grazing mine. "I can change the reservation no problem if you want to go somewhere else. I'm not trying to make this difficult for you."

"You're not," I tell him truthfully. "You're making it too good. Ruining all future first dates." *Shit. Stop talking, Isabella Andrews.*

The corners of James's mouth turn up. "How nervous are you?"

"Extremely nervous," I rattle on.

"Why?" His one hand moves to my hip, sliding up to rest in the dip of my waist.

"Because I don't want to ruin this with you. And I haven't done this in a long time. And I'm not sure I know how to anymore."

"You're doing great, baby." He drops his head, pressing a kiss to the side of my neck. It sends a blanket of goosebumps over my skin and I gasp. "Relax, Bella," James murmurs. "Tell me more. Just keep talking."

"I want to go to Carter's with you," I admit. "I want to do all the things you planned. It's just weird, sometimes, having had certain experiences already with someone else. And I don't know what to make of that."

James pulls back and his eyes search mine. "Do you regret them? The past experiences?"

I shake my head slowly. How can I regret them? Being with Jerry, even though it ended awfully, still brought me Miles.

I expect James to be put off but instead, he smiles. "Good. I don't either. I have no regrets about my past, Bella. But I also don't want to have regrets about my present. I want to try this with you."

I bite my bottom lip, losing myself in his eyes. "Me too."

"So we go slow. We do this at our pace, at what we're comfortable with. We just need to communicate, babe. You can tell me anything; you're not going to scare me off and you're not going to offend me. Our situation, it's unique. And we're both still working through a lot of painful things." His hand finds mine once more. "But I want you."

"Me too, James. More than you know," I admit, my body relaxing under his touch, my mind clearing from his words.

"Oh, I have a pretty good idea." His eyes flash and I smile. My pelvis tilts upward to meet his and I almost groan at the contact. He's already hard, wanting me the same way I want him.

"Take me to dinner first," I joke.

But he doesn't laugh. "Of course, Bella. The night is young." With that, James presses a kiss to my mouth. It's sensual, soulful, and I dive just a little bit deeper into this thing between us.

"We keep doing this in the wrong order," I murmur when he pulls back.

He smirks, shaking his head again. "Nah, we're just doing it in our order."

"Yeah," I agree, liking the sound of that.

I step out of the house with James and we walk to his SUV. By the time I click in my seat belt, all of my reservations have dissipated. I no longer care what anyone except me and the man sitting next to me thinks. Our relationship is ours and we're going to grow it the best way we can. Together.

CHAPTER 11
JAMES

I'm out of my element with Bella Andrews. Not because she's drop-dead gorgeous. Or because she's intelligent, compassionate, and great with my kids.

Nope. I'm out of my league because being with her makes me feel whole again. She rearranges my broken into a mosaic that's healing. Her presence both roots me when I feel uncentered and injects a lightness into the heavy my life has become. In a way, she found me, and reminded me of the man I used to be. The teammate I was before. The father I always swore I'd grow into.

She smiles at me across the table at Carter's and my chest twists, a complicated tornado of emotions. Does desiring Bella the way I am lessen my commitment to Layla? Am I ready for this next step? If we take it, is it too soon? Does Bella look at me and see a new future? Or a distraction from her painful past?

"You look very serious," she comments, calling me out.

I smile and lift my wine glass. "I'm just thinking."

"About?"

"Pretty heavy stuff for a first real date."

She laughs, the sound tugging at my heartstrings. It's the

same sweet music of that first night, easy and melodic. "Good thing we've done everything backwards so you can confide in me instead of keeping it all bottled up." She lifts an eyebrow in challenge and relief rolls through me.

She's right. Of course she is.

I lean forward, my hand reaching for hers as I lower my voice. "Sometimes, it scares me. How much I feel for you. It just seems…" I trail off, trying to organize my thoughts so I can explain them coherently.

"Too much too soon," Bella supplies.

"Yes," I breathe out. "I don't want to feel like this." I press a hand against my chest. "Guilty and worried and anticipating the worst. Because when I'm with you, Bella, you make me feel like *me* again."

She bites her bottom lip, tilting her head to study me. "You feel guilty because of Layla?"

I nod slowly, hating that I'm admitting this to her. Hating that I even feel this way. It's been over a year and while Layla was my partner in all things and I loved her with every fiber in my being, I'm finally realizing there's enough room in my life, in my heart, to love Bella just as ferociously. Is that what this is? Love?

The thought should scare me. Instead, another piece seems to click into place and I feel…settled.

"Why the worry?" she asks.

I brush my thumb over the back of her hand. "Things happened so quickly between us. We're both unpacking a lot of hurt, a lot of feelings. Sometimes I don't know if we're building something meant to last, if you even want that, or if it's just for this phase of our lives. If we found each other at a moment when we need each other the most."

Bella lets out a sigh and I realize she was holding her breath. "Does it matter? If we end up growing old together or if we're just helping each other get to the next level of healing?"

My heart beats frantically as a wave of terror grips me. Does it matter? "Kind of," I admit. Staring straight into her deep blue eyes, I say, "I'm falling for you, Bella. It's come out of left field and I didn't plan it but there it is. I'm in so deep with you and I'm terrified you don't feel the same."

Surprise ripples across her expression as she leans forward, our faces only inches apart, our voices hushed. The din of Carter's fades away as I study Bella. The longing in her expression, the lick of heat in her eyes, the purse of her lips. What is she thinking? Is she happy? Excited? Or did I scare her away?

Her fingers tighten around mine. "James," her voice is quiet and a sinking sensation settles in the pit of my stomach. Dammit. I was too forward, too brazen, too—

"I'm falling for you too." Her voice is barely more than a whisper, and I have to lean even closer, my ears straining, to make sure I heard what I think I heard.

"You are?"

She nods, the sweetest smile curling her lips. "I never thought I'd find this again." She gestures between us. "I never thought I'd ever meet anyone who would look at me and not see a train wreck." Tears swell in her eyes and my heart breaks a little at all the hurt she's endured, at all the pain her ex-husband piled on top.

"You're not a train wreck, baby. You're real, Bella, and trust me when I say this, real is the sexiest damn thing a woman could ever be."

She smiles even as a tear rolls down her cheek. "I'm scared too. It's like always waiting for the other shoe to drop. Because this, with you, it seems—"

"Too good to be true."

"Too much too soon," she repeats.

"But you want this? With me?" I press for the clarification. Are we on the same page? Are we moving in the same direction? God, I hope so.

"I want this with you. All of it and all of you for all the days," she murmurs, as clear a declaration as I've ever heard. Hope replaces my concern, filling me back up with a happiness I only seem to feel with Bella.

"Good," I say. My grin splits my face and I can't stop it. I don't want to. "I know I did it all wrong with you, Bella, but I want this too."

"You did it all right," she says. "We were never going to have the traditional, do it in the right order, check all the boxes, kind of romance, James. We've both been through too much. We've both been holding ourselves back from happiness for too long."

Her words pack a powerful punch because, is that what I've been doing? I think back to the past year, to my teammates' subtle attempts to drag me out, to Maia's not-so-subtle demands to keep living. Yes, I suppose I have been denying myself happiness because when I felt it, the *guilt* wrecked me. "You make me happy again, Bella. I don't know what the future holds for us. I don't even know where we go from here. All I know is that when I'm with you, I feel happy. And I haven't felt that in a long time."

She presses forward and places a kiss against my mouth. "I feel the same, James. Let's just, do us."

"Do us," I agree, liking the sound of that. With Bella, there's no pressure. There's no checklist or mind games. There's just us, two imperfect individuals, trying to find our way to a better tomorrow.

Together.

"Have you had a chance to look at the menu?" Our server appears at the end of our table and Bella blushes.

I squeeze her hand once before releasing her fingers and easing back in my seat. "Yes," I say to the server. "Thanks."

Bella and I order our steak dinners. Now that the serious conversation, the tough topics, that have been lingering in my mind all week are settled, it's easy for me to relax. To embrace this happiness I've been denying myself.

"To you, Bella Andrews. You saved me." I lift my wine glass in her direction.

She clinks her glass against mine and grins. "You saved me too, James."

We drink to each other and to our blossoming relationship. Once our entrees arrive, we settle into a natural conversation. We talk about the twins, about hockey, about Bella's career trajectory and future opportunities as a children's therapist.

We share funny stories of our friends and siblings. We laugh easily, smile constantly, and after a round of cocktails and dessert, are surprised that we've been in Carter's for nearly four hours.

As we exit the restaurant, I reach for Bella's hand like I've been doing it for years. "Ready to go home?"

She glances up, her eyes bright. She winks saucily and I chuckle. "I've been ready for a while now, James."

My chuckle is cut short as heat flares in her eyes. I feel it race through my body like a live wire. "Me too. Come on." I tug on her hand and we run through the parking lot to my SUV.

We're both laughing and breathless by the time we reach it.

I grin at her and she smiles at me and for a snapshot, the whole world looks clear again. I'm right where I'm supposed to be, with the right woman by my side.

I help Bella into the car and slide behind the wheel, suddenly desperate to get home.

HER EYES FLARE as she eases back against my bed. It's not the first time Bella's been in my bedroom but it's the first time I've had her in my bed and I take a moment to appreciate that.

"You're gorgeous." I reach for her, hooking my palm around the back of her ankle so I can unzip the killer boots she's rocking. When I first saw her in them, I had to stifle back my groan. But after a night of such honest conversation, and a few drinks, I take my time to admire every inch of her.

I pull the zipper down slowly as Bella perches up on her elbows, watching me. Her gaze darkens and she bites her bottom lip. Jesus, she's sexy without even trying.

When her boots drop to the floor, I reach for her waistline and roll her tights down her legs until she's clad in a black scrap of lace and a black dress that's hiked up around her hips.

"Your turn," she murmurs.

I smirk, kicking off my shoes and popping the button on my jeans while she shifts onto her knees to unbutton my shirt. When my shirt floats to the floor, she releases a shaky exhale. I shed my jeans next and she tugs her dress over her head, discarding it. When we're both in our underwear, we drink each other in.

It's different than our first night. That night, everything was desperate and a little bit clumsy. Hot with a current of neediness. Tonight, we move slower. We savor and linger, letting our eyes wander, allowing our touches to soak up the moment.

Bella reaches for me and I lean forward, kneeling on the bed until she falls back beneath me and I hover over her frame. Her dark hair spills around her face like a fan, like a halo, lighting up my personal angel. The one who brought me back from the brink, the one who's made me whole again.

She tips her chin up, her eyes boring into mine. I lower slowly, my lips meeting hers in the sweetest of kisses. Her knees drop open and I settle in between her thighs, my hand swiping up her side to wrap around her breast. It's the perfect size for my palm and as I squeeze and touch, she deepens our kiss, arching up into me.

Fuck, it's heady. Being with Bella, having these sensations coursing through my body, having these feelings unraveling in my chest. I drop even lower, my tongue slipping in between her lips and dancing with hers. Her hips tilt upward to greet mine and her core presses firmly against my dick, already rock hard and desperate to get inside of her.

She moans, I groan, and our languid pace picks up. I kiss a trail down the column of her neck, loving it when her fingers grip my hair and tug. I yank down the cup of her bra, my mouth watering at the rosy pink of her nipple. I pull her breast into my mouth and suck, getting buzzed off her sweetness. Her hand grips the back of my head, pressing me even closer as I lave her breasts with attention.

With a quick flick, I pop her bra open and pull it off, leaning back so I can take her in. Jesus, she's perfect. Pert, round breasts, her nipples pointing straight at me, begging to be touched. Her slim waist flares into hips I want to sink my fingers into. And her legs, long and lean, wrap around my lower back, filling my head with all sorts of dirty images. Desperate scenarios. I peel her panties off next, unhitching her legs just long enough to remove the lace.

"Want you, James."

"Need you, Bella," I tell her the truth. "Need you to come for me first." I lower myself once more, snaking down her body. My fingers trail over her skin, featherlight, as I stroke her. My lips blaze a trail of heat until my head is in between her thighs. I part her core with my tongue, my hands settling on her inner thighs and prying them open.

She drops back, arching her back and moaning aloud. "Oh God, James."

I love the need in her voice. I love that I'm the one making her thighs tighten up, causing her breathing to intensify.

"That's it, Bella," I blow against her sensitive flesh. I drag my tongue through her folds, slowly, savoring the taste of her sweetness against my tongue. She glistens for me, wet and begging, and when she groans again, I settle into a rhythm. My mouth works her over as my fingers plunge into her heat. Bella cries out and I quicken the pace. It doesn't take long for her to shatter, breaking apart in my hands, against my lips, right before my eyes in the most beautiful display of pleasure I've ever witnessed.

Bella is uninhibited, unashamed, and I fucking revel in it.

"Oh God, James," she says again.

I love the sound of my name on her lips, in that voice. I lose my boxer briefs and grip my dick. It's already pulsing in my hand as I slide my hand over my shaft twice, pumping it slowly. Bella's eyes widen and nearly roll back in her head as I drag the tip through her wetness, teasing her.

"Please, James. I need you," she says, her voice tight and strained.

I reach into my bedside drawer and grab a condom from a box that Panda stashed in my hockey bag. At the time, I was pissed at him for being so damn insensitive but now, I could hug him for having some responsible foresight.

I roll it on, noting the way Bella watches intently, her face glowing, her teeth nibbling her bottom lip. When I'm fully sheathed, I line myself up at her entrance. "Ready?"

She flops back again, her eyes finding mine. "Yes, please."

I grin. "You're a good girl, Bella Andrews." I push to enter her, practically seeing stars. "And so fucking tight. Wet."

"For you," she murmurs, her hands covering her breasts.

"Fuck," I swear as she plays with her nipples, rolling them between her fingers as I plunge forward.

Once I'm all the way in, I take a deep breath, steadying my hammering heart rate. Bella moans again and I pray to Jesus that I can last long enough because damn, having her writhing below me is already more than I bargained for. Other than the night after Taps, with Bella, I haven't been with a woman since Layla.

In this moment, it all seems to catch up with me because I'm suddenly desperate, my body burning from the inside out for her touch. For her sweetness. For *her*.

I slide in and out several times before increasing the tempo. Bella and I fall into a rhythm, her meeting my thrusts, me working her over steadily.

"Yes, James. Right there," she cries out, her fingernails digging into my hip, her thighs clenching.

I grip the headboard with one hand as I pound into her, my eyes trained on her face. I take in every expression that flits across her face and let it fuel me, fill me up with so much light and goodness, that when we break apart, her first and me a few seconds later, my body feels like air and my mind settles.

Completely and totally.

I collapse forward and roll Bella in my arms. We're both panting, our limbs in a complicated tangle we're both too drained to work out.

"That was incredible," she says.

"You're incredible, Bella. Fuck, you're, you're everything." I kiss her ear, pulling her closer against my chest.

She wraps her arms around mine, gathering our hands against her hot skin. "I'm falling for you, James." She shifts slightly, just so our eyes can meet. "Don't let me hit the ground, okay?"

The vulnerability in her eyes undoes me, the thread of fear in her voice twists something deep inside my soul. I know the courage it takes to open yourself up again after a devastating loss. I know the type of trust it takes to do what we just did and be sincere about it. I would never put Bella in a position to question if this, us, is a mistake.

"Never, baby," I promise, dropping my lips to hers. I kiss her slowly, soulfully, with promises and intentions and plans for a future I've been too scared to envision.

She turns in my arms, until our chests our pressed together, our heartbeats thrumming in unison. In an instant, I harden against her leg and she giggles against my lips. I reach for her, sliding my fingers over her center. "You're wet again."

"And you're hard," she replies.

"So fucking hard for you," I admit.

Her arms snake around my neck and she pulls me into her embrace, kissing me deeply. "Let's do that again, James."

I laugh softly and kiss her back. "Anytime you want, Bella. Every time." I roll her again, until I'm on my back and she's perched above me. Her eyes haze over with lust, her hair falls around her shoulders, wild and tangled. She grips my shoulders as my hands find her hips.

"Condom," she tells me and I reach for a new one and pass it to her.

I smirk as she rips it open with her teeth, skillfully cleaning me up and rolling on a fresh condom. Then, she lowers herself over me with painstaking slowness that has my eyes rolling back in my head.

"This time, it's my turn," she says saucily.

"Fuck yeah," I agree, turning myself over to Bella's touch.

She rides me hard and deep and I love every second of it.

CHAPTER 12
BELLA

Waking up in James's arms is like a half-forgotten dream. One I want to sink back into and play out until its conclusion. His arms envelop me, his scent soothing. The breath on the back of my neck tickles and the weight of his hand against my stomach roots me to this moment.

For the first time in years, I haven't woken up before dawn to run. This morning, I didn't need to. My body doesn't feel restless and antsy. My mind is calm and quiet. It's an achievement I've been striving for for a long time and I savor the feeling.

Stretching slowly, I feel a delicious soreness that fills my head with images from last night. The heat in James's eyes when he tucked a strand of hair behind my ear, the way his lips parted when he entered me for the first time, the words he murmured at Carter's. *I'm falling for you, Bella.*

A smile skates across my lips and I snuggle deeper into his embrace.

They're words I never thought I'd hear again, words I knew better than to wish for. Who could love a half-woman like me? Broken, scarred, and desperate to both live in and never return to the past.

I'm falling for you, Bella.

But God, do those words fill me with a lightness that makes me feel like I'm floating. On the other side of tragedy, I also know better than to take those words for granted. Nothing in this world is a given and when you find a person, a someone, who understands the darkest parts of your soul and doesn't try to change them, doesn't try to change *you*, it's nothing short of a miracle. After the past few years, I can use a miracle and I'm thankful mine appeared in the form of James Ryan.

I turn slowly, careful not to wake him. When our noses are nearly touching, I smile again, studying his face. Stubble shadows his jawline and a slight whistle rings out on his exhales. His eyebrows are dark and thick, his mouth lush, the cleft in his chin sexy. In sleep, he's almost too pretty to be the formidable, serious defenseman he's known as.

"You're staring," he murmurs, his voice thick with sleep.

"Your eyes are still closed," I reply, grinning, because I can't *not* smile when I'm around him.

His eyes flutter open and his lips curl. "I could feel you."

"Really?" I ask, skeptically.

He nods, kissing the tip of my nose. "For a second, I thought I dreamed it all."

"I know what you mean."

"But then I started to wake up and I could feel your soft skin." He swipes his fingers over the small of my back. "Your warmth"—he dips his head closer to mine—"and I just knew you were watching me. Creeper."

I chuckle, shaking my head. "I was admiring you."

He meets my gaze, his smile lopsided. "Well in that case…" He presses even closer and I can feel the length of him against my thigh.

My hand moves lower and I drag my fingers up his shaft.

"Christ," he murmurs. "You're too good to be true, Bella."

I shift my weight so I can press myself even closer to him,

skin to skin, heat to heat. "I'm not taking any of this for granted." I roll on top of him, straddling his waist.

He swears softly, his eyes hazy with lust and sleep and want. "Trust me, baby. Neither am I."

"Good." I flip my hair over my shoulder and lower my face to his, kissing him slowly, before trailing down his body. His neck, his muscular chest, his tight abs.

James's fingers find my hair and tangle there, alternating between sharp tugs and sweet brushes. His breathing increases, his limbs locking down. I love that I can affect him like this. His reaction fuels me, filling me with a brazenness, a confidence, I haven't leaned into in a long time. I feel sexy, desired, *wanted*.

By the time my lips close around him, he's desperately hard with need and I'm nearly panting with want. I want to make him feel good, I want to light him up, I want to claim him. The same way he claimed me—body, heart, and soul.

We spend the early morning hours wrapped up in sheets, caged in by pillows, lost to the world outside of James's bedroom. It's perfect and I revel in every sweet second of it.

"PANCAKES OR WAFFLES?" he asks, handing me a mug of coffee.

I'm sitting on the kitchen island, one of James's T-shirts hanging off my shoulder. "Waffles. You?"

"Same. Ocean or Lake?"

"Ocean."

"Lake."

"No!" I groan. "Really?"

He snorts, slipping onto a barstool. "What's wrong with the lake?"

"I just feel like beach people are my people."

James rolls his eyes.

"Lakes have too many flies," I point out.

"The ocean is too unpredictable."

"It's fun!" I retort, taking a sip of my coffee. "City or country?"

"Country."

I gasp.

"What?" James asks, his eyes wide with amusement.

"We have nothing in common."

"You prefer the city?" He gapes.

"Any day of the week."

"Why?"

"It's…people. Life."

"Nature is life."

"Oh no, I forgot you guys camp," I mutter.

He swears. "You don't like camping?"

"I've never been."

James groans. "Bella, you haven't been living."

"I beg to differ." I point at him. "Going off into the middle of nowhere—"

"National parks aren't nowhere."

"You're going to make me camp, aren't you?"

His eyes dance. "And fish."

I laugh. "Do the twins really like all these activities?"

"They do."

I sigh. "Then I'll give it a try. But"—I point at him—"I'm not sleeping in a tent. And there needs to be bathrooms. Real ones, not a hole in the ground."

James snickers, shaking his head at me. "This summer, we're going camping, baby. Swimming in the lake at dawn and hiking at dusk."

I make a face but inside, I'm excited. As much as I'm not a nature girl—and I'm one hundred percent not, unless it's the artificial nature of five-star hotels—I want to camp with

James. Just because of how excited he looks at the prospect of introducing me to it. Because of how much he seems to truly enjoy it.

I want to do something I've avoided for years because it's important to him. If that's not love, then I don't know what is. Besides, if he's talking summer, he's making plans for our future. Together.

I hide my smile behind my coffee mug. "I'm in."

His eyes flick up to mine and hold. "Me too."

I clink my coffee mug against his and take a sip, still fighting the smile on my lips.

Because even though we both agreed to camping, we really agreed to a hell of a lot more than that. We agreed to the future.

"SO, YOU'RE DATING," Dr. Carlisle concludes during our session.

I smirk. "I have a boyfriend, Dr. C," I joke and he cracks a smile, his eyes warm.

"I'm happy for you, Bella. This is a big step. Huge, really."

"Yeah. But it doesn't feel that way. It feels more natural, like an organic extension of everything we've been through, shared together."

Dr. C nods. "And Milly and Mason? How do they feel about it?"

Here, I falter, biting my bottom lip.

"Ah," Dr. C surmises. "Are you planning to tell them?"

"It's kind of new…" I sigh. "But yes, I'd like to tell them. Of course I don't want to keep James and me a secret. Because we're not doing anything wrong."

Dr. Carlisle raises an eyebrow with an *are-you-seriously-asking-my-permission* quirk to it. "Bella, there's no right or wrong in these situations. Grief and loss affect people differently and how they process, heal, and move forward happens incrementally. With different time frames. Do you feel like you're doing something wrong?"

"No."

"Are you worried about what Milly and Mason will think?"

I nod, picking at a hangnail. "I don't want them to think I'm trying to take their mother's place."

"Then you need to explain that to them and *show* them. Continue to honor their mother the way you have been. Allow them to feel the way they feel and help them navigate the new feelings that may arise if your presence in their life takes on a different meaning. Or title."

"Yes, you're right. I need to talk to James about it. Make sure he wants to tell them too, figure out how…it's just, it's so new and fragile and I don't want to mess things up."

"If having honest conversations messes things up, then is this really the type of relationship you want?" Dr. C poses wryly.

I roll my eyes and shake my head. "You got me there, Doc."

He smirks. "Have you given any more thought to our discussion regarding family? How you envision creating or being part of a family?"

I nod slowly. "I have. To be honest, I can see myself being part of the Ryans. I have since the beginning, since before James and I even started…this." I gesture around the room. "I just, I want to belong to something larger than myself. I want to have those emotional connections and tight unit where we know we can count on each other for anything. And yeah, I'd still like to have a baby one day. I'd love to be pregnant again, to feel those little kicks. But it's not a deal breaker. You were right; there are a lot of ways to make a family. Sometimes, I get so caught up on what I lost that it's hard to imagine anything than the life I was supposed to have."

"That makes a lot of sense, Bella. I'm glad you're clarifying things for yourself. And it's normal to cling to what was, to what you once thought would be. But maybe, this is the life you're meant to have."

"Yeah," I agree, smiling. "Maybe it is."

I wrap up my session with Dr. Carlisle, his words rolling through my mind. Since moving in with the Ryans, I feel a lot more settled in my life, in my future. My conversations with Dr. C have taken on a glimmer of hope, of possibility, when they used to be firmly rooted in getting through the day. I'm proud of the progress I'm making and I say as much to my parents when I call them next.

After our chat, I check in with my brother. Colton is four years older than me but one would guess fourteen with how much he worries about me.

After everything that happened with Jerry, Colton stepped up in a big way. He took me to grief counseling, where I first connected with Dr. Carlisle. Colton encouraged me to go back to school, to pursue a career in psychology, even as I clung to the life I already knew: nanny-ing. The more I clung to my past, to the world I recognized, the more he tried to lend his support. His relationship with his long-time girlfriend suffered, until they broke up. He spent his summers in Boston with my parents, even though he was a teacher in Maryland. Colton is more than my brother, he's my very first friend. My day one. And as much as I miss him, it's a relief that after the first year of losing Miles, my brother resumed his own life.

Having him pause his life to support mine as it crumbled was the most thoughtful thing he could have done. But his actions left me reeling with guilt on top of the emotional cocktail already dictating my days.

"You sound good," he tells me after we've chatted for a few minutes.

"I'm doing well," I reply honestly.

"And this new family? The Ryans?"

"They're pretty great. James and I hit it off and the twins are amazing."

"What about the mom?" Colton asks.

I work a swallow. "She passed. Almost two years ago."

My brother swears, his tone heavy with sorrow. "I'm sorry to hear that."

"It's been really hard for them."

"Are you sure it's not too much for you?" Colt asks, always worrying about me.

"I'm sure. If anything, connecting with James, talking with Milly and Mason, it's been…healing. Kind of cathartic. I've been able to take a step back from my own grief and support them. It's going to sound silly but we've all been…helping each other heal. Even Dr. Carlisle is happy with my progress."

My brother is quiet for a few moments and I know he's trying to read between the lines, fill in the gaps of what I'm *not* saying. But no way in hell am I telling my brother that I'm sleeping with my employer so I remain silent until he sighs. "Good. That's good, Bells. As long as you're happy…"

"I am. Now, tell me about you. What's going on in your life?"

As my brother fills me in on a woman he recently started dating, the kids in his tenth-grade literature class, and some of the things his buddies from college are up to, I kick back in a chair and relax.

Glancing around the living room, I feel settled. Relaxed and at ease in a way I haven't in a long time. Being here, with the Ryans, feels *right*. It's as if things clicked into place and I'm not running anymore. Instead, I'm staying and staying feels pretty fantastic.

JAMES ORDERS in Thai takeout for dinner. Milly and Mason are exhausted from a fun sleepover at their aunt's house so we decide to keep it low-key. Sitting around the coffee table with takeout containers, Mason pulls out the board game *Clue*.

"I haven't played this in years!" I exclaim.

"I've never played," James admits sheepishly.

"You're going to love it, Daddy." Milly opens the board while Mason picks out the game pieces. "You have to discover who killed Mr. Boddy. What weapon was used for the murder. And what room it happened in." She points to the library and then the Conservatory.

"Here are the weapons." Mason shakes out the candlestick followed by the lead pipe.

"Who bought you this game?" James asks warily, his eyebrows pulling together.

"Aunt Maia," Mason replies, not missing the way his father is taking in the board game.

I snort. "It's a classic."

James shakes his head. "I'm sure. When I was a kid, I was too busy playing hockey to ever play any of these classic board games. I used to think my dad was too strict but now I think he was onto something..."

I laugh. "Come on, it will be fun."

"Yeah, Daddy," Milly echoes me. "It will be fun." She snuggles closer to my side, practically sitting in my lap.

I brush her hair out of her eyes, smiling up at James.

His expression changes, a tenderness rippling over his face. We exchange a knowing glance, an understanding look. One that reenforces everything that's changed in the past twenty-four hours.

One that fills me with certainty that this time, I'm making the right choice.

I'm taking a step forward.

CHAPTER 13
JAMES

In the space of a few weeks, my life changes.

Being with Bella, being intimate with her, flips my perspective. The early mornings streaked with worry are replaced with an easygoing lightness. Breakfast becomes a family meal again. Getting the twins ready for school becomes a fun part of the day instead of a frantic chore to try to make it out the door on time.

Afternoons I used to spend watching game reels or getting in an extra workout, anything to focus my spiraling thoughts and avoid self-pity, are spent wrapped in Bella's embrace. Lazy lovemaking followed by late lunches.

The dark nights I used to beg for sleep to quiet my mind and end my restlessness are spent watching old sitcoms and new action movies, with Bella next to me on the couch.

While we're careful to maintain a professionalism in front of the twins, by the end of the following week, it's getting harder to not touch her, to not kiss the back of her neck, to not ask her a personal question when they're home. Bella asked me when we should share our relationship with the twins and I clammed up, unsure how to proceed.

How do I ease them into understanding that I'm dating

someone? Will they be angry? Hurt? Confused? Will they hate Bella? Or worse, me?

Looking for advice, I run it by some of the guys on my team. They're all unanimous in their decision to tell the kids. In fact, they're truly happy for me, smacking me on the back and telling me that I've made a fantastic choice in Bella.

Over the past few weeks, she's brought the kids to more of my games and all of the wives and girlfriends embraced her like she was one of them. Even before she really was one of them.

As much as my teammates' approval soothes some of my concern, it doesn't alleviate it entirely. Because the guys are like my brothers, of course they have my back. They want to see me happy. But maybe they're not looking at the situation from the perspective of Milly and Mason.

For that, I need to touch base with someone who would put the twins' best interest before mine. I need to tell Maia.

I swing by her house after practice in the middle of the week, knowing it's her day off from working at the hospital. Nerves skate up my spine and I spend an extra five minutes idling in her driveway, my fingers tapping out a beat on the steering wheel.

I shouldn't be this nervous. I'm a dedicated father, a good provider, a man who loved her sister with every part of me. Still, telling Maia that I'm now seeing Bella, my kids' nanny, is a delicate subject. Thoughts on how to broach it swirl in my head. I'm so lost in my own mind that I jump when a tap sounds from the passenger window.

I whip my neck to the side, snickering when I spot Maia next to the passenger window, bundled up in a massive scarf, with two mugs of coffee in hand. I unlock the car door and she slips inside, passing me a mug.

"Thanks," I say, taking a sip. The bitter roast quiets some of my thoughts and I lean my head back against the headrest.

"I was starting to worry about you. You look like you're

going to tell me you got traded to Los Angeles and are taking Milly and Mason away..." she says half-jokingly but I hear the concern in her voice.

"No," I say quickly, shaking my head. "It's nothing like that."

"But it *is* bad news," she murmurs, watching me.

I blow out a deep breath.

"Oh my God! Are you sick? Is one of the twins ill?" she asks quickly, panic blazing across her face.

"No, no, of course not," I rush to reassure her, placing a hand on her wrist. "I'm making a mess of this."

Maia takes a deep breath, her dark eyes flashing the same way Layla's used to. Since Maia is so much younger than Layla, I never realized how similar they look. They always resembled each other, were clearly sisters, but now that Layla is gone, Maia seems to hold so many more of her features.

"What's going on, JR?"

I take a deep breath. "I've come to tell you some news, some changes in my life. And I don't really know how to say it."

"Just blurt it out."

"I'm dating someone."

Maia freezes, her eyes swinging to mine. For a beat, she's frozen and then, her laughter erupts.

I lean back, the back of my head hitting the window. I reach to rub at the spot as I stare at my sister-in-law like she's lost it. Is she upset? Is this one of those disbelieving reactions to the news I shared? Is her laughter going to morph into tears in a second? "Maia," I say slowly.

"Oh gosh, JR, jeez," she wheezes out, pressing a hand over her heart. "You really scared the shit out of me and, well, to tell me that," she chuckles, "that you're dating..."

I wait for her to finish her thought but she doesn't. She just keeps laughing and shaking her head.

Slowly, her laughter dies down. Maia runs the back of her

hand over her eyes and takes a sip of her coffee. Clearing her throat, she turns toward me and nods. "Okay. What's her name? How'd you meet her?"

"Hold up," I say, squinting at her. "You need to explain what the hell that"—I wave a hand in her general direction—"was about."

"Honestly? Relief. I thought you were going to tell me something truly awful but to learn that you're dating, that you're living again, it's a big, big relief."

"Relief," I repeat, not believing her.

She nods. "Mom and I were really starting to worry about you. You seemed so down all the time, so sad. Which, of course, is normal. But your life was just becoming this routine. No joy, no socializing. Just work and home, work and home." Maia shakes her head. "No one can keep that up forever. We all need people, companionship, emotional connections with others. It's important, JR."

"You talked about this, about me, with Zainab?" I ask slowly, wondering how my mother-in-law would feel about me *dating*.

Maia nods. "Of course. With your parents gone, we consider ourselves your strongest support system. Still, we hoped you would meet someone…"

"You did?"

Maia smiles. "Is that so hard to believe? We want you to be happy, JR. Whole. All of us do…"

"Yeah, but, you know I loved, love, your sister, right? I mean, I would never want to disrespect Layla or dishonor her memory."

Maia chuckles. "That's what you're worried about? JR, anyone with eyes could tell how much you cherished Layla. And how much she adored you. You guys were the most amazing couple, real relationship goals. If I'm being honest, I used to be a little jealous of how effortless things seemed for you guys. Trust me, no one would ever think that you were dishonoring what you and Layla had, the family and the life you built. But JR, you're supposed to keep living.

You're supposed to heal and find good again. Love. It's natural and Mom and I would never want less of a life for you because Layla passed." Her eyes fill with tears and one spills onto her cheek. She flicks it away with the backs of her knuckles, offering a soft smile. "Trust me when I tell you, my sister would want you to choose love again over constant heartache. She would want that for you and she would want the best of you, the whole you, to raise the twins. Not just pieces and shadows."

I shake my head in disbelief. "I thought you'd be upset. Or angry."

"Never." She takes my fingers and squeezes them. "Tell me about her. Is it serious?"

"I, it's…new. But yes, my feelings are very strong. I wouldn't—"

"Date someone casually. I know. With you, it's always all in or nothing. Layla used to joke that you were a man of extremes."

I smile, remembering how she used to tease me about that too.

"What's her name?" Maia asks. "How'd you meet?"

"She's, well, it's Bella."

Maia's eyebrows fly up. "The nanny?"

I nod.

Maia's eyebrows snap back together, her eyes narrowing. "And you're sure about this? It's not just some natural extension of living together, raising the twins together or—"

"It's for real," I cut her off, not wanting her to think that Bella and I would take a risk like this just because it's easy. "Trust me, I fought against it, tried to avoid her, kept her at arm's length… The truth is, I met Bella before she came to nanny for the kids. I couldn't have been more shocked when she showed up on the doorstep to interview. But she was the best person for the job, the most qualified, and the twins took to her immediately."

"They adore her," Maia agrees, smiling at me. "That's good, JR. Really."

I blow out the breath I didn't realize I was holding.

"To be honest, it makes me feel better that you met Bella before. That you guys were interested in each other for real and not just because your lives overlap so much."

"It's definitely a lot more than just the convenience of it. I…I'm falling for her, Maia. She makes all the aspects of my life better and I miss her when we're not together."

Maia's expression softens. "I'm happy for you."

"Thank you," I say, truly touched that she means it. "I don't know how to tell Milly and Mason."

"They don't suspect?"

"I don't know," I say slowly, thinking over the past week. "There were a few instances this week where Milly looked at me funny or Mason looked like he wanted to ask something. But neither of them came out and said anything directly. I don't know if it's a good or a bad thing that the woman is Bella. But I want to be honest with them. Do you think it's too soon? How do you think they'll react?"

Maia blows out an exhale. "I honestly don't know, JR. That's a tough one. I'm not sure how the twins will take the news but what I do know is that if they learn about you and Bella from anyone who isn't you, it's going to hurt a hell of a lot more. You need to talk to them. You need to be honest and upfront about your feelings. It has to be you."

"I know. I agree with you. I just, I don't want to flip their worlds upside down when they're finally doing so well."

Maia smirks at me. "I don't relish your position."

I snort. "Thanks, Maia. One day, you'll have kids and—"

"Not anytime soon," she cuts me off.

I lift an eyebrow but Maia shakes her head, not taking the bait.

"Talk to them, JR. Be honest and upfront with them. For too long, we all hid Layla's illness from them. I know at the time, we thought we were doing the right thing. Maybe we were…but the one thing I learned from everything that happened is that being honest, sharing information, matters. Choosing how to feel about something matters. Tell them and then, let them feel what they feel. Just be there for them."

I think over her words, nodding slowly. "Okay."

She takes another sip of her coffee. "You know once the twins know, Mom is going to expect Bella to come to Delaware for Christmas."

I snicker, knowing she's right. Marrying Layla was like hitting the in-law jackpot. I don't know anyone who has the type of relationship with his in-laws that I have with mine. After my parents passed when I was in high school, I yearned to belong to a family again. Layla's family became mine from the moment I met them and I've never taken that for granted.

"We'll take it step by step," I say slowly.

Maia laughs. "Tell that to Mom after she has a stocking made for Bella."

I chuckle with her, some of the weight I was carrying around dissipating. Maia's approval makes my future with Bella seem that much more realistic. I'm not building castles in the sky, dreaming of wild hopes. I'm turning my dream into my reality.

CHAPTER 14
BELLA

"Need you, Bella," James's voice rumbles over the shell of my ear.

I turn toward him. Even half-asleep, my body is drawn to his like a moth to a flame. His mouth is hot against my skin, his stubble prickly against my neck.

I moan, arching into his touch as he slips his hands under my sleep shirt and over my skin. When his palm closes around my breast, I waken fully, my eyes finding his in the dark.

"You're home," I murmur.

"Just walked in."

"How was the game?" I ask, as he kisses the sensitive flesh where my neck rounds out into my shoulder.

"We won." He keeps kissing a trail over my throat.

"Congratulations."

I feel James's mouth curl into a smile against my skin. My fingers rake though his hair, pressing the back of his head more firmly against my body. "The twins—"

"Are fast asleep," James explains, tugging the tie on my sleep shorts and rolling them down my body along with my underwear. "I missed you, baby."

I settle back against my pillows. "You did?"

James's hand slides up my leg, slowly. When it reaches the apex of my thighs, it stops and he swipes two fingers up my core, through the wetness already waiting for him.

"I missed you too," I murmur.

He laughs. "I can tell." Then he slips his fingers inside his mouth and sucks my sweetness, grinning wickedly as he pulls his fingers out with a loud smack.

My gaze is already at half-mast at that little display and when James reads the heat in my eyes, desire flares in his. We move at the same time, removing clothes, our breathing ragged. Our sweet and lazy of the past week kicks up into sexy and needy as we reach for each other. Our mouths crash together in a hungry kiss, wrought with delicious promises and sinful intentions.

I shush James twice, reminding him that we need to be quiet but it's hard to remember as his body coaxes the most delicious sensations from mine. James and I lose ourselves in each other and somewhere over the course of the night, we find ourselves too.

As the darkness eases into dawn, I realize that I don't want to hide my relationship with James. I don't want to keep my newfound happiness under wraps when I feel almost drunk with the need to shout it from the rooftops. Being with James has restored a part of me I thought I lost and I don't want to conceal it. I want to celebrate it. Rejoice in him. Rejoice in us.

As the first rays of sunshine flicker across my bedroom wall, I turn toward James and open my mouth. But his finger comes up and presses against my lips, silencing me.

"I've been thinking," he starts slowly and my stomach twists, nerves and anticipation rolling through me. "I'm ready to tell the twins. I want to."

I smile against his finger and he removes it.

"What do you think?" he whispers.

"I think I like this idea very much," I tell him truthfully. "I want to be with you, James. But they're the heart of this family and I want to be honest with them."

He kisses me deeply, pulling back only to stare into my eyes. "Me too, Bella. I love you."

Pure joy radiates through my veins as I smile at him. "I love you, too."

Then, we make love again as the sun rises on a new day and the next chapter of our together begins.

THE FOLLOWING days are busy with extracurricular activities and hockey games so James and I agree to tell the twins this weekend, when he returns home from a game. We're in the kitchen, eating lunch, before he flies out for two days.

Snow falls thickly outside the window, blanketing the ground in white.

"What are you going to do while I'm in Milwaukee?" James asks. "Maia is keeping the kids overnight on Wednesday. You should do something with Selina. Go out to dinner."

I wrinkle my nose. "I picked up Selina's shift at Taps that night. She has an audition."

James frowns, turning toward me. "You did? Why? You don't need to be working all these hours. I mean, you pretty much work all the time here." His frown deepens as he considers his own words. "Do you need more time off? You should do something fun with your friends."

I shake my head, forcing a smile. I try to keep my voice light. "It's fine. I like working at Taps. It's fun."

James gives me a disbelieving look.

"Besides, I want to help Lina out. She's been so great to

me, letting me live with her for stretches at a time. Trust me, it's no big deal," I reassure him, not adding that I like to keep busy. It's how I cope; it's how I've been dealing with all the things I don't want to think about for years now. Sure, my sessions with Dr. Carlisle have curtailed a lot of my need to throw myself into things. But I'm still adjusting.

While being with James has placed my life on a new trajectory, it hasn't erased all the things I'm still working through. After long days surrounded by incredible kids, in a house that is truly a home, I still sometimes long for the family I don't have. Will Milly and Mason ever consider me a motherly figure?

Being with James eased a lot of my hurt, but it also raised a lot of new questions. What does my future look like? Do I have a place in his family? In their home? As more than just the nanny?

When you're sitting in someone else's home, no matter how much you love it, no matter how much you revel in it, it's still someone's home. It's built from their dreams and hopes. It's wrought with their plans and ideas.

Since Jerry and I divorced, I never had a space that was just mine. I never had an opportunity to truly create a place for myself to think and reflect. I never had that because I didn't want it, in fact, I ran from it. The best way to keep those old hurts and devastating memories, the quiet longing and needy desires, under wraps, is to stay busy. Filling in at Taps provides that and when Selina asked if I could cover for her, I jumped at the chance.

James pushes my hair over my shoulder, looking down at me with worry in his eyes. "You sure? You're not taking on too much?"

I smile at his concern, hearing an echo of Colton's words. "I'm sure." I tip my chin up and kiss the underside of his jaw. "Don't worry about me. Go to Milwaukee, win your game, and when you come home, we'll tell the twins our news."

He smiles but it doesn't reach his eyes. "Okay. But if you need anything, you call me."

"I'll be fine."

He sighs. "I know. I just, I worry about you when you're on your own."

His words cause me to pause. "Why?" I ask slowly.

His hand cups my cheek, his thumb drawing a line down the center of my chin. "Because I love you, Bella."

Even though he's said the words before, they still turn my body to mush. "I love you too." I lean back so he can drop his head to kiss me again.

He glances at his watch and groans. "I need to head out. I'll see you in a few days."

"Be careful," I remind him, slipping off the barstool so I can follow him to the door.

He pauses in the foyer. Intensity burns in his eyes for a long moment before he grips my hips and pulls me flush against his body. James kisses me deeply, causing my head to swirl. When he releases me, he grins wickedly. "You be careful," he says instead.

Then, he shoulders his bag and lifts his hand in a wave before leaving. I close the door behind him, rolling my back against it as I take in the Ryan home.

In many ways, it feels like my home too. But is it? Will a home James built and brought to life with Layla ever truly be mine?

I shake the thought away. First, we need to tell the twins about us. How will they react? Will they hate me?

Christmas is only a few weeks away and James invited me at Maia's urging. But I've held off on agreeing until we talk to the twins. Will they want me to celebrate with them? Go to Delaware and stay at their teta's house over the holidays? Or will that be overkill? Will it hurt too much? Will they think I'm trying to replace their mother?

I sink to the couch, my thoughts tripping over each other.

That's the last thing I'd ever want to do. Everything I know about Layla Ryan and her family is good. She was a beautiful, intelligent, compassionate woman. An amazing wife, a phenomenal mother, a wonderful person through and through. I'd never try to take her place. But is there room, true space for me, in the Ryan family? In James's, Milly's, and Mason's lives? Can their love for me coexist with their love for Layla?

I hope so.

I lean back on the couch, checking the time. I don't have to pick the twins up for several hours. Suddenly, the weight of the empty house presses in on me. My thoughts begin to spiral as different scenarios about us telling the twins play out in my mind.

My fingers swipe across the keypad of my phone as I debate messaging Dr. C for a session. No. I pull my hand away and close my eyes. I just spoke with him last night and I'm making progress; I'm moving forward. I can handle this.

I blow out a shaky sigh, hating that this many years later, I still struggle to sit idly. I still jump at the chance to pick up Selina's serving shifts at Taps or Jolene's.

I force myself to stand and head into the kitchen. I tidy up from James's and my lunch before doing a deep clean of the entire kitchen, throwing myself into the task. When the countertops gleam and I can see my reflection in the stainless steel of the refrigerator, I close my eyes in defeat. Because it wasn't enough. Restlessness still courses through my veins. Heading to my room, I change into workout clothes.

Then, I pop in my ear pods, select a high energy playlist, and head to the basement where James has a home gym with a treadmill. I run until I can barely breathe, until my lungs burn, and my legs feel like jelly. I run until my thoughts quiet and my concerns ease.

That night, after I tuck Milly and Mason into bed, I climb

under my duvet and let sleep claim me. I'm so exhausted that I sleep through my alarm the following morning.

However, when I wake up and read the message on the screen of my phone, I wish I slept even longer.

JERRY

Bells, we need to talk.

CHAPTER 15
JAMES

Milwaukee is a tough loss and it rests on my shoulders. I didn't stop a shot the way I should have. It was my failure on the ice that let Milwaukee take the lead and when the final whistle blows, shame burns through me, layered with guilt.

We've been having one hell of a season and skated onto the ice too damn confident for our own good. We get our asses handed to us, both on the ice and afterwards, when Sims gets into it with their center. Smarting from bullshit calls, a rough game, and my screw-up, both teams jump in and the fight, over minutes after it begins, leaves us all in a piss-poor mood.

The flight back to Boston is mostly silent, with a thread of tension tugging throughout the entire team. Everyone is frustrated with our game time performance, annoyed by the stupid fight we let ourselves be dragged into, and exhausted.

When our plane lands in Boston on Wednesday evening, even the light fall of snow irks me. It's another reminder that the holidays are upon us, that it's another Christmas without Layla, and that Bella still hasn't given me a final answer about celebrating with us in Delaware.

I'm cranky, tired, and desperate to be home with Bella and the twins. I grab my bag and head out to catch the team bus back to the arena. As I step up into the bus, I remember that the twins are sleeping at Maia's and Bella is filling in for Selina at Taps.

I swear under my breath, drawing a look from Panda.

"What's wrong?" he asks, sliding into the seat closer to the window so I can sit beside him.

I plop down and shake my head, feeling my jaw clench. "Nothing. I'm just in a shit mood."

"We all are." He shrugs. "But something else is bothering you."

"I just remembered the twins are at Maia's tonight."

"Isn't that good? You can get that hot ass nanny all—"

His words die in his throat as I pierce him with a look. Fury rolls through me, an intense feeling I'm not used to having toward one of my teammates.

"Shit," Panda mutters. "You and Bella are for real, huh? I'm sorry, James." He raises his hands in surrender. "I thought you guys were just playing house, that you were easing back into the dating pool and didn't want to stick your dick in a puck bunny or—"

"Stop. Talking," I cut him off, my anger blazing. Panda's one hell of a hockey player but his reputation off the ice couldn't be farther apart from mine. Where I'm the family man, maybe too strict and serious, he's the wild playboy who hops from bed to bed. Still, I can tell by the regret in his gaze that he didn't mean any harm. He talks a lot of shit before he thinks and this is another one of those times.

Panda clears his throat. "It's for real, then?"

"It's for real," I confirm, my jaw tight.

"How'd the kids take it?" he asks, hitting at another sore subject.

My mood sours further, irritation mixing with my anger. "We haven't told them yet."

"Oh," Panda says, snapping his mouth closed.

Finally, silence. I turn away from Panda, debating if I should move seats. But after a few breaths, even his silence, which I wanted only moments before, grates on my nerves.

"Why? You think it's too soon?" I turn back toward him.

He opens his mouth but no words come out. His gaze is wary and I blow out a sigh.

"Be honest. I want to know what you think," I say in a calmer tone.

"I think you should have told them already. It's been going on, what, a month?"

"More or less," I say, not wanting to add that I *knew* Bella before she ever became our nanny.

"If Milly or Mason find out from anyone but you, it will shatter them. Bella's the first woman, you know, maternal figure, they've really connected with since Layla passed, right?" He clears his throat again, scratching at his cheek. He's uncomfortable.

I frown, wondering where the hell he's going with this. "Yeah. I mean, there's Maia but Bella is the first woman to step into a dedicated, caretaking role, since Layla passed."

Panda nods, the movement jerky. "They might feel protective of her. And it could be hard because their feelings for Bella could complicate their feelings for Layla."

"What do you mean?" I ask.

"I mean, it's hard to trust, to let someone in, after someone close to you dies. If they find out that you're keeping something like this, something big from them, and it involves the woman they're coming to think of as their safe haven, it's going to hurt. You need to be honest with them."

"We were going to tell them this weekend," I say, my eyebrows bending together as I study Panda. He seems jittery, nervous.

He shakes his head. "No, you need to tell them now, by

yourself. They might not feel comfortable voicing their concern in front of Bella."

"Concern?"

Panda nods, gripping the back of his neck. "Look, I could be way off base here but when my dad started dating again after my mom…" He pauses to glance out the window. Whatever emotion he's struggling with is gone by the time he turns back around. "He dated my sophomore English lit teacher. She's now my stepmom and I love her. But back then, fuck, it was hard, James. Ms. Green was *my* teacher, *my* person. I confided in her a lot after my mom died and then, all of a sudden, she was his. I'm not saying Milly or Mason is going to have that issue but for what it's worth, I'd be upfront."

I nod slowly, processing his words. "I never even considered…I didn't think of it like that."

"Yeah," he breathes out.

I look up, meeting his eyes. "I'm sorry about your mom."

"Thanks." Panda forces a grin. "I was fourteen at the time. So, older than the twins but…

"Yeah."

"Cancer sucks," he mutters, his tone hard. He turns to stare back out the window.

"Yeah."

I think about Panda's words until we arrive at the arena. I fist bump him goodbye and wave to my other teammates as I make my way to my SUV. Panda's advice, his experience, leaves a sourness in my stomach, darkening my already shitty mood.

I stow my bag and slide behind the steering wheel, ready to put this week behind me. I just want to go home and sink inside of Bella. Tangle up with her until this cloud passes.

Except Bella is still at Taps. I glance at the clock. 9:30 p.m. Things are probably picking up now. Even though I know she'll be too busy to talk, I point my SUV in the direction of the bar. I can sit and have a beer, wait for her to finish up the shift.

I pull at the collar on my shirt. Going to sit in a bar brimming with Hawks fans after a crap game isn't the smartest decision but I know seeing Bella will help clear my mind and improve my mood.

I park in the Taps parking lot and jog to the front door, ducking my head from the snow. I push inside and pull up short as I scan the bar for Bella. My breath catches in my throat and I see red when I spot her, leaning over the bar, hugging a man I've never seen before.

He's grinning at her like she's the most important person in the world to him and she's letting him hold her in a tight embrace instead of pushing him away.

What the fuck?

Insecurities I haven't felt in years rock through me, leveling me in a second. Is this Jerry? Is this the guy who dragged my girl through fucking hell after she buried her son?

I stride toward the bar, another thought popping into my mind.

Is this a new guy? Someone she never mentioned? Someone she dated after her divorce?

The man pulls back and stares into Bella's eyes, frowning at whatever he reads there.

They're too fucking familiar to be mere acquaintances. Why the hell is he still touching her?

I don't notice the patrons at Taps. The *tough loss* and *sorry about the game* comments roll off my shoulders. They don't even register because I can't think about anything except this fucker's hands on my Bella.

My hands are nearly shaking with anger. My stomach is roiling with fear. Am I going to lose her? Did I read everything wrong? Who the hell—

"James!" Bella gasps when I enter her line of vision. She's

surprised to see me and that pisses me off too. Didn't she think I'd come for her after the plane landed? Didn't she know she'd be the first person I'd want to see after *that* loss? She smiles, her face lighting up, which confuses the hell out of me.

I stop in my tracks, my hand planting in the center of the bar.

Bella's smile slips as she tries to gage my mood. Good luck, I don't even know how the fuck I feel right now, other than fuming. Anger, bitterness, and downright hurt laces my blood, causing my head to spin. My ability to reason disappears and I'm left *feeling*. Too many awful things. I wish they'd fucking stop.

"Hey, this is James?" the man asks.

I sneer at him, my other hand curling into a fist.

I note the recognition on Bella's face as she finally clues in that I'm fucking furious. Her hand on the dude's bicep clenches and she blurts out, "Yes. James, this is my brother, Colton."

What. The. Fuck?

Her brother?

Coldness sweeps through me as I start to process her words. Immediately, my face falls slack. The hot fire from seconds ago burns up into nothingness. What the hell is wrong with me? I just wanted to deck a guy, a man I don't even know, for hugging Bella hello. I doubted if my girl was what, *cheating*, on me? For hugging a guy in public?

And it's her brother.

I clear my throat, embarrassment and shame rolling through me. I uncurl my fist, swipe my palm along the material of my dress pants, and hold it out. "Hey. It's good to meet you, Colton."

"You too, man." He shakes my hand, his eyes sizing me up.

I stand a little taller, trying to keep my expression neutral.

"Thanks for being so good to my little sister," he adds, an easy smile slipping over his face.

Lucky for me, he seems to have missed the moment of my near meltdown.

I force a chuckle. "You've got it backwards. Your sister's been looking out for me and my family."

"Yeah," he agrees, sitting on a barstool. I take the seat next to him and Bella slips away to fill two pints. "I've heard a lot about Milly and Mason."

My eyebrows lift. "You have?"

"Yeah, Bells adores them."

"We all adore her," I respond, automatically.

He nods, thanking Bella for the beers she drops in front of us. She wrinkles her nose at me and tips her head down the bar where a customer is calling out for her.

"Don't tell him any embarrassing stories, Colt," she warns. But her eyes are trained on mine and I read the concern shadowing their depths.

Is she worried about her brother and I not getting along? Does she wish I hadn't met him? Sure, Bella's spoken about her family before but she's never mentioned my meeting them. Not the same way I've been trying to include her in my world, inviting her to Christmas with my in-laws. Should I be reading into this?

Pebbles of discomfort, of worry, start to stack in my stomach. I clear my throat. "Bella didn't mention you were coming to visit."

Colton takes a swig of his beer. "She didn't know. I wanted to surprise her. This time of year"—he shrugs—"it's hard for her, you know?"

I nod, my mind racing. Does he mean Christmas or something else? Miles's birth occurred in November. What happened in December?

"Jerry and she were never going to last," Colton lowers his voice, shooting me a knowing look. Except I have no clue what he's talking about. "But the divorce still stings. Especially because of how ugly it all got. I just, I wanted to be here for her. She's been quieter lately, not sharing as much, always rushing me off the phone." He shakes his head like he's missing a puzzle piece. "But she looks a hell of a lot better. Healthier, happier." He frowns and I realize that Colton has no idea about Bella and me.

She hasn't told her family yet.

Well, neither have I. I mean, I told Maia but the twins still don't know. My insecurities flare back to life. Was Panda right? Will they be hurt by my dating Bella? And how come I'm going to tell my kids when she hasn't even told her brother?

And what the hell did Colton mean about things with Jerry getting ugly? What *really* went down between them?

I pick up my beer and take a swig. I can feel Bella staring at me from down the bar but I don't turn to meet her gaze. Suddenly, my anger bleeds out. It's replaced by a coldness I'm more familiar with. I reach for the numbness, gripping it with both hands.

Maybe Panda was right. Maybe I keep thinking of this thing between Bella and me as a "we," an "us." But maybe Bella isn't all in the way I am. How many things about her life do I not know?

"Bella has been an incredible addition to our family," I say for her brother's sake. I keep my voice light, my tone level. "We're lucky to have her."

Colton grins, one side of his mouth pulling up. "That's good to hear, man. You have any sisters?"

Maia flashes through my mind and even though she's a sister through marriage, I nod.

"Then you know how it is," Colton continues. "I'll never not worry about her. The past few years have been unkind to Bells. I mean, really, how much hurt is one person supposed to shoulder?" He shakes his head, his expression forlorn. "But

I'm glad to see her here, like this." He tips his chin down the bar. "It's nice to see her smile again. Hope we can convince her to re-enroll in her PhD program next."

PhD program? I know that Bella studied children's psychology and education. I know that she still considers a therapy-centered career. But I didn't know she was completing her PhD. I didn't know that at some point, she dropped out of the program and never went back.

I turn to glance at Bella, chatting easily with a customer. She's rocking the same smile I noticed on the first night I saw her. Open, polite, charming. But her eyes blaze with the same emptiness I despise. With a loneliness I thought I was chasing away.

Suddenly, Taps seems to close in on me. All the things I was starting to believe in seem flimsy and ring false. My stomach plummets and my chest tightens. I drain my beer and place it back on the bar. I just want to get the hell out of Taps. I want this day to be over. I don't want any more drama or heavy bullshit.

What the hell happened between when I left for Milwaukee and now? The lighthearted and easygoing vibe of last week is gone. Now, I just feel overwhelmed and… drained. Too exhausted to think over all the things about Bella I *don't* know. While I've been confiding in her, sharing parts of myself and my family, telling her that I *love* her, she hasn't even mentioned that she has a brother?

I frown at Bella for a long moment. She turns and offers me a soft smile, a silent plea in her eyes to let her explain.

I tip my chin at her before gesturing toward the door.

Her expression falls.

"Good meeting you, Colton." I hold my hand out for her brother.

He smacks his palm in mine, giving it a warm shake. "You too, James. Thanks for keeping an eye on my sister. Hey, you want to grab a bite with us? She's getting off early tonight since it's not too busy. We're just going to head to the diner around the corner."

I smile at Colton, appreciative of his offer. But if he traveled all this way to surprise his sister, then they should have some time together. Besides, it seems like Bella has some personal things to work out before she and I can even discuss the massive elephant that just walked into the room. "Nah, I'm okay. You guys should get caught up. Thanks though."

"Another time then."

"Another time," I agree.

I don't turn around as I walk to the door of Taps. All of the things that have been eating at me pull me under, too overwhelming to process. All of my failures, all of my guilt, all of the uncertainties that I live with each day, minute to minute, swallow me whole.

I can't handle another rejection, another disappointment, on top of everything else. So, I don't bother with a second glance or a final goodbye. But I feel Bella's eyes on the center of my back and know she's confused by my behavior.

Well, I'm bowled over by hers.

The door closes behind me and I step back into the snow, swearing at this shitty day that seems endless.

CHAPTER 16
BELLA

I wring my hands together as Pete tells me to take off early, to grab a bite with my brother who has patiently sat at the bar and watched bits of my life unfold all evening.

Nerves rattle in my veins and a slickness coats my stomach, making me feel nauseous and light-headed. Why did James leave? Why didn't he say goodbye? Are we over?

No, that doesn't even make sense. He just had a tough loss, a hard day…

He doesn't even know about Jerry's message.

Still, the rationalizations do little to quiet my mind.

Images of Jerry, storming out of our house, the storm door banging behind him, the rain beating relentlessly, cloud my mind. Two years ago, this week, I signed the divorce papers that Jerry waved around like a victory flag.

His callousness cut deeply. His disgust with me, with my weakness, ran through my veins like molasses, slowly, steadily, sluggishly. By the time he was gone, a *fuck you, Bella,* howling with the wind, I was numb.

Too numb to cry. Too emotionally burnt out to feel the acute pain of another failure. Never a mother, not even a wife.

I hardly remember the days that followed save for my big

brother's presence. Colton showed up on my doorstep, my parents close behind, and showed me the greatest compassion as I broke apart in his arms for the second time in two years. Dad helped me pack up my house and sell it, splitting the profit with Jerry, as we agreed upon. Mom helped me perfect my resume and search for a new job, telling Colton to ease up when he pleaded with me to go back to school and pursue children's psychology full-time.

But Colton saved me and seeing him walk into Taps tonight quieted some of the unsettled energy that surges this time of year. Even more so now that Jerry contacted me. What does he want? What could we possibly need to talk about?

I could reply to his message and find out but…am I ready for that?

"You hungry?" I ask Colton, untying my apron and folding it into a square.

"I can always eat, Bells."

I smile at him and he grins back and a quiet voice whispers *you're going to be okay*. God, I hope so.

The snow is falling heavier now and Colton and I make a run for it, shrieking through the thick flakes like we did as children, until we find shelter in the little diner around the corner.

We sit in a booth, snowflakes dropping past the window next to us, and drink hot coffee. We feast on Belgian waffles with a side of eggs.

"You look good, Bells," my brother murmurs. His eyes, the same cerulean blue as mine, pierce me with a knowing look.

"I'm in love with him," I admit.

If he's surprised by my admission, he conceals it well, ducking his head and hiding his smile behind his coffee mug. "He's in love with you too."

"He's angry with me," I say instead, not wanting to let the hope I was starting to lose myself in surge again. Not tonight, when James's behavior threw me for a loop. Not now, when Jerry's message and the week of my divorce, two years old and a failure still too fresh, prickles at me.

"Why didn't you tell him about Jerry?"

I shrug. "What's to tell?"

Colton sighs. "If I ever get my hands on that son of a bitch—"

"He messaged me," I say quietly.

"What? When?" Colton leans forward.

"Late last night… I saw it this morning."

"What the fuck does he want?"

I shrug.

"Bella."

I look up. "He was grieving," I say, not sure if I'm trying to convince myself or my brother.

"Don't you dare defend him." Colton glares at me, his jaw clenched. "That piece of shit put his hands on you, Bells. His fucking hands on his *wife*. The things he said to you, the way he acted—"

I hold up a hand, silencing my brother. Jerry's words, barbed wires and blades, cut through me all over again at the reminder.

You're nothing. A wasted-up failure that even biology deserted. How could you lose our son? How could he die? I don't want you anymore, Bells. No man will.

For weeks, starting at the one-year anniversary of Miles's death, Jerry ranted and raved in a drunken stupor. His heart had been obliterated, his life twisted into something tragic and unrecognizable. He spat anger and breathed fired while I curled into myself, an unfeeling, numb shell of a woman unfit to be a mother. His anger broke one night in a startling shock of violence, a backhand across my face, that left both of us reeling. Jerry's eyes were wild before he broke down in a fit of sobs, apologizing to me and swearing at himself. That was the night we knew we were done.

Jerry walked away without a backward glance. But in the aftermath of our devastation, his cruelty and my indifference, I drowned in insecurities. I lost my way, my will, my purpose and I've only started to find my footing again with James and his family.

Old habits die hard and confiding in the man I now love about the emotional scars I bear from the man who once loved me is a hurdle I haven't yet cleared.

"You can't move on if you're not honest with him," Colton says quietly.

I meet his gaze, hating the sympathy ringed in pity I read in his eyes.

"Everything you experienced, everything that happened afterwards with Jerry, it changed you, Bells. For the past three years, since, since Miles, you haven't been living. You've just been existing, biding time. For what?" Colton leans forward, reaching across the table to clutch my wrist. "That man, James Ryan, cares about you. I could tell the second I saw him walking toward us, looking like he wanted to knock me out."

I snort and Colt grins.

"Trust me, Bells. The only way through this"—he squeezes my wrist—"is to feel it. You can't keep everything bottled up forever. You can't reach for numbness all the time. Closure is a good thing and as much as I hate Jerry, and as much as I don't want you to talk to him, if you think it will help, maybe you should respond to his message. All I know is, you need to let someone in. And I will always be that person for you but I think you should give James a crack at it too."

My eyes burn with tears I won't let fall. Colton's voice cracks and I hate how much hurt I've dragged him and my parents through over the past few years. "I want to forgive Jerry for me, not for him. It's something I used to speak with Dr. Carlisle about. I *want* to move forward. And sometimes, that's hard when I still feel so angry and…bereft, about the way things ended with Jerry. But I don't know how to tell

James that. He's dealing with his own grief," I murmur, not wanting to share just how deeply Layla's death cut him. "He's still coming to terms…"

"What better person to help you through yours? You can support each other. But the only way to do that is to be honest. Really, truly honest."

I nod slowly, wetting my dry lips. "What if he rejects me?"

Colton tilts his head, the corners of his mouth curling upward, at odds with the blaze in his eyes. "You've survived and endured a hell of a lot more than a guy's rejection, Bells. You can get through anything." He leans back in his seat, his hand releasing my wrist. "But he's not going to reject you. The guy I met tonight wants to step up for you. You just need to let him."

JAMES IS ALREADY ASLEEP, his light snore whistling through the dark, when I let myself into the house. I hesitate in the doorway to his bedroom, shifting my weight from one foot to the next.

Colton's words echo in my ears. My brother was right. Since losing Miles, I've been in a strange space, existing but not really living. Going through the motions but not engaging with the day, not being truly present for any of it.

I work to ward off the hurt. I run to keep my restless energy in check. I move in with families who need me so I can be useful and not have to examine the emptiness of my own life too closely.

For three years, this has been my norm but if I want a real chance with James, a real shot at a future and a family and happiness, then I need to start letting him in. Dr. Carlisle can't be my primary sounding board, not if I want to belong to a family the way I do. That means making myself vulnerable and I finally feel like I'm at a place where I can do that. With James.

I start right now, by peeling off my snow-covered jacket and letting it fall to the ground. Next, I shimmy out of my jeans, pull my shirt over my head, and tug off my socks. I take a deep breath and do something I've never done before. I climb into James's bed in the middle of a weeknight, when he's already asleep, and press my cold toes against his warm legs, snuggling into his side like a child seeking comfort.

He opens his arms, his eyes still closed, and I roll into them, my body relaxing into his. I let out a deep sigh and allow my eyes to close.

"I'm sorry," I breathe out, kissing his forearm.

"Shh. We'll talk tomorrow. Sleep now, baby," James murmurs.

I melt into him, my worries easing, my hurt abating, and do as he says. I slip into a peaceful slumber that's cut short by a shriek that nearly rips my heart out of my chest.

CHAPTER 17
JAMES

"Why is Bella in here?" Milly screams the following morning.

My eyes snap open as adrenaline shoots through me, causing me to wake up in an instant. My head swings from my daughter's horrified expression, her eyes wide, her mouth hanging open, to the panicked eyes of Bella, still in bed next to me, practically naked.

Fuck. Shit. I messed this up so fucking badly.

Maia appears behind my daughter, calling out to Mason to stay where he is down the hall. She shoots me an apologetic look that I barely register before planting her hands on my daughter's shoulders and steering her out of the doorframe. Milly kicks at Bella's discarded clothes as she leaves.

"Shit," Bella murmurs, holding the sheet to her chest as she sits up. One bra strap slides down her shoulder and bile rises in my throat.

My daughter just caught me in bed with her nanny. I look around the bedroom as if seeing it for the first time. The framed family photos Layla set out on the dresser, the same white, linen duvet she purchased the year she fell ill wrapped around Bella's chest.

Jesus, what must Milly think? What is Maia telling my kids? What the hell am I going to say to explain this?

I narrow my eyes at Bella, Panda's advice coming back to me. *Make sure they hear it from you.* This is so bad.

I scramble from the bed, pulling on a pair of sweats and throwing Bella's clothes at her.

"What are you doing in here?" I ask, my tone heavy with accusation.

She shrinks away from me, her expression dazed. "I thought, I wanted to talk."

I huff out a breath, shaking my head. Right now, my focus needs to be the twins. I don't have time to hash things out with Bella; I can't worry about whatever the fuck last night was. I need to see Milly and Mason. "Right, well, that will have to wait. Get dressed. I'm going to talk to my kids." I turn away from her before the hurt in her eyes, the devastation rippling over her face, can persuade me to stay even a moment longer.

I swipe a T-shirt from the top of my dresser and pull it on as I leave the bedroom, closing the door behind me, and leaving Bella alone in a sea of sheets.

I bound down the stairs, my heart racing and my ears ringing, as a million excuses that I know won't cut it flash through my mind. I stop short in the doorway to the kitchen, meeting Maia's worried eyes on the other side of the kitchen counter.

My kids are eating cereal with their backs to me. Milly's shoulders are stiff, her posture perfectly straight, and I can tell she's trying to school her emotions. Shit.

"Hey guys, how was your night at Aunt Maia's?" I try for cool.

Milly whips her head around, glaring at me with malice.

I look to Mason who shakes his head at me.

"Guys," Maia says calmly, leaning down to rest her elbows on the island. "Your dad wants to have a serious conversation with you. Let's give him a chance to explain some things, okay?"

The twins grumble their agreement and a swell of gratitude for my sister-in-law rises in my chest. Maia walks toward me, lowering her voice as she nears. "I'm sorry. I thought you wanted me to drop them off before school. Otherwise, I could have just taken them but I'm filling in for a shift and—"

"No, it's okay. I overslept. Don't worry about it," I reassure her, tipping my head toward the door. "Go to work and I'll call you later."

"Okay," she agrees, biting her lip. She glances over her shoulder at the twins' backs but doesn't say anything else before she slips out of the house, the lock on the front door catching behind her.

I blow out a deep breath and rub my hands together. What the fuck is my game plan? Why does this suddenly feel like the most difficult conversation I've ever had with my kids? Surely, we've been through worse than my starting to date. Haven't we? Will the kids see it like that? Or will they see this next step with Bella as some kind of betrayal to Layla?

Suddenly, I wish I had been upfront with them from the beginning, even if it seemed too soon. Maybe Panda was right. Maybe my not telling them from the start has shaken their faith, their trust, in me. The thought rattles me and I force myself to round the island and face them before I spiral further.

"Milly, Mason," I start, meeting each of my kid's eyes. Milly looks like she's about to burst into tears. Mason's expression is more impassive, his eyes curious. "Bella and I were planning to talk to you guys this weekend. I never meant for you to see that, to find out the way you did." I glance at Milly but she averts her gaze, scraping her fingernails against her palms, the way she does when she's anxious. My heart breaks for my daughter and I hate myself for being such a selfish man, for falling so goddamn short as a father. "I'm sorry," I lower my voice but Milly doesn't meet my eyes.

"The truth is, I met Bella before she became your nanny," I continue, garnering the attention of both of my children. "We were…friends, from before. This new part of our relationship"—I gesture to the doorway, to all that transpired outside of the kitchen this morning, before yanking on the back of my neck. Fuck, this is hard—"well, it's new. I was trying to figure out the best way to tell you, that's all. But Bella and I are… we're dating."

"You always say honesty is the best policy," Mason accuses me.

"You're right. And I'm sorry I wasn't honest from the beginning but I'm being honest now."

He shovels a spoonful of Cheerios into his mouth in response.

I glance at Milly. The tears she fought so hard to keep at bay have spilled over.

"Oh, Milly," I race to my daughter's side, wrapping her in my arms. "It's okay, sweetheart. Everything is okay. I know you're upset. You can feel however you feel. Angry, sad. Just talk to me, Jellybean."

My daughter sobs in my arms and Mason glares at me like I just told him Santa isn't real. An overpowering sense of helplessness crashes over me and unworthiness floods my limbs. I don't deserve these kids. How could I mess things up so badly for them? Of course it's too soon to start dating.

How the hell was Panda right? They needed to hear about Bella from me, not find us tangled up in bed together.

Failure and anger, already at an all-time high after yesterday, buzz through me as I shush Milly, brushing her hair away from her forehead.

"Are you and Bella getting married?" Mason asks suddenly.

"What? No," I say.

"Are you having a baby?" he asks. "Making a new family?"

Milly freezes in my arms and I bite my tongue. "No, of course not. Why would you even think that?" I ask my son. Wanting to reassure him further, I blurt out, "The three of us will always be a family. Forever."

Mason shrugs, clinking his spoon against the side of his cereal bowl. But the sound is closely followed by someone clearing their throat in the doorway.

I turn toward the kitchen entrance, with Milly still clutched in my arms, to witness the blood drain from Bella's face.

Could this morning get any worse?

"Bella," I say slowly, watching as a wall shutters over her eyes, concealing her hurt and replacing it with that aloofness I can't stand.

"I just, I wanted to see you guys. To say I'm sorry for how this morning started out," she says in a flat tone, her fingers twisting together in front of her body.

Mason shrugs. "S'okay."

But Milly doesn't lift her head and her unwillingness to look at Bella has me tightening my hold, keeping my daughter shielded.

Bella catches the movement and her expression wobbles, her eyes taking on a sheen of moisture that she rapidly blinks away.

"Why don't you take today off?" I suggest. "I'm going to keep the kids home from school today. I think we need to spend some family time together."

"Oh, sure. I mean, of-of course," Bella stutters, her expression too locked down to read. "I'll, um, check in with you later?"

"Yeah. I'll, I'll call you," I say before looking back to Milly. I hear Bella slip from the room but I don't bother looking up.

How can I meet her eyes when I've made such a mess of

things? My chest aches when I hear the front door close a minute later. A few weeks ago, I told Bella Andrews that I fucking love her.

Now, I do absolutely nothing to stop her from walking out of my home. From walking out of my life. Because why would she want this? As much as I care for Bella, the needs of my kids, especially at their tender ages, will always come first.

What woman would want to come second, always after the family a man built with his first wife? Bella deserves more than I can give her. She deserves a man who will always choose her first, who will give her the babies her heart desires, who will create a family with her.

I cling to that thought so I don't run after her. Instead, I squeeze my eyes closed, drop my cheek to Milly's hair, and pray.

May God forgive me for all the hurt I've caused.

May Layla forgive me for falling in love with Bella.

May Milly and Mason forgive me for pushing her away.

CHAPTER 18
BELLA

"Has James reached out since you left?" Dr. Carlisle asks, his voice too calm for the panic racing through my limbs. I've been on high alert all morning, since the moment I walked out of the Ryan home. Even now, a few hours later, I feel nauseous with adrenaline and worry.

"Nothing." I rub the back of my hand over my cheek. "What if we're over?"

"Do you truly believe that?"

I shake my head. "But he said 'the three of us will always be a family. Forever.'" My voice breaks. "Does that mean there's no room for me? That I'm just…here."

Dr. Carlisle regards me seriously. "I don't know. And as much as your mind is racing right now, you don't know either. Has James ever given you a reason to believe that there's no room for you?"

"No. But that was also before he told his children about us."

"True. But he didn't tell his children as much as his children found out by—"

"Yes, I know," I cut him off, not needing to revisit the

visual of Milly's horrified expression at finding James and me in bed together.

"He could have said it in the moment. There was a lot happening. He was trying to assure his children," Dr. C points out.

"I know you're offering logical explanations, Dr. Carlisle. But none of them *feel* logical to me."

"You're hurt."

"Yes."

"But you still need to talk to James."

I huff out a sigh.

"Where are you now?"

"Selina's. My brother is here too."

"I'm glad you have a support system right now, Bella. Focus on that. Focus on the good, on the progress you've made. You need to keep yourself in the present and not let past experiences or emotions bog you down. Why don't you have some lunch and check in with me later today?"

I sigh but nod in agreement.

After I hang up with Dr. Carlisle, I enter the living room of Selina's townhouse. She and my brother are seated on the couch, watching me expectantly. No doubt, they're waiting for an explanation since I flew through the front door over an hour ago, tears streaming down my cheeks, hollering about a session with Dr. C.

"What happened?" Selina asks as I begin to pace in front of the couch.

"Talk to us, Bells," my brother says gently, but I hear the undercurrent of worry in his tone and it causes my guilt to rise.

I stop suddenly and face the two people who repeatedly show up for me. "Milly walked in on us."

Selina gasps and Colton's mouth falls open.

"Oh God, how much did she see?" Lina asks.

My brother swears.

I shake my head. "Not like that. We *were* in bed together—"

Colton slaps his hands over his ears.

"But we were just sleeping. It was early this morning," I add.

My brother drops his hands but gives me a look.

"She didn't take it well," Lina surmises.

"That's an understatement." I resume my pacing. "She screamed and cried and wouldn't even look at me when I came into the kitchen. James asked me to take the day. He's keeping the kids home from school so their *fa-family* can spend time together," I stammer, mentally cursing myself for tripping over the word *family*. That's a definite red flag that Selina and Colton pick up on.

That slip of the tongue let them know just where my head's at.

It's fucked up. I feel like I got TKOed. I can't repress all the messy feelings bubbling inside of me enough to ensure they won't spill over. As much as Dr. C helps me sort out my thoughts, this time, they're still a complicated jumble.

I feel like I'm about to rip wide open and all the ugliness is going to pour out, drowning everyone and everything in its wake. Washing away the hope I've clung to, wiping out the good I wished for.

I plop down on a chair across from the couch, the fight suddenly seeping out of me. I drop my head into my hands and draw in an inhale that burns.

"Oh my God. Oh fuck. I've messed this whole thing up," I cry out.

In an instant, Colton is at my side, pulling me into his embrace similar to how James held Milly this morning.

"You're okay, Bells."

"No," my voice cracks. "No, I'm a mess." I wipe my eyes and look up, meeting Colton's eyes. "You were right. I can't keep bottling it up. I can't keep reaching for the numbness. It's too much." I gesture to my body, where all of the feelings and emotions I fight against reside, growing stronger, sweeping through me like a hurricane.

"Shh." My brother rubs my back soothingly. "You don't have to figure it all out right now."

I give him a sad smile. "But you were wrong too. James isn't ready to step up for me. He can't. He needs to step up for his children, for his family, first. Even though I hoped it might be different, even though I thought it *was* different, there's no room for me there."

"Bella," Selina starts but I shake my head.

"I need to get my head on right. I need to take some time to...think. To just be with all the shit swimming in my mind. How can I be a partner to someone else when I don't know what I want anymore?"

Colton and Selina remain quiet and their silence confirms it. *I can't.* If I want to be with James, I first have to be okay with myself. And I haven't allowed myself the time, the space, or the grace to do that since losing Miles.

"Have you responded to Jerry?" Colton asks.

Selina's eyebrows disappear into her hairline and she shoots me a look.

I shake my head. "No. I don't know if it's better to hear him out or ignore him. I don't know what the heck I'm doing anymore..."

"You should hear him out," Selina says, surprising me.

"And you should talk to James too," my brother adds.

"Sure," I agree. But my voice is devoid of emotion. First, I reach for my safety net and message Dr. Carlisle again.

JERRY APPEARS on Selina's doorstop like an apparition. Even though I knew he was coming, I'm still surprised to see him. I pull the door open before he can knock and his hand drops to his side, his eyes widening as they drink me in.

I step back and he slips in from the cold, shaking out his coat and scarf. I hang them in Selina's hall closet wordlessly. I'm relieved Selina coaxed my brother into going for dinner after he refused to leave me alone with Jerry. It took a lot of convincing, but Selina finally managed to drag him away. I owe my friend a lot. Plus, she's allowing me the full use of her townhouse as I try to get my life in order.

"It's good to see you, Bells." Jerry's voice is deeper than I remember. His hair is thinning but he looks good, mostly the same. Blue eyes, blond hair, and a trim physique.

I keep staring, waiting to *feel* something. Attraction, nostalgia, anger. Mostly, I just feel relieved that we're about to get this conversation over with. Maybe it will offer the closure I need to let go of some of the anger I carry from our broken marriage and bitter divorce.

"Would you like a coffee?" I ask.

"Sure," he agrees, following me through the townhouse and into Selina's kitchen. She already brewed a pot, knowing we would end up here, and I pour two mugs, fixing his the way I did every morning for over five years.

When I place it in front of him, he whispers his thanks and takes a tentative sip, his eyes finding mine over the rim and holding.

I force myself to sit down on a barstool next to him. "What would you like to talk about?" My voice is even, too formal for a history as complicated as ours.

Jerry stares at me for a long beat before ducking his head and clearing his throat. "I'd like to apologize to you, Bella. Fuck, it sounds so stupid just saying it because I owe you so much more than an apology. But I am truly, truly sorry for the pain I caused you after we lost Miles. I am sorry for being a selfish drunk. I'm sorry for slapping you that night and for all the disgusting things I said to you for weeks before then." He holds my eyes as the words pour from his mouth, sincere and truthful.

I lean back, unprepared for such an honest apology. I've never known Jerry to make himself vulnerable, to accept any blame or shoulder any responsibility for his actions. I blink slowly, my eyebrows drawing together. "Thank you," I murmur, surprised by how much his words mean to me.

"I went to therapy…afterwards," he adds.

"Me too. I still talk to someone."

Jerry nods and clears his throat. "Is it helping?"

"Yes," I admit.

"Good. I did anger management too."

"Really?" I clamp my mouth shut, staring at my ex-husband. "You should have."

"I know. I'm also in the program."

I frown.

"AA," he clarifies.

"Wow," I mutter, surprised that Jerry accepted so much responsibility to turn his life around. He's a very different man than the one I was married to. "Is this one of your steps?" I gesture between us.

He nods, clearing his throat again. "It is but that's not the only reason why I'm here."

"It's not?"

"No." Jerry smashes his lips together and the temperature in Selina's kitchen suddenly drops.

A cold dread drips down my spine as my awareness sharpens, adrenaline filling my mouth with a metallic taste. My nerves buzz and I feel restless, desperate to throw myself off the barstool and out into the street. To run until my legs give out and my lungs burn.

"I, I met someone," he says tentatively, as if he's not sure how I'll react.

My eyes widen, waiting for him to continue.

"She's, well, we're having a baby."

My eyes close and it takes me a full minute to understand that the wetness on my cheeks is tears.

"I'm sorry, Bella. I'm so fucking sorry for everything. I'm sorry I wasn't there for you after Miles…you deserved better, Bells," Jerry rushes to add.

I lift my hands to my face to wick away the tears. "We were both grieving, Jer. But the way you…" I pause, shaking my head.

"I know."

"You buried my self-esteem. You made me feel unfit to be a mother, a wife. To be a fucking woman," I snap, my anger coloring my words. I hold on to it, the anger. It's a hell of a lot safer than the hurt that's swimming in my veins at his admission. Why the hell does he get to be a parent when I don't? Why does Jerry get a family and I get to be alone?

"I know. The way I treated you was—"

"Reprehensible."

"Worse."

I blow out a deep breath, forcing myself to look at him. To study him and see, really *see*, the regret in his expression. "When is she due?"

"February."

I nod. "And the baby, is it—"

"He."

A sharpness cuts through my chest, like a knife sliding through a tenderloin. The sting is sudden and instead of receding, an ache grows. "Is he okay?"

Jerry nods. "Michelle encouraged me to seek you out. To recognize how unfair I was toward you. She didn't want to bring our baby into the world without my acknowledging just how painful losing Miles was. Is."

"And what about you? What do you want?" I ask, frowning at him. He's here because his girlfriend told him to call me? All that proves is that she has a heart and he's still a selfish bastard.

"I want your forgiveness. It's okay if you don't want to give it. I understand, really, why you wouldn't. But I, I want to be a man worthy of being a partner, a father. I want to be a dad Miles could have been proud of."

Tears are streaming down my face now, a torrent of them too rapid to quell. "You kicked me when I was already down."

"I know."

I roll my lips together, my thoughts a furious swirl. Even though a part of me wants to hurt Jerry with callousness the way he did to me, a larger part of me wants to move on from this. So, I tell him the truth. "I think you're capable of being a good father. The guy I married never would have gone to therapy. Or anger management. The fact that you're taking these steps means you want to be better. And I still remember you from when…when I first got pregnant. You were so happy. I remember the tiny baseball glove you bought and the baseball cards you pulled out of your parents' attic. You changed after…after Miles. But if you're in the program, if you're trying, really trying with Michelle… I think you have a chance to do it right, Jer."

Jerry's eyes spark, a hesitant hope in their depths. "Really?"

I nod. "Yeah. There was a time when you were happy and hopeful and so damn proud. I hate the way things ended between us. Sometimes I think back and think we weren't ever suited to make a go of this." I gesture between us, shaking my head. "Not the way we both wanted it to be. But you're not a bad person, Jerry. You lost your way. It's…it's good of you to try to make amends." I clear my throat, staring directly at him as I say the words that free me just as much as they release him. "I'm saying this for myself more than I am for you. I want to move on. I want to get rid of the anger I feel toward you. I don't want the shadow of you, of our marriage, to continue to play a role, even a small one, in my future. So..." I let out a deep exhale. "I forgive you."

Tears well in his eyes, his face crumpling. "Thank you, Bella. That means more to me than you know."

It's strange, seeing a person you spent so much time with, someone you poured so much of yourself into, and viewing them as a stranger. I don't recognize the Jerry sitting beside me but I like him better than the man I was married to.

I tell him as much and he lets out a small laugh.

"I'm sorry I wasn't better to you. I'm sorry I wasn't there for you the way you needed."

"Thank you."

"I hope you find what you're looking for, Bella. I hope you discover happiness. You're all good, all light. Any kid would win the lottery to have you for a mom. You were meant to be a mother and I hope someday, you are."

My sob echoes in the kitchen, loud like a clap of thunder.

Jerry reaches out and wraps his arms around me. I cry on his shoulder and his tears fall into my hair. We hold each other for a long moment before I pull back, wiping my face, and he stands from his barstool.

I trail him to the door, my emotions bubbling under the surface of my skin, ready to burst forth.

But I don't feel the edge of desperation the way I usually do. I don't want to run. I don't want to hide. I want to cry until I feel peace instead of numbness. Clarity instead of chaos.

"I think I needed this," I tell Jerry. "The closure."

"Me too," he admits, offering his signature lopsided smile. "Take care of yourself, Bells."

"You too." I pull the door wide open and freeze.

Because James is standing on the porch, his hand lifted to knock on the door.

As soon as he sees my tear-stained face, a blaze of fury rolls over his. His features lock down, menacing and fierce, as he growls at Jerry. "Who the fuck are you?"

CHAPTER 19
JAMES

The tears on Bella's face, the hurt in her eyes, makes me feel sick. I glare at the fucker standing across from her and even though he hasn't answered my question, I know it's him. Jerry.

My hands clench into fists and an unmatched ferocity rocks through me. Never before have I felt so out of control, so wildly angry. Did he hurt her? Why is she crying?

"Who the fuck are you?" I repeat.

The guy glances between Bella and me but he doesn't look nervous. He shakes his head imperceptibly and says, "I meant what I said, Bells." Then he moves to walk around me but my arm darts out, my hand grabbing his shoulder.

He freezes, not in fear. In fact, the look he gives me is filled with understanding that confuses me while notching my anger higher.

"James." Bella's voice pulls my attention. When I focus on her, the guy blows past me, bouncing down the steps. I turn to watch him make his way toward a car parked on the street, memorizing the make and model in case he brings trouble in the future. "What are you doing here?"

"What?" I turn back to Bella.

"How'd you find me?" she asks, stepping back so I can enter Selina's townhouse.

"I figured you'd be with Selina. I asked Pete for her address."

"Oh."

"Who was that?" I point toward the street as Bella closes the door.

She blows out a heavy sigh, confirming my suspicions. Still, I need the words. I need to hear her say his name. "That was Jerry."

"What the fuck was he doing here? What did he want? Did he hurt you?" Questions rattle off my tongue, more like demands, as I step toward her and place a hand on her arm.

She shakes off my touch and I frown, not liking how aloof she's being with me when *he* clearly had her teeming with emotions. "He came to apologize. To make amends."

"Amends?" I ask harshly, not understanding what the fuck is happening right now. I came over here to talk to Bella about Milly and Mason, about the future of our relationship. And she's...sobbing over her ex-husband?

Fear disguised as anger rips through me and I grip the back of my neck, squeezing hard enough for it to hurt.

"He's"—her voice cracks and uselessness rolls through me —"he's having a baby."

"Son of a bitch," I swear.

"No, it's okay. I mean, I'm happy for him."

"You don't look happy," I say, releasing my hold on my neck and letting my hand fall. Knowing Jerry's having a child with someone else eases some of my jealousy and I blow out a deep breath, reminding myself to keep a cool head.

"It was hard to hear," she admits. "Especially since the thing I want most in the world is to have a family."

I nod but her words are like being steamrolled by a Mack truck. Of course she wants to have a family. It's the same thing I strived for after my parents passed. That sense of belonging, that feeling of knowing, without a shadow of doubt, that you are connected to something larger than yourself. That's partly the reason why Layla's family means so much to me; they accepted me as one of their own from the start. I shake my head, the exchange from this morning in the kitchen flooding my mind. The words I said, the look on her face.

How did I not realize sooner that this is a fundamental need for her? How much about her and her past do I not know? Insecurities rise to the surface as I recall meeting her brother in Taps last night. He mentioned her divorce, her PhD program. Why didn't she tell me about these things? Why didn't she trust me with them?

Too much too soon.

Bella's words come back to me. Is she right? Did we rush into this?

"Why are you here?" she repeats, her expression guarded, her voice uncertain.

I sigh, reaching out again and placing my hands on her shoulders. "I needed to see you."

She dips her head. "How's Milly? Where are the twins?"

"Confused," I admit. "She was surprised to see us together and to be honest, I'm not sure how she feels about it. Maia's fiancé took them to the movies."

"Of course," Bella agrees. "It must have been a shock for her and since I'm not her mother…"

She lets her sentence trail but now that I'm aware of it, I hear the silence for what it is. *I'm not her mother because I'm not part of your family.*

"Are you okay?" I ask her.

"Where do we go from here?" she responds, letting my question dangle.

"I don't know," I admit quietly, feeling my stomach twist as the words shatter the air. "It's going to take Milly some time to get used to us."

"Is there an us?" Her voice is small but her eyes hold mine, unwavering.

"I'd like there to be." I grasp her fingers in my hand. "I love you, Bella. I can't just turn that off. I just think we need to…tread carefully."

"Right," she replies automatically.

I frown, feeling like I'm missing something. Something big. "What's going on? What aren't you telling me?"

She chuckles, the sound exasperated. "James, just be honest with me. Milly being uncertain of us is an issue, isn't it?"

I nod, because yeah, my daughter struggling with my dating, with my having a relationship with Bella, isn't something I'm going to overlook. I'm not capable of it and up until this second, I didn't think Bella was either.

"I just, I thought I was becoming a part of your family," she murmurs quietly. Tears fills her eyes and my stomach twists at the sight of her hurting. "I thought we were building something together."

"You are. We are."

"Do you want more children?" she asks out of left field.

"What?" I frown, staring at her. "I don't know. I never…I never thought about it before."

"Right. Because you already have kids." She tosses an arm in my direction, as if that settles is.

"Don't put words in my mouth," I say, starting to lose my patience. "I never thought about it because I was never in a serious relationship, talking about the future, the way I am now. If you want to discuss having children—"

"Or adopting."

"Or adopting, then we can do that. But not tonight, not when we're both upset and wading through all of this." I gesture to the room at large, as if that will clarify all the things we're now dealing with.

Bella glares at me but behind the anger in her eyes is a fear that scares me. "Do you think Milly is upset because you're dating *me* or because you're dating in general?" she asks quietly.

"I don't know."

"You can tell me the truth."

"I am. I didn't get much out of Milly." I narrow my eyes at her, unable to get a pulse on her emotions. She's all over the place.

"I think we should respect her concerns and give her... time."

"Time?" I repeat.

"Did you have another suggestion?" she asks, crossing her arms over her chest. Her posture is suddenly defensive, her voice holding an edge I don't care for.

I shake my head. "No. But, I don't want to call things off with us either. I'm still planning to take the kids to Delaware for the holidays to be with Layla's family. It will be good for them to spend time with family and to have a break from Boston, from all the traditions Layla used to do in the house."

"Okay."

"Okay? That's all you're going to say. You still haven't given me an answer about spending the holidays with us and I still want you to come, if you'd like."

"What do you want me to say?" She shrugs. "You've made a decision that's right for your family and now you've told it to me. And...I don't think that's a good idea, given everything that's going on."

"What the hell is happening here? It's like I don't even recognize you right now. I thought we were in this together. I thought we were building a future together."

"Milly hated seeing us together, James!" Bella shouts, throwing her arms in the air. "She hated seeing me in her mother's bedroom. And can you blame her? I'm not her mother. I'm not anyone's mother. I want to be part of a family.

And this morning, you made it really clear that you already have one. That there's no room for me."

"That's not true, Bella. I didn't mean for it to… just, calm down. Let's—"

"Don't tell me to calm down. My feelings are valid. What you said to Milly and Mason this morning—"

"Was me trying to reassure them."

"So, you lied to them? Either you think I could belong to your family or not."

"I know that." I squeeze her fingers again in an attempt to take the sting out of my words. Leading her into Selina's living room, I sit on the couch and tug her down beside me. "What's going on, Bella?"

She shakes her head. "I can't keep existing in this limbo, James. Either we're together or we're not. I respect Milly and I understand that she may need time. But I'm not emotionally strong enough to live in your house, care for your children, see you every day, and not be together. And I'm not at a point where I can continue a relationship with a man who doesn't want the same things as me. I want a family. To be part of a family. I don't want to be an outsider, existing on the edge."

Her words are absolute and direct, an ultimatum underlining her tone that causes me to rear back. "I can't make those decisions right now and you know it. So, what are you really saying?"

"I'm saying, I need you to be honest with me. Are we in this together or not? Can we desire the same things for the future or no?"

I narrow my eyes at her, irritated how she's glossing over everything. Boiling down huge issues into mere sentences. "Honesty? You want to talk about honesty? Why was Jerry here, Bella? Did he just randomly show up? Why didn't you tell me about how ugly your divorce was? Or how about you shed some light on why you run every morning, like a junkie addicted to heroin? Pushing yourself until you're ready to collapse?"

She pulls her hand away from mine and glares at me. "That's not fair. That has nothing to do with you. With us."

But now I'm angry. How dare she think I'm not in this with her? When I'm right here, still asking her to celebrate Christmas with my family. Still wanting to work through everything and have her live in my home. "Doesn't it? It's like I don't even know you sometimes. You only let me see the pieces you want and sidestep the rest."

"That's not true. You've *seen* more of me than, than anyone else. Even Dr. Carlisle thinks so." She bites down hard, rolling her lips together.

I narrow my eyes, my anger spiking. "Who the hell is Dr. Carlisle?"

Bella hangs her head and mutters, "He's my therapist."

I throw a hand in the air, an incredulous chuckle dropping from my lips. "And you didn't think that was something you should mention to me? To confide in me about when I've shared every fucking thing with you? Everything. And I come here tonight to find fucking Jerry standing on the other side of the threshold." I stand up from the couch, walking a few paces away to put space between us, to clear my head. This conversation is going all wrong.

Everything about today is all wrong.

I whirl to face Bella. "I love you, Bella. I am in love with you. And as much as you want to sit here and try to paint a picture where I'm not all in the way you are, I call bullshit. Becoming a family, having children, adoption, those are conversations we would have eventually discussed. As our relationship progressed, it would have naturally come up. But no, until I met you, I never considered marrying again. The thought of having more babies never crossed my mind. But those future hypotheticals have nothing to do with right now.

You've never been as invested in this relationship as I've been. If you were, you would have opened up about your baggage a hell of a lot earlier. You would have trusted me the same way I trusted you. We were planning to tell my *children* about us when you haven't even told your parents. Your brother. Does Dr. Carlisle know?"

Bella's eyes flare, her mouth dropping open. "That's not fair, James."

"None of this is fair." I gesture between us. In my pocket, my phone buzzes and when I slip it out, Maia's name flashes across the screen. I swear, shaking my head. "I gotta go. I'm leaving for Delaware on Wednesday. I'll see if Maia and her mom can help with childcare so you can have some time off. Go home for the holidays, see your family. Will I see you when we get back?"

She nods stiffly, averting her gaze. "In the new year, I'll stay at the house when you're traveling but I can't live with you guys anymore."

I chuckle humorlessly. "So that's it? You're pumping the brakes, just like that?"

She glares at me, her blue eyes glittering like hardened gemstones. "Consider it self-preservation. I'm already in too deep with a family that was never going to be mine."

Her words pummel me, a jab to the temple I never saw coming. I back away slowly, holding up a hand in defense. "Merry Christmas, Bella," I mutter as I near the door.

She holds my gaze until I open the door and slip outside, into the cold winter night. I don't feel the drop in temperature though because inside, I'm blazing, an inferno wreaking havoc on my nervous system.

What the hell just happened? Why did Bella push me away? How large and looming are the demons she's battling? Why wouldn't she tell me about Dr. Carlisle and therapy?

The realization that she's withheld a lot more than I have

cuts deep because I thought I could trust her. I thought we were moving forward together, helping each other heal.

Instead, I feel like I did waking up in that hotel room over the summer—foolish, embarrassed, and ashamed. Lost.

CHAPTER 20
BELLA

The ocean waves of the Pacific crash against the California coastal bluffs, spraying sea and salt into the air. I grip the neckline of my robe tighter as I step out onto the balcony. The temperature, a balmy 50 degrees, is much warmer than Boston but still, I feel cold. I have since James walked away, leaving me to stare into the void, the rush of my anger and hurt cooling into a frozen tundra that still hasn't thawed.

"You hungry?" Colton appears beside me, shielding his eyes from the sunshine as he turns toward me.

"No thanks."

"You have to eat, Bells."

I nod, even though I haven't had much of an appetite lately.

My brother sighs. "Why don't you call him?"

"And say what?" I don't tear my gaze from the ocean, the swirling whitecaps and fog layering on the horizon. The Pacific is a complicated, dangerous sea that can drown you as quickly as it can infuse your soul with joy.

Over six years ago, I married Jerry on a beach much like

this one. I gazed into his eyes and thought I saw my forever staring back at me.

I snort, my thoughts too depressing to be ironic.

"You're still working for his family, Bells. Unless you decided to call it quits on that too?"

My neck swivels toward my brother at the sharpness in his tone. It's unlike Colton to tough love me when I'm feeling so low. I narrow my eyes but he crosses his arms and lifts his eyebrows, waiting for my words.

"No, I'm still working for the Ryan family."

"Right." Colton nods. "Because disappearing on Milly and Mason, after all they've been through, would be a pretty shitty thing to do. And my sister wouldn't—"

"I'm not bailing," I snap.

"No, you're hiding. Again."

I push away from the railing and throw my hands up in the air. "What does everyone want from me? I'm hiding, I'm running, I'm numb... I don't know how the hell to be, okay? What do you want me to do?"

"I want you to try." Colton's voice is raw, scraped with emotion and jagged with the hurt of seeing me hurt. "I want you to stop pretending everything is fucking fine. Stop going through the motions of your goddamn life and embrace it. Feel something. Let it move you and break you and put you back together again. Because I can't do this anymore, Bells." He points at me. "I can't keep trying to hold you together if you're not going to at least try to be some goddamn glue."

Colton storms off the balcony, the screen door sliding closed behind him. I sigh and turn back to the ocean. He's right. Deep down I know he is. After James left, my brother and Selina returned to find me sobbing on my knees. At first, they thought Jerry had hurt me again but after I managed to get the whole story out, they both looked at me with a mixture of pity and judgment that made me recoil.

Milly's a child. She needs you now more than ever. Don't give up on them just because things with James are complicated. Why haven't you told James everything? He doesn't know that Jerry hit you? He doesn't know about the anxious thoughts and the need to run? About Dr. Carlisle?

I didn't have any good responses because deep down, they're right. All of them, James included.

Colton decided I needed a time-out. Space and a chance of scenery to clear my head, be alone with my thoughts, and decide what I really want to happen next. If James and I have a future, will Milly and Mason want me as a stepmom? What do I even want to do with my life anymore?

Should I finish my PhD program to pursue the career I always thought I'd have? Is it still the career I want?

Can I make things right with James? Does he still want me? Can he forgive me?

Colton and Selina convinced me to take a time-out and my parents fully supported this decision. By the following after-noon, Mom and Dad had rented a place on Hermosa Beach, not too far from Los Angeles. Selina had packed up some of her clothing and toiletries, with Colton promising to purchase the rest. And I'm beachside in December, soaking up sunshine and trying to ease my tears.

I close my eyes and let the wind blow across my face. Instead of breaking down the way I would have a few years ago, I focus on my breathing. I let the sea soothe me. I let my thoughts wander, flitting in and out of my mind in their own time.

I am not the woman I was then. I have grown. I have endured years of therapy and coping mechanisms. I have survived the worst of whatever could happen, whatever will happen. And I have persevered.

James was right. I am real and there is nothing more beau-tiful than that.

My lips part and an anguished scream bursts forth, piercing the air for a heartbeat before it's swallowed by the wind. But releasing the hurt makes room in my chest for other things.

Like grace. Hope. A desire to do better, to be better.

I don't know how long I stand at the railing, staring at the ocean. But when I return inside, Colton is seated at the dining table, a lunch spread out.

He quirks an eyebrow, giving me a look. "You ready to figure out what comes next?"

I nod, sitting across from him and taking a sip of the sparkling water. "What do you think I should do?"

Colton flashes his lopsided grin. "I think you should call Dr. Carlisle."

I snort.

"You've been through a lot, Bella. But you can't keep punishing yourself for losing Miles, for divorcing Jerry. It's time for you to make a new plan, one that centers on your happiness, on creating the future you'd like to live."

I nod slowly, considering his words. "Yeah."

I look down at the plated food, a strip of salmon, a kale salad, some potatoes. Then I pick up my fork and take a mouthful, allowing myself to appreciate the good food, allowing myself to be present in this moment.

I will never be worthy of a man like James or a family of my own if I'm not willing to make myself whole. It may have taken me a long and twisted road to arrive at this point but my next step forward is done with intention. It is taken with a promise to myself.

To be a person Miles would have been proud to call Mom.

After lunch, I pick up the phone and call Dr. Carlisle.

IN THE FOLLOWING DAYS, I hold multiple sessions with Dr. Carlisle. I spend stretches of hours walking along the beach, staring at the sea. I talk, I cry, I force myself to confront so many of the things I've kept buried for years. Since speaking with James about Miles, I find it easier to remember that time in my life with a flicker of gratitude for the baby I was able to hold, even for a moment. Slowly, I'm able to think of Miles's presence as the blessing it was instead of the tragedy it became.

Christmas comes and goes. My parents fly out for a few days and we gather around the dining table, catching up and laughing at old memories, the way we used to in too many years past. The entire holiday leaves a bittersweet taste in my mouth but as the days pass, the sour turns sweet.

I send Milly and Mason gifts and trinkets from the beach to let them know I'm thinking of them. That I haven't forgotten them. That I will be back.

I'm eating breakfast one morning, waiting for Dr. Carlisle to call for our morning session, when my phone beeps.

JAMES

Merry Christmas, Bella. Thank you for the gifts for the kids. You didn't have to send anything.

My thumb brushes over his name on the screen and a swell of longing fills my chest. God, I miss him. I wish I had been more honest and open with him from the start. I wish he knew the depth of my agony. Maybe he would have understood? Maybe I wouldn't have needed so much intervention to set myself on the right path.

BELLA

Merry Christmas! It's no worries. I miss them. Hope you're all enjoying Delaware.

JAMES

We miss you. How are you?

We. Does that mean him too? I hope so.

BELLA

I'm okay. Sorting through some things. It's long overdue.

JAMES

???

BELLA

I'll see you in the New Year.

JAMES

We should talk.

My stomach twists at his words. Jerry's message from weeks ago flickers through my mind. Will talking to James do more good or harm at this point? What will I even say to him? Am I ready to have the real conversation, the one where I leave all my cards on the table, and allow him to see the depths of my vulnerability?

I blow out a deep breath and pick up my coffee mug. I take a long sip and let the bold roast center me. Right now, I need to focus on the matter at hand. A ringing sound and a pop-up window on the screen of my laptop alerts me to Dr. Carlisle's call.

BELLA

Soon. Have a good day.

James's name flashes across the phone screen a second later but I ignore his call, place my phone facedown on the table, and accept Dr. Carlisle's invitation to talk.

JAMES

Are you okay?

BELLA

I'm getting there.

JAMES

Please, talk to me, Bella. I'm worried
about you.

BELLA

Don't be. I'm right where I need to be.

JAMES

Are you still coming back in time for the
Detroit game? Are you visiting your parents?

BELLA

Yes, I'll be back in time for the Detroit game.
Are the twins having fun with their
grandmother?

JAMES

Yes. They are thrilled to spend time with their
new baby cousin too. I'm back in Boston but
Maia is going to stay in Delaware with them
this week and bring them back on Tuesday.

BELLA

That's great. It's good to have family you can
count on. I'll be back in town next weekend.

MINUTES PASS and I wonder if James is going to respond.
I turn in my bed, reaching over to the bedside table to place
down the book I was reading and flick off the lamp. I'm tired
but a ripple of satisfaction runs through me. With each

passing day, I feel more balanced and less agitated. I'm building a toolbox with methods to use when the anxiety swells. I'm learning how to cope and discovering more about the life I'd like to lead.

The shift from last week to today is tangible. Of course I know I'm not perfectly healed. I know this is more about the journey than the destination and that I can get better but not necessarily be well. But I'm on the path. I'm putting in the time. I'm being honest and I'm not shying away from the feelings, as mentally draining and emotionally gutting as they are. With each sunrise, I feel a little more settled, a little less restless, a bit more whole. My runs have lost some of their intensity, the need to physically exhaust myself has lessened. I am making progress. I hit a bump in the road and now I'm realigning. Dr. Carlisle says this happens sometimes and the important thing is to keep going, keep moving forward.

JAMES

You can still count on me.

James's message surprises me and I read it three times to make sure I'm understanding it correctly. But I know he's being honest. I know that right now, if I called him and needed him, he'd drop everything to show up for me. I smile at the thought, the realization a comfort. But I'm not ready to let James in yet. Soon, but not yet.

BELLA

I know. We'll talk soon.

JAMES

I hope so, Bella. I'm ready when you are.

I smile again, a little thrill zipping through me. I miss James Ryan more than words can express. I hope I can be worthy of him once more. I glance at the time, realizing it's already after midnight in Boston. I yawn and tap out one last message.

BELLA

Good night, James.

JAMES

Sweet dreams, Bella.

CHAPTER 21
JAMES

Indecision and frustration weigh on me as I stare at Bella's text messages from last night. She's erected a wall between us, a barrier I can't scale no matter how hard I try.

"Hey." Austin sits down on the bench in front of me.

"Hey," I reply, dropping my phone into my practice bag. I look around the locker room, realizing we're the only two left.

"Want to grab a beer?" my team captain asks.

I grin and shake my head. "Am I that obvious that you're suggesting beer before a game?"

"Game's tomorrow. Come on. Taps?"

"Sure." I nod, grateful for the distraction.

Austin and I leave The Meadow together, catching up from the holidays. He tells me about how his family spent Christmas with his girl, Chloe, and her family. Sure, the Merricks and the Crawfords go way back, from when Austin and Chloe were kids. But as Austin explains how they blended their holiday traditions, I recognize just how important it is to keep old memories alive while continually adding to them and making space for new ones. A hollowness spreads through my chest at the realization that I never made enough room for Bella and her past in my world.

She wants a family and I never considered how that would look. Not for the first time, I wish I was open with Milly and Mason from the start. I wish I better understood Bella's desires and the twins' expectations before I started envisioning a future that might not align with everyone else's.

I think about that as I drive to Taps.

When Austin and I are seated at the bar, with fresh pints set out before us, Austin tilts his head toward me. "Lay it on me, man."

"It's really not that bad," I say.

"You've been in your head all week."

I sigh, tipping my chin in acknowledgement. This past week, I have been a little lost, and not even the promise of hockey and the allure of the ice has been able to draw me from my thoughts. "Bella and I…" I trail off, unsure what to say.

"What happened?"

I swear and Austin raises his eyebrows. I quickly fill him in on everything that transpired since Milly caught Bella and me in bed together. "And now," I conclude, "I realized how much I don't know about her. About her past. I mean, I show up to Selina's place and Bella's crying, looking at her dirtbag ex-husband like he's worth a damn. I know nothing about their history. It just…it fucking sucks that she's kept her guard up around me while I've let her in."

Austin takes a swig of his beer, his expression carefully neutral. "Where is she now?"

"Spending the holidays with her family. But that's another thing. She promised she'd never ghost me and…I know she didn't just leave. It's not like she won't respond to my messages or anything. But when things between us got tough, she ran."

"You're angry," Austin notes.

I shrug, picking up my pint. "I'm hurt."

"Because she took a time-out?" he asks.

"Because she doesn't trust me. Not the same way I trust her."

"Have you guys talked?"

"She says we will but she's not ready yet. I need to respect that."

"Yeah, you do," Austin says and I look at him in surprise. He offers me a small smile. "It sounds like she's working through a lot. I know you feel like she wasn't as upfront with you as you were with her. But if she let you in, even a little bit, it means she trusts you. It's just harder for her, and if she's working through that, then she obviously needs the time and space to do so."

"Shit," I swear. "I think you may be right." Even Bella admitted that I've seen more of her than anyone else. Does this mean she's spent the past few years suffering in silence? The thought makes me ache for her on top of all the loss she's experienced.

"How are the twins handling it?" Austin tips back his beer and polishes it off.

"They're doing okay. They've been distracted, being in Delaware with Maia and their teta. They're there until next week and I think the space from Boston, the time with their family, has been good for them."

"That's good."

"Yeah. I miss them though. I wish I understood Milly's reaction more. Why is she upset about Bella? Not that she shouldn't be; I just want to understand the root of her concerns. To help her clarify them so we can work through them."

"Are the twins in therapy?" Austin asks.

"Huh?" I look up. At the surprise on his expression, I wince, and recall the folder I tucked away in the kitchen junk drawer after Layla passed. "No, but maybe I should make an appointment for Milly?"

"It can't hurt. You can try a family session too," Austin advises.

I nod slowly, wondering how the hell I didn't think of this sooner. "Yeah. Okay, thanks, Austin. I have a teammate from college whose wife is a children's therapist at Bellevue."

"Worth making a phone call."

"Yeah. It is. Thanks, man," I say seriously. Then, I grin and clasp his shoulder. "You're one hell of a captain, Cap."

He shakes off my touch and flips me the bird but he's smiling too.

I turn toward Pete and order another round.

I RETURN HOME THAT EVENING, acutely aware of how quiet it is. I miss the twins but I miss Bella too. I plop onto the living room couch and kick my feet up on the coffee table, glancing around the space. Layla's smile stares down at me from a framed family photo on the mantle. The twins' artwork is framed on the wall to the right. We built a beautiful life here and now that life, the one I knew and clung to, has passed. It was agonizing and awful and brought me to a crossroads.

For too long I gave up on trying to find happiness. I gave up on a lot of things. But existing isn't the life Layla would want for me. In fact, she'd probably be disappointed if I didn't strive to set a better example for Milly and Mason. If I didn't aspire to try again, to be open to new possibilities, to allow myself to fall in love.

Of course, I'd never do anything to hurt my daughter's fragile emotional state, but I also can't abandon my feelings for Bella.

What is she working through now? Does she even want

me after everything that happened between us? Does she still want us?

What about the twins? Are they open to the changes that my being in a relationship with Bella would bring? Could they ever view her as their stepmother?

My phone rings and I swipe it off the coffee table, sitting straight as Maia's name flashes across the screen. That flicker of panic, the one that sparked to life when I became a dad and has only increased since, burns through me.

"Maia, what's wrong?" I answer.

She snorts and I can picture her rolling her eyes on the other end of the line. "Nothing, JR. Nothing is wrong."

"Oh." I settle back into the couch cushions. "Okay. What's going on?"

"Well, I just had a chat with my favorite niece and she shed some light on a very interesting conversation."

I freeze, gripping the phone tighter. "Is Milly okay? Is it about Bella?"

"Milly's fine," Maia says gently. "And yes, it's about Bella."

I bite my cheek to keep from blurting out a million questions. In a strange way, it's as if my recent thoughts somehow conjured up this conversation with Maia. Things are about to come full circle, this conversation is about to answer all the unknowns I've been contemplating.

"She's scared," Maia says.

"What?" I ask, my eyebrows dipping.

"Milly's scared that if Bella becomes too close to you all, a part of your family, then she'll die like Layla." Maia's voice cracks on her sister's name and my chest squeezes at the pain in her tone. At the fear my poor baby girl has been trying to swallow down, not knowing how to confide it in me.

"No," I say, my voice layered with emotion. "No, she would have told me…"

"She didn't know how. JR, I think on some level she

knows it doesn't make sense but she can't help the fear, the anxiety, she's experiencing."

My stomach twists and I feel physically ill. My conversation with Austin flares to life in my mind as I recall other conversations. Conversations I had with childhood psychologists after Layla's death. Words like bereavement, loss of control, depression, post-traumatic stress, avoidance. Words I overlooked at the time because I was a single dad drowning in grief.

But now…how many signs did I miss? How much did I not recognize?

"Jesus," I mutter, feeling like I'm caught in a riptide. I'm way out of my depth here and that familiar feeling of failure overwhelms me. "I let her down."

"No, no you didn't, JR. You couldn't have known," Maia tries, her tone compassionate.

"I'm her father, Maia. I should have seen the…the signs. I should have talked to her more about Bella. When she ran out of the room crying that morning, I didn't listen the way I should have."

"You did your best," Maia refutes. "You're a good dad, JR. Parenting isn't easy and single parenting is something else entirely."

I blow out a sigh, shaking my head. "How's she doing?"

"She's good. Right now, she and mom are baking maamoul."

I smile, recalling the shortbread cookies filled with dates that Layla loved to bake during the holidays.

"Can I talk to her?" I ask, not wanting to interrupt her time with her teta but also needing to hear her voice.

"Of course." Maia calls out for Milly.

"How's Mase?"

"He's great. He's having a good time, loves being with the baby. I think he misses you. And Bella. But he doesn't have the same worries Milly is struggling with. Hang on, here she is."

"Thanks, Maia. For everything."

"Anytime," my sister-in-law says. In the next breath, the sweetest voice I've ever heard comes through the line.

"Hi, Daddy," Milly says.

"Hey, Mil. How're you doing, sweetheart?"

"I'm good."

"You having fun?"

"Yes, I'm baking with Teta. Amo Zein is taking Mase and me to the movies later."

I snort, betting that Layla's brother Zein, a new father, is desperate to get out of the house for a short while. His son has colic and I know it hasn't been an easy transition for the first-time parents. "That sounds awesome. If Amo Zein falls asleep, go easy on him."

"I will. I miss you, Daddy."

"Miss you too, Jellybean. Aunt Maia is bringing you home soon."

"Will Bella be there?"

I sigh, not sure how to answer that question. Bella said she'd be back by the time we play Detroit but…she hasn't said anything since. Should I look for alternative childcare? Should I ask Maia to come with me and the kids to Detroit?

"I really miss her," Milly adds.

"You do?"

"Yeah. I-I thought if you and Bella got married, then something would happen to her. What would we do if she died too?"

I swallow past the lump in my throat, my hands nearly shaking. "That's not going to happen, baby girl."

"But how do you *know*? Mama used to say you can't predict the future."

"Well, that's true. But what happened to Mama doesn't

happen to everyone. Have any of your friends lost their mommies?"

"No."

"See?" I point out gently.

"But now Bella's gone anyway. I cried too much and she left."

My heart breaks for Milly. "That's not true either, Jellybean. Bella just had some things she needed to take care of."

"So, she's coming back?" she asks hopefully as my stomach sinks.

"I hope so," I answer truthfully.

"I hope so too, Daddy." She sighs and then, "Can't you fix this? Make her come home? You always protect your team, right?"

Emotion builds in my throat, making it difficult to swallow or speak. I clear my throat and grip the phone until my knuckles ache. "Right. I'll see what I can do, okay, Mils?"

"Okay. Here's Aunt Maia."

"Love you, Jellybean."

"Love you," Milly says.

"JR?" Maia comes back on the line.

"Did you hear all of that?" I ask.

"I did," Maia says slowly. "Are you asking what I think you should do?"

"I'm not opposed to hearing your two cents," I joke.

"Bring her home, JR. I know it hasn't been easy but...if you love Bella, she must be pretty special. Don't pass her up because of your past. Or hers."

"Yeah," I agree, clearing my throat again. "I'll see..."

"Call her. Then let me know what you need from me. Anything I can do to help, I'll—"

"You already do more than you should."

She laughs. "We're family, James. This is what family does."

"Thanks, Maia."

"See you soon."

"See you. And thanks." I hang up the phone and force myself to stand.

Pacing around my living room, I try to make sense of everything that happened. Milly trying to manage her anxiety, trying to process her mother's death. Mason, desperate to be back in a stable family environment, his uncle and baby cousin providing stability and a sense of merriment that I've been short on. Bella, away for the holidays, barely speaking to me, and still slaying demons.

I enter the kitchen and dig through the junk drawer until I find the folder I'm looking for. Then, I dial the number handwritten on the bottom.

"Bellevue Psychology, how may I direct your call?"

"Hi, may I please speak with Dr. Haley?" I ask.

"Certainly. May I ask who's calling?"

"This is James. James Ryan," I state.

A moment later, a friendly voice I recall from college floods the line. "James? I'm so glad you called."

After I make an appointment for Milly to meet with my college teammate's wife, I make appointments for my family to see another therapist.

Then, I dial Selina and ask for Colton's number. As soon as she sends the contact, I call him.

"Hello?" he answers on the first ring.

"Colton? It's James. James Ryan."

He snorts and for a second, I'm worried he's pissed off with me too. But then he says, "It's about time you called, man," and I breathe a little easier.

"How is she?" I ask.

"She's getting there…"

"I need to see her."

"Why?" he asks, and even though his questioning is impeding my plan, I respect the way he looks out for his sister. It provides a slice of comfort to know that someone is looking out for Bella the way she deserves.

"Because I love her and I want to bring her home," I say, my voice even, my sincerity blatant.

Colton is quiet for a moment before his chuckle sounds out. "Happy to hear it, man. Better get your ass down to SoCal. We're in Hermosa Beach."

"What?" I laugh, surprise rocking through me. Bella's in California? I don't know why but whenever I pictured her with her family for the holidays, I imagined a quiet family gathering around a dining table in snowy Massachusetts. Not a waterfront condo on the beach.

"Yep," Colton says, rattling off the information.

"I'm booking the next flight out."

"Send me your flight details. I'll see you at the airport."

I recognize the olive branch for what it is and thank Colton.

Then, I book a flight, pack a bag, and head to the airport to see my girl.

CHAPTER 22

BELLA

Seagulls squawk and the ocean rumbles as I walk down the coastline after dinner. The sun is slowly setting, painting the sky in brilliant oranges and golden hues. The wet sand clumps beneath my feet and the ocean runs over my toes, washing away my sins and easing my guilt.

I miss James. I miss Milly and Mason. I miss Miles.

These long hours and short days to myself have been both cathartic and restorative. I've let go a lot of the past, putting to bed many of my issues with Jerry since I finally received the closure I needed from our divorce.

I've also allowed myself the chance to envision a future free from guilt, shame, and shortcomings. That future includes James and the Ryan family no matter how I think about it. As much as I hope James and I can continue our relationship, I won't ever put my romantic hopes before Milly's emotional well-being. In a handful of months, Milly and Mason have become so dear to my heart and I would never want to hinder their grieving process or jeopardize their future happiness.

I stop to pick up a seashell, my fingertips running along the jagged edge. It's white with hints of blush and splashes of a deeper mauve. It's beautiful in a completely imperfect way that causes me to smile. I tuck the shell into my pocket just as I hear my name.

What is Colton doing down here?

I turn slowly, my hair whipping back as the wind hits me square in the face.

A man is jogging toward me, barefoot, in a pair of sweat shorts and a hoodie.

One of his hands is lifted to his mouth as he calls my name again and my knees almost buckle.

"James?" I call back, surprise exploding in my chest.

But it's most certainly him, running toward me with an urgency I wouldn't believe if I wasn't witnessing it with my own eyes.

He slows as he nears, the ocean spraying up over his legs as the tide rolls in.

"What are you doing here?" I ask, my hands dropping to my sides. I watch his face closely, trying to piece it all together by the emotions flitting across his expression.

But it's impossible.

Because he looks hopeful, earnest, and concerned all at once.

"I always protect my team," he states.

"What?"

"I came to bring you home," he says clearly, like it should be obvious.

I frown and James closes the last bit of space between us, reaching for my hands. His hands engulf mine, his fingers squeezing tightly. I shuffle forward, a sigh falling from my lips at the warmth he provides, at the glow his presence alone casts me in.

"Home?" I repeat, bewilderment rocking through me.

James's expression softens, the moonlight rippling over his face. "Home. I miss you, Bella. I love you. I know we had a rocky start. I know we did everything backwards. But I'm not giving up on us and I came here to see if you feel the same way. If you're ready to come home and figure out the next part together."

Emotion swells inside of me, causing tears to gather in the corners of my eyes. "But, but what about Milly and—"

"A misunderstanding."

I press my lips together, my eyes wide as I wait for James to continue.

"She was scared. Afraid that if we got together, you would die like—"

"Her mother," I say, realization dawning. Of course she was scared. How did I not see it sooner? This is what I studied and when I needed it most, I didn't recognize Milly's concern for what it truly is—fear.

"It's a bit irrational but—"

"It's not," I cut him off again. "It's completely natural for children affected by loss to feel like so many aspects of life are out of their control. It makes them want to cling to the parts they have some say in." I shake my head. "Poor Milly. I should have seen it."

"That's how I feel too. She's my daughter and I let her down."

"How is she?"

James smiles. "She misses you."

The tears spill over and I dip my head.

"Hey, don't cry." James's finger curls under my chin, lifting my face to meet his. "Don't cry, baby. Just…talk to me."

"I miss her too. I miss you all. I just felt so confused, so overwhelmed and…the space has been good for me," I admit.

James nods slowly, uncertainty fanning out over his face.

I take another step forward, our chests nearly brushing when we inhale.

"I've already lost more than I ever imagined and it devastated me. But I learned that I have more control than I realized too. I'm not willing to lose you, James. I don't want to live without you and your family. I don't want to give up on us, especially not over a miscommunication."

"I know," he responds, his hand lifting to cup the side of my face. His hand spans my cheek, his thumb tilting my face upward until his eyes meet mine with an intensity that takes my breath away. "I love you, Bella."

"I love you too, James." I smile, biting my bottom lip. "But I should warn you, I'm an emotional train wreck."

A soft smile glances off his mouth as tenderness flares in his irises. "I should warn you, I'm done being left in the dark. We need to do better, Bella. We need to *talk* about things, especially the things that make you run away."

"We need to trust each other," I agree.

"Can we start now?" he asks hopefully.

I nod and James brushes the pad of his thumb along my bottom lip.

"I was hoping you'd say that," he murmurs as he lowers his head.

When his lips meet mine, I close my eyes and melt into him. He kisses me slowly, our mouths exploring, our touches sweet. James and I kiss under a dusky sky on a beach in California and this time, I don't try to plan out our forever, I just savor the moment. Because this moment, with this man, is already everything.

COLTON IS PERCHED on the couch, his suitcase packed, when we enter the condo.

"Heading somewhere?" I joke, my laughter fading as I note the seriousness in his eyes.

But Colton laughs as he stands and gestures between

James and me. "Glad you guys kissed and made up. That's my cue to head out."

"Wait, what?" I ask, stepping forward.

Colton grins, his eyes clear. "I'm happy for you, Bells. Now that your man showed up, it means I can head home to my life. And you can move forward with yours."

"You don't have to—" James starts but Colton holds up a hand, stopping him.

"I'm glad you called, James," Colton says and that missing piece of the puzzle snaps into place in my mind. "My sister is lucky to have a man like you in her life. But you're also lucky as hell to have a woman like her."

"I know," James agrees, making my heart warm.

"You guys need to talk and I don't need to be here for that part," Colton says lightly, gripping the handle of his suitcase. "Honestly, I don't want to be."

James laughs.

"Sort it all out now. Enjoy a few days at the beach. Eat some good food," Colt continues.

I snort.

My brother smiles at me. "I ordered you takeout."

"Breakfast for dinner," I say and Colton winks, knowing it's my favorite.

"Come here." Colton opens his arms and I step into them for a hug. "You're okay, Bells. You're more than okay," he whispers in my ear.

"Thank you for everything, Colton." I squeeze him tightly.

He kisses the top of my head and releases me. Then he turns and shakes James's hand. "Take care of her."

"I will," James promises, his voice serious.

Colton nods once. We walk him to the door and say one final goodbye. Before James can close the door, our delivery arrives and we both laugh.

We carry in the takeout boxes and plop down on the living room floor, making a picnic with the coffee table between us.

"This was nice of Colton," James says conversationally.

"I'm sure he's just relieved to not have to listen to me cry anymore," I joke.

But James looks up sharply. "No more tears, Bella. From here on out, we need to talk to each other. Be honest."

"I know," I agree, pulling out packets of syrup and ketchup.

James lifts an eyebrow. "Jerry?"

I sigh, scrubbing a hand over my face. "He came for closure. He's having a baby, he's in rehab, and he's completing his steps."

"Making amends."

I nod.

"For not supporting you after Miles passed?" James asks slowly, his gaze sharp upon my face.

"For that," I agree. "And for…being abusive." I watch the color drain from James's face, his body freezing until he's so still, I can't even hear his inhales.

"What happened?" he asks slowly, his jaw clenched so tightly I wonder if it's going to crack.

"After Miles, Jerry had a hard time."

James's eyes narrow and I forge ahead.

"He turned to alcohol and the drunker he got, the more nights his drinking went unchecked, the uglier the things he would say were. It quickly became an emotionally abusive environment, with Jerry cutting me down every chance he could. I was almost too numb to react. But then one night…" I pause, blowing out a deep breath. James's hand reaches out, settling on my leg for support. I offer him a small smile but his expression remains unchanged. "One night, he hit me."

"Fuck," James breathes out. Even though I know he knew it was coming, I think hearing me say the words makes it a hell of a lot more real in his mind. "Were you okay? What happened?"

"He backhanded me across the face and I fell into the

stove, banging my hip." My voice is even, devoid of emotion. It's strange but when I think back to that night, I can envision it with perfect clarity. But it's almost as if I'm watching the scene unfold as a spectator, observing everything from above, as an out-of-body experience.

"I told him we were getting divorced the following day. That was the last straw and we both knew there was nothing left of our marriage to salvage. Jerry went downhill pretty fast after that and I was too…heartbroken, numb, empty, to care. I threw myself into work. Into caring for the children of other families. I picked up every shift Selina would give me. I ran every morning, and most nights as well, until I felt like vomiting. I did everything I could to ward off the feelings that threatened to drag me under. I didn't want to feel. I didn't want to cope. I just wanted to…"

"Disappear," James supplies.

I nod, hating the heartache that bleeds from his eyes. "Yes. I've been in therapy since Miles passed but after Jerry, my sessions picked up. Dr. Carlisle has helped me manage my thoughts, my anxiety, from the beginning. Slowly, my running lost some of its intensity. I've been able to think about the future, about being part of a family, about career options, with an open mind again. And then, everything got better, more hopeful, after I met you."

"That night at Taps," James says slowly, "that was a turning point for me."

"For me too. That's why I left. I, I was scared. I felt too much for you. All the emotions I spent months, years, burying, were right there, at the surface and I ran."

James's grasp on my leg tightens. "I understand, Bella. More than most people, I truly understand."

"I know you do."

"But if Jerry comes near you again," he growls, "I'll—"

"That won't be necessary. Jerry is part of my past now." I place my hand on top of his and squeeze.

His expression is tortured and I know it's hard for him to reconcile the scenario in his mind with him not reacting to it. But he doesn't need to because I already did. I've finally put that chapter of my life to rest and it's freeing to move forward without it hanging over me, like a black shroud threatening disaster.

"No more running away," he murmurs. "You promised you wouldn't ghost me again."

Shame swims in my stomach as guilt rises in my throat. "No more running."

James shifts forward onto his knees, our food forgotten. His mouth covers mine and I lean back, my hands planting flat against the floor to brace against his sudden shift.

His mouth is desperate against mine, needy and hungry. His fervor ignites a passion, low in my belly, that gathers and blazes the longer he kisses me. I revel in the possessive edge of his touch, feel beholden to the glint in his eyes.

James pulls back, his breathing ragged. He buries one hand in the hair at the back of my head and guides me down slowly, until he's hovering over me.

"I won't let him hurt you again, Bella."

"I know."

"And I won't let you disappear."

"I hope not, James."

"I won't lose you, Bella. That means talking about things, compromising."

I nod, biting my bottom lip as his gaze intensifies.

He dips his head and presses a long kiss against my lips. When he pulls back, he murmurs, "You are part of my family. And having more children isn't off the table. It never was. It's a conversation I want to have. It's something I'm open to… with you only." His eyes search mine.

I blink away my tears, as hope swells inside my chest. "We'll talk about it," I whisper.

"Yeah, baby. We'll talk about everything."

"You're my home, James. I'm not going anywhere without you by my side."

"Good," he bites out. Then he dips his head again and kisses me passionately.

I moan into his mouth and arch into his frame, meeting his every kiss and touch with my own.

We have sex, hot, heady, and frantic on the living room floor, with the ocean waves sounding through the open balcony door and the night sky surrounding us.

Then we relocate to the bedroom, where our touches linger, our kissing soothes, and our lovemaking turns sweet and blissful.

When the sun rises over the Pacific, we collapse on the couch and eat cold waffles and iced coffee.

It's the best morning after I've ever had and when I tell James, his laughter fills me up with love.

CHAPTER 23

JAMES

Easton takes a slapshot that glides into the corner of the net, securing our lead over New York. The fans are on their feet, cheers ringing out through the arena. I pump an arm in the air and skate toward my teammates, smacking their helmets and congratulating East.

When I glance into the stands, my eyes automatically zero in on the family box where Bella and the twins shout and dance, jumping up and down. Their faces are painted with excitement, their eyes glow, and a sense of peace flows throughout my body.

It wasn't easy getting to this point. I've endured a hell of a lot of heartache and an alarming amount of self-doubt. My ego has taken too many hits to count and for a long time, I felt like I could barely keep my head above water.

But the past few months have changed everything. Meeting Bella Andrews was the turning point I needed, even if I didn't recognize it at the time. Spending time with her, getting to know her, watching her interact with Milly and Mason clarified my priorities and restored my faith in love.

I pause on the ice, unable to turn away from the scene. Bella has her arms around Milly and Mason, squishing them into a hug that has the three of them cracking up. She's been a force of positivity in their lives, helping Milly navigate her grief and anxiety, supporting Mason as he dives into new challenges.

When I hired Bella at the start of the school year, I hoped for a seamless transition. I never anticipated that the bartender from Taps would weave her way into the fabric of my family with invisible thread, becoming a part of us.

She looks up and our eyes hold, the noise and chaos of the arena freezing for a moment. Bella smiles, her face lighting up, and gratitude rushes over me.

I lift my hand, she tips her chin, and we both honor the moment. Because moments like these, where everything clicks together, where suddenly you can view the world with a sharper, crisper lens, where health and happiness and love trump every little thing, are rare. We both know that and we both savor them whenever they flare up.

"I love you," she mouths to me. I blow her a kiss that Milly catches and giggles.

Then Noah smacks me on the back and my focus returns to my team, to the game.

I play the last period hard, going all in on every play. Knowing my girl and my kids are in the stands, that my family is watching over me, I play like I will forever. Like my days as a hockey defenseman nearing forty aren't numbered.

I play like I did as a kid, savoring the sweep of exhilaration that floods my stomach when I catch sight of their cheering faces.

In another season or two, it will be time to hang up my skates, but knowing that I get to go home and build a life with my three biggest fans makes it a hell of a lot sweeter.

We win the game and the applause is deafening. I let myself get lost in the swarm of my teammates, in the locker room joking and after-game interviews. I enjoy every part of the process because at the end of it, when I push through the locker room doors, my family is waiting for me with open arms and sweet kisses.

"Good game, Daddy!" Milly clasps her hands, jumping up and down.

"Thanks, Jellybean." I tug on the end of her ponytail, leaning over her head to kiss Bella.

She returns the kiss and for a second, we forget ourselves. Mason's gagging interrupts the moment but when I glance at him, he's laughing and Milly is beaming.

While the past month has been its own type of transition, with Bella moving into my bedroom, losing the nanny title, and becoming part of our family, it's trending in the direction we all hoped it would. With each passing day, and weekly therapy sessions, the bumps we endured smooth out a little more. Milly and Mason lean on Bella for support when they need it and she gives her love easily, helping them in any way she can.

"Pizza?" I ask the twins.

"Definitely," Mase agrees, linking his fingers with Bella's.

I lift Milly and place her on my shoulders as we stride toward the parking lot.

"Can we get ice cream too?" Milly asks.

"Now you're pushing it, Mils." I tap her knee.

"But we're celebrating," Mason explains.

I chuckle, thinking they're going to reference the Hawks win.

Instead, Milly surprises me by saying, "Yeah, Bella starts school on Monday."

Bella laughs but I catch the way her expression softens. During our marathon-long conversations in California, she mentioned wanting to finish her degree. While I was supportive from the start, Milly and Mason really drove the issue, encouraging her until she signed up for two courses this semester. She's joining in a little late as it's already

February, but her professor made an exception after she assured him she would catch up.

"Well, that's true," I agree. "I guess if it's for Bella going back to school…"

"And your game," Mase adds. "Nice win, Dad."

"Nice save, Mase," I joke.

Bella's laughter grows.

"So pizza and ice cream?" I amend as we near the SUV.

"Yes!" the twins shout.

I place Milly back on her feet and the twins scramble into the back seat.

"You believe that?" I ask Bella, touching her hip. "Your return to the classroom just upstaged my win."

She grins, wrinkling her nose. "I taught those kids well."

I shake my head, smiling back. "They're lucky to have you."

"They're lucky to have us," she amends, leaning forward.

I kiss her hard as snowflakes begin to fall. I feel the curve of her mouth against my lips as she smiles.

"What's so funny?" I whisper.

She pulls back, her eyes flashing with merriment. "Today is one of my favorite Saturdays."

I grin at the happiness in her expression. Bella truly understands that magic happens in ordinary moments, that the best days are usually unplanned, that love is life's greatest gift. "Mine too." I kiss her one more time before opening the passenger side door. "Come on, we're going for pizza."

"And ice cream," Milly reminds me.

And ice cream. Sometimes, the simplest celebrations hold the most meaning.

Sometimes, the mundane moments change everything.

I slide behind the steering wheel and point the SUV in the direction of our favorite pizzeria. The twins talk and laugh in the back seat, playing some game with rules I don't fully understand.

Beside me, Bella glances out the window, a serene smile on her lips.

I reach over and take her hand, lacing our fingers together.

She squeezes her hand, the pressure gentle, the flash of her eyes knowing.

We've traversed a long road. We've climbed a lot of hills. It was rarely easy.

But as my family's happiness surrounds me, I can say it sure as hell has been worth it.

EPILOGUE

BELLA

Three Years Later

"That's it. You got it!" James claps his hands, his eyes zeroing in on the puck as it slides down the ice.

Mason skates quickly, weaving and zooming, until his stick connects with the puck. He brings it up the lane and flips it to his teammate for a goal.

"Nice! Yes!" James hollers out.

Next to me, Milly rolls her eyes and I laugh. Annie gurgles in my lap, clapping her hands, her hat riding low on her forehead.

"How many times do you think he'll say 'nice'?" Milly whispers next to me.

I chuckle and shake my head. "Ms. Milly, your dad is an encouraging coach. He doesn't want the boys to get burned out."

"He's too easy on them," she says, the judgment in her tone amusing me.

James hung up his skates after last season and we all sort of held our breath, wondering what he was going to do next. For a few months, he puttered around the the house, taking on several DIY projects that resulted in Milly and Mason begging me to intervene.

Luckily, as Mason's hockey team began to take off, the league was in need of more experienced coaches. James volunteered and landed the job, trading in his hockey stick for a whistle. He's great at it, encouraging the boys while improving their skills, keeping up team morale while pushing everyone to work harder.

"Nice work, guys!" James's voice rings out.

This time, Milly and I glance at each other and burst out laughing.

"Okay, fair. We need to tell him to pick a new word," I agree.

"Right?" Milly's eyes light up.

In my lap, Annie sneezes and Milly reaches out to tickle her sister.

About two years ago, James and I tied the knot. Six months later, we became pregnant with Annie. It was a decision we talked about at length, as a family, but when it actually happened, we were all delightfully surprised. None more than Milly and Mason, who were over the moon to have a new baby of their own.

Our little brood is growing, changing, and challenging James and me daily. But I've never felt more settled or happier in my life. I love being a mother to all of my children. I revel in the early mornings, taking an easy jog with Annie in the stroller to shed some of the baby weight but also to maintain mental clarity.

I've taken a year of maternity leave but finally became a psychologist. I work with teens and adolescents who have experienced trauma and easily lose myself in my work. In many ways, I've become a motherly figure to many children and it's a role I relish but take with a great deal of responsibility.

A lot of changes occurred for the Ryan family in the past

few years, but all of them have moved us closer to our new norm. Our growing family. Our prosperous careers. Our relentless gratitude.

"Nice game, boys!" James claps and Milly groans.

After the team finishes their post-game chat, James and Mason meet us near the arena exit.

"*Nice* job, Mase," Milly says.

Mason snorts and James narrows his eyes.

"You really overdid it today, Dad," Milly explains.

James looks to me. I nod, ceding Milly's point.

Mason chuckles. "But I had a *nice* time."

James groans. "You two are too young to give me grief like this," he grumbles, reaching for Annie. "That's why you're my favorite," he tells Annie, lifting her above his head. She kicks her little feet and a moment later, spits up, the white fluid gliding down James's cheek.

Milly and Mason howl with laughter. Who am I kidding? I join in, cracking up along with them.

"Come here, sweet girl." I reach for Annie as James grabs a wipe from the stroller and cleans his face.

"I'm outnumbered," he mumbles.

The kids and I smirk.

"Pizza?" I ask.

"Yes!" The twins high-five each other.

"And ice cream," Milly tacks on.

James narrows his eyes. "What are we celebrating?"

Milly's mouth drops open and she stares between us. "Our anniversary."

"Anniversary?" I question, my brow furrowing. What am I missing? Did I forget a date?

"Yeah," Mase says, shouldering his hockey bag that he had dumped at his feet. "Three years ago, today, Bella moved in with us for real."

Recognition dawns on James's face and emotion swims in his eyes as he meets mine. "That's right."

"It was the day we became a family," Milly adds. "The day that changed everything."

I smile at my family, momentarily overwhelmed with emotion. "I can't believe that was only three years ago."

"We should definitely get ice cream," Mason says. "To celebrate."

"Right," James snorts.

"Pizza and ice cream," I declare, buckling Annie into her stroller.

Behind me, I hear the twins high-five again.

James steps up behind me, his frame shadowing mine. "Three years, baby."

I look up and smile. "Best three years of my life."

"I love you, Bella Ryan."

"I love you more, James. Now let's get this celebration going before Annie's nap."

He chuckles. "I love it when you sweet talk me."

I swat the back of my hand against his stomach.

We walk as a family toward our ride, a minivan now. In many ways, our lives have stayed pretty consistent. A constant state of parenting, hockey arenas, and too much laundry to ever fold. But in many others, the entire world opened up the morning I became James's.

My whole future suddenly appeared before me, unblemished and promising.

I stepped into it with scars on my heart but hope in my soul. And grew a family I'm prouder of than anything else in the world.

THANK you so much for reading Bella and James's story! I hope you fell in love with them and their journey. For more

Boston Hawks reads, don't miss *The Heart Chaser*. Luca Pandatelli's story is packed with heat and second chance vibes!

THE HEART CHASER

PROLOGUE - LUCA

A bead of sweat rolls over the swell of Abbi's breast, sinking lower and disappearing into the material of her dress. I can't tear my eyes away if I want to. Who am I kidding? I sure as fuck don't want to.

I bite my bottom lip and continue to stare, unashamed when she turns in my arms and grasps my chin, realigning my focus to her face.

"You're staring again," she murmurs.

"It's hard not to."

She tries to fight her smile but loses. "Well, stop being so obvious about it," she warns playfully.

I smirk and shift on the barstool, which is tough to do considering her ass is grinding against my lap as she reaches across the bar and picks up two more tequila shots that Pete, the bartender, placed down. Damn, I'm ready to get out of Taps and take Abbi Walsh back to my place, my bed, for round two. Night two.

A body bumps into my side and I turn, a lazy grin rolling over my lips when I spot my captain's girl, Chloe. She's also Abbi's best friend and I can tell by the nervous way she tucks a strand of hair behind her ear that she's worried about her girl.

Ah, to have a reputation that precedes me. Usually I prefer it that way but tonight…tonight, I'm breaking my own damn rules. I never go back for seconds but something about this woman makes me want another taste.

Not just want…*crave*.

"We're going to head out," Chloe says, gesturing toward Austin. "Do you guys want to come with?" She keeps her eyes trained on Abbi and I press my lips together not to laugh.

"I'm good, Chlo. Swear it," Abbi replies. Good girl. I slide my hand higher on her leg, my fingers gripping at her inner thigh a smidge tighter than necessary. Her ass settles more firmly against my hard length and I cough back a groan.

"Don't worry," I tell Chloe. "I'll take care of our girl." I'll take care of her all right. Images of last night, taking Abbi in the center of my bed, up against the door to my closet, then again, in the shower, flicker through my mind.

Chloe leaves with Austin and a moment later, Abbi turns again, her lips just grazing mine. "You ready to get out of here?"

"Fuck yes."

She giggles, the sound sweet. But I'm not interested in sweet. I'm interested in tonight, this moment, with this woman. I signal for Pete to close out my tab and slip my phone from my back pocket to order an Uber.

Abbi and I step out into the sticky heat of July together. While I normally prefer the winters—I live in Boston, bred in Philly—right now, I'm grateful for the heat. Because Abbi Walsh rocks curves for days and they're barely concealed in the tight, crochet dress she's wearing like a second skin. It should look hideous, like something my Nonna Angie would knit. Instead, it's sexy as fuck, clinging to her curves. It's nude colored and by the hard nubs of her nipples, it's clear that she's got nothing on underneath.

I help her into the Uber and slide in beside her, my hand once again planting on her thigh. This girl is like a drug, one hit and I already want more. It's disconcerting, this feeling. I don't know whether to run from it or lean into it. But it's just one more night, right? Abbi's only in town for a bachelorette party weekend. Then, she heads back to Hoboken, New Jersey and I get on with my life: my family, hockey, and girls with no drama.

She checks her phone, oblivious to the thoughts running through my mind, which is a bit of an ego check. Usually, women are desperate for my attention. Hell, they even do stupid shit like make out with each other, to get it. But not Abbi.

Nope, this chick played it cool from the moment I met her, uttering some bullshit about being into players and not the game. A flicker of annoyance runs through me when I recall she doesn't watch hockey. How the hell does one not like the greatest game ever invented?

I narrow my eyes, studying her expression. Her plush lips have tightened, her carefree expression from Taps now pinched. I glance at her screen but the letters swim.

"More bachelorette drama?" I joke, since the party ended last night with all the girls going in different directions.

She sighs heavily and stuffs her phone back into the tiny bag she's toting around. "It's nothing. Just my boss. Work stuff."

I snort. "Work? It's"—I lean forward to glance at the time on the car's dashboard—"one a.m. on a Saturday night. Tell your boss to fuck off."

I expect her laughter but when she glances at her lap, I know that whatever is going on is more than that. Curiosity flares through me but the uncertainty in Abbi's expression has me biting back my words. I get it; I'm not usually a sharer either. Who wants to discuss feelings and crap when we could spend our time doing better, more interesting things?

"Hey." I reach out, lifting her chin. "Forget work. Let's just have fun, okay?"

She holds my eyes for a long moment. So long I begin to feel hot under her scrutiny. And not hot and bothered hot. Hot like itchy hot…like Abbi can see past the veneer of bullshit I like to coat myself in so I don't have to do the whole feelings and crap bit.

"Okay," she murmurs finally.

I flash her a grin followed by a wink. It's a relief when she settles more firmly into my side and I wrap my arm around her shoulders, hold her close. Not that this will go anywhere but for tonight, it feels nice to have a woman like Abbi under my arm.

It feels a hell of a lot more natural than it's supposed to.

Fuck. My body is weightless. Right now, I'm not in my bed, my legs tangled in my duvet, but in the middle of the Atlantic, floating along the tops of waves. I glance out the corner of my eye at Abbi. Who is this sexy temptress who managed to make my body break apart like *that*?

How was I supposed to hold on when she shattered on my cock, calling out my name like I was some kind of god, her eyes wild and reckless? A small ring of vulnerability edged her irises, which should have scared the shit out of me. Instead, I reveled in it and let her trust push me over the edge.

I swallow thickly, reaching out to pull her naked body

against my chest. I'm not usually a cuddler but Abbi's leaving tomorrow, and for the first time in my life, I want the night to extend well into the following morning. I want to soak up all these little moments I usually rebuff.

On my nightstand, her phone buzzes and she blows out a sigh.

A wave of jealousy rises in my gut, intense and unprecedented. I bite down hard, trying to dispel the unpleasant emotion. At least Abbi didn't answer the call.

I press a kiss to the back of her neck, my tongue darting out and catching her earlobe. She sighs, contentedly this time, and I savor the swell of pride that rises in my chest.

Buzz. Buzz.

"Who keeps blowing up your number?" I ask.

"Damn." She moves to answer it which irks me.

I flop back onto my pillow and watch as she swings her legs to the side of the bed and swipes the phone up, her movements jerky.

"I told you not to call me again," she bites out through clenched teeth.

At that, I sit straight up, moving toward her. But she tosses out a hand, keeping me at arm's length, which I both respect and despise. Is some dick giving her a hard time? Harassing her? Or is it a one-night lay who won't take a hint?

Unease followed by frustration blows through me and I'm instantly awake, all my former orgasmic bliss dissipating. Now, I'm on edge, tense and tuned into every little emotion that flits across Abbi's face.

Her dark hair hangs like a sheet down her naked back. All long, shiny locks I want to run my fingers through. I reach out and play with the ends of her hair, wanting to touch her in some way. Have her connected to *me* because I can't stand the thought of her having a one-night anything with someone else.

"I'm not joking around, Phil."

Phil? Who the hell is Phil?

"You're making things harder for me," she admits, her voice strangled.

In the next moment, she pushes off the bed and strides into the bathroom, the door closing behind her.

The vibe in my bedroom changes drastically, the temperature dropping as if all the heat went with her. I fall back against my pillow, my frustration spiking. More than anything, I want to stride into the bathroom and demand… what? That Abbi answer my questions? That we keep in touch after this weekend?

The door to the bathroom opens and I look up as Abbi walks toward me, full hips, pert breasts, and a scowl. My dick hardens beneath the sheet as a flood of desire hits me, my need to remind her just how good it can be between us skyrocketing.

"You okay?" I ask, genuinely curious.

Abbi tips her chin at me and climbs back onto the bed, swinging a leg over my body.

She collects my hands in hers and pushes them over my head, her hair and breasts swinging into my line of vision as she leans forward. "Ready for round two, Luca?"

I nod, my throat too dry to form words. I want to ask her what happened, but I can barely think when she rolls her hips over mine. Abbi Walsh knocked me off my game real fast and right now, I don't care. I want to fall in line while she calls the shots.

"Everyone calls me Panda," I admit for no reason.

The corners of her mouth curl. Not quite a smile but no longer a scowl. "I like Luca."

"I like it when you say it, too."

She lowers her face slowly and when her lips meet mine, I bite lightly on her lower lip, egging her on. She kisses me hard, passionately, and I revel in it, letting her set the pace this time. It's aggressive and delicious. Intense and fierce.

Shit. Being with Abbi Walsh leaves me reeling.

"You're ruining me," I pant out, half joking but half not, after we've both climaxed for the third time tonight.

She chuckles. "That's the point."

"Who's Phil?" I ask, my voice light, but I'm more than just curious. I'm fucking desperate to know who the hell he is and more importantly, what he means to Abbi.

She gazes at me over her shoulder, turning fully until her upper body is splayed across my chest. Her eyes catch mine again, searching. At first glance, they're ordinary brown. But on closer inspection, they're not brown at all. Flecks of gold, sprinkles of green, the tiniest infusion of blue… She's got eyes like a marble. "Phil's a long story," she says finally.

"You in trouble?"

"I hope not."

I frown, hating her vague responses when two weeks ago, I would have high-fived her for them. But not now that I'm *leaning*. Now, I want more. "What's going on?" I ask quietly, my fingers lightly swiping up her back.

She freezes under my touch before relaxing again. "I made a mistake. At the time, I didn't think… I never expected things to turn out the way they are." She shoots me a half smirk but her eyes are too big. A glint of fear rings her irises. "You ever do something when you knew better?"

I nod slowly, mentally flipping through the mistakes I've made. There's a lot but the latest is thinking I have a chance with the beautiful brunette before me. I have no clue how to be the kind of guy a woman like Abbi would want. She's motivated, intelligent, and sincere. It's only been two nights and the things I feel for her have ballooned into something bigger than the weekend. "Yeah," I murmur, tilting my head to study her. My thumb traces her lip. "But the worst was not being there for my family the way I should have, the way I knew I should have, when I went off to college. I knew my siblings counted on me for a lot, they have since my mom passed when I was in high school. But I wanted my freedom and when I finally got it, I went all in. Kind of left them behind." Regret colors my words. Even though I've since made up for that wild period of my youth, tenfold, showing up for Pop, my stepmom, and my brothers and sisters constantly, that slip in judgement still pricks at me.

"Your mom passed?" Her eyes widen, her voice dropping.

I nod. What the hell am I doing? I rarely, if ever, talk about my mom. I clear my throat. "I was fourteen."

"That must have been hard," she says and I'm grateful she doesn't flip me some apology just because it's what you're supposed to do.

"It was." I press my lips together but a moment later, more words slip past. "At the time, when I was first recruited to play Division One, I thought my actions were justified. By then, Pop had already remarried." I tip my head toward Abbi. "He married my high school English lit teacher, which is a whole other story. But Ms. Green was kind of my person, my sounding board, after Mom passed and when she started dating Pop…"

"Things got weird?"

"Definitely strained," I agree, hating how angry I was with Pop during that time. "It wasn't until later that I realized it was mostly selfishness on my part."

"Or coping," she says, surprising me. Her eyes take on a faraway look. "My parents died too."

"Both of them?" I ask in disbelief, her story shining my past in a different light. One a hell of a lot less bleak than I usually consider it.

She nods. "My mom when I was twelve. She was incredible." A soft smile touches her lips before it falls, a hardness lining her face. "My dad, well, he hasn't been in the picture in a long time. He walked out on us when I was eight for his new family, the one he was building when he was still married to Mom." She turns away and I can tell she's trying to school the expression on her face. When she speaks again, her voice is direct, hard and cold, like a bullet. "I heard from his other family that he passed two years ago."

My throat tightens, a wave of empathy rising. I don't want Abbi to think I'm pitying her, especially since I know how much it sucks to be on the receiving end of pity, but my chest squeezes at how much she's lost. My hand stills in the center of her back. "That sucks, Abbi."

"Tell me about it."

"Must have been really fucking tough."

She shrugs. "My gran raised me."

I wrap my arms tighter around her, hating that she stiffens. "Is she, do you see her often?"

She blows out a breath, relaxing slightly. "As much as I can. She's in a nursing home now. Her health has declined over the past few years. She's the closest person in the world to me and it's weird knowing that when she…well, it'll just be me then."

Swallowing becomes difficult as the emotion clogging my throat grows at Abbi's words. I have a loud, rambunctious family and while we're usually too involved in each other's lives, I've never considered the alternative. I've never even thought about if I didn't have my siblings and their kids around. "Have you ever reached out to your dad? Your…half-siblings?"

Her face falls and her eyes swim with moisture. What the hell am I doing? This is supposed to be casual and now… now, I feel sick that my questions are causing her pain. I'm about to tell her to forget it when she responds.

"Once," she whispers, wicking away a tear with a knuckle. "Sorry."

"Don't be. What happened?"

She lets out a big exhale, her eyes studying mine intently.

"I tracked him down. Showed up at his home. It was my junior year of high school and I just got my license. He didn't even live far away, only three towns over from mine. All those years, I thought he was in California or Texas or someplace different. I made up all these stories about him in my head, excuses to explain why he never came around, made an appearance at my birthday parties, spent a holiday with me. And he was right…there."

I pull her closer and kiss the side of her head as anger builds in my veins.

"I parked across the street and just…watched. His new wife was pretty. His kids were small. And after they had this picture-perfect dinner at their dining table, he came outside to throw out the garbage. I approached him and…I don't know why I'm telling you this. It doesn't matter."

"Yes, it does," I say, my tone soft. "It matters, Abbi."

She wets her lips. "He asked me what I was doing there. He asked if I have any respect for him, for his life, his family." She winces, and more tears fall. "He told me I was a mistake and my presence would mess up his life, the good thing he had going on. Basically, he discarded me as easily as the trash bag."

Fuck. My stomach clenches at the expression on her face. Hot anger burns through me and even though I never met her father, I hate the man who gave her life and didn't stick around to see her embrace it. "He never deserved you."

She bites her bottom lip, trying to force a smile. "You don't even know me."

"I know you deserved a hell of a lot better than what you got." What kind of man steps out on his family? On his kid? I frown as my sister Nikki's life flares to mind. My worthless brother-in-law left her a few months after their first child, Valentina, was born. My other sister, Justine, lost her husband too. But Dean was one of the greatest men I've ever known, and his being killed by a drunk driver cut my entire family off at the knees.

Abbi sighs and presses her palms against my chest. A wariness fills her eyes and I can relate; we're both sharing more than we bargained for tonight. "Sorry, I just made that a lot more real then—"

"No," I cut her off, tapping her ass. "You're just being honest."

She shrugs, her eyes serious. While I should change the subject, distract her from the too real thing we're doing right now, I move closer. I *want* her words. Her thoughts. Her goddamn feelings and crap.

"You ever want more than one night?" she asks, reading my mind. "More than just the moment?"

"We've spent two nights together," I remind her.

She bites lightly on my index finger and I pull my hand back, laughing. "Are we having *the* talk, Abs?"

At this, she laughs, amusement flaring in her eyes. "No, Luca. I'm not asking you how many women you've slept with."

"That's a relief." I grin saucily, but at the seriousness in her expression I continue to share. "But I thought *the* talk was more about commitment?"

Abbi chuckles, dipping her head in acknowledgement as something I can't read flares in her eyes. "Definitely not ready for that. You know me, I'm just over here keeping things light."

I laugh with her since we just had one crazy intense, serious conversation. "Yeah, that's you."

She smirks, but her eyes remain pinned to mine.

"To answer your question, not really. I know what my reputation is and I do nothing to help it. Women know exactly what they're getting when they climb into my bed." I wince at how the words sound when they're out in the space between us.

Abbi's eyes dim and my chest tightens, uncomfortable. I clear my throat and toss out more unexpected honesty. "But with the right woman, yeah, I'd want more. Doesn't everyone?"

Slowly, she nods. "I just don't want to be naive," she says quietly. "Every time I trust a man..." She trails off. "Well, it never works out the way I think it will."

I hate the sadness that streaks across her expression. I hate the failure that flares in her eyes because I've seen my sister Nikki wear it on too many occasions.

"Hey." I pinch her side. "You're not naive, Abbi."

"You barely know me, Luca."

I shake my head. "That's not true. I know that you growl when you—"

"All right," she cuts me off, her hand slapping over my mouth. But she's laughing and that makes me feel like I just saved a game by catching the puck at the buzzer.

I roll her until she's settled beneath me. Dipping forward, I drop a kiss to her mouth. "Everything you've showed me of yourself this weekend has been the opposite of naive. You're independent, you know what you want, and you're not afraid to ask for it. You're a good friend, putting up with that bachelorette bullshit. You're loyal, worrying about Chloe the way you do." I pause, realizing that I'm gazing into Abbi's eyes like I want to fall into them and stay awhile. I brush her hair back from her face. "Don't beat yourself up, babe. Not about things in the past that can't be changed."

I lower my head and kiss her again, wrapping her up in my embrace. I keep my arms around her as I doze off to sleep, the buzz of alcohol, the intensity of our connection, catching up with me.

I wake early the following morning, mostly from habit. I need to get up, get a run in, have a smoothie. But when I glance at my bedmate, with her tangled dark hair and long, black eyelashes, I don't want to leave the bed. *Her.*

It's an intense realization because it's the first time I've had it. I've seen firsthand how much love, real love, destroys a person. First, my Pop, when Mom died. Then, my sister, Nicole, when her husband took off. I've watched the loss of Layla devastate my teammate James and held my sister Justine as she wailed over Dean's lifeless body.

Of course, there's happy examples too—Noah, Easton, and Torsten come to mind. Jesus, even Cap is shacking up with Chloe now.

But when you're raised in a house overflowing with love and light, with laughter and fun, and the matriarch of the household, the glue that holds it all together, is suddenly gone, the shadow stamps out all the remaining glow.

I watched Pop fall apart until he met my stepmother. I watched Nicole break when she learned her husband was cheating on her while she was pregnant with their first child. Since then, I've stepped up for my family in all the ways that matter. I don't have the mental bandwidth to be a man for anyone else. Most days, I don't want to be. But today…

I brush Abbi's hair back from her forehead, grinning at the soft snore that whistles from her nose. I wish I didn't have so much fun with her this weekend. I wish I didn't like her so damn much. Because a part of me wants to see her again, even knowing it's a dangerous step. Could we keep in touch? Be…friendly? It's not like she won't be coming to Boston to visit Chloe.

When she's in town, could we kick it? Have some drinks and laughs together?

I chew the corner of my mouth, liking the way she looks in my bed. Liking her sexed-up hair and the makeup smudges underneath her eyes.

Her eyes flutter open and a slow smile covers her lips as she catches me watching her.

"You're checking me out pretty hard," she calls me out.

I smirk, crawling closer to her luscious lips. "I've got something else that's hard."

She squeals as I wrap her up in a giant hug and kiss her.

"I need to brush my teeth!" She pushes at my chest. "Morning breath."

I laugh and shake my head. "Not letting your ass out of this bed until you have to go."

She sobers for a second, stilling in my arms. "I had fun this weekend, Luca."

"Me too, Abbi Walsh. But it doesn't have to just be this weekend. You could, you know, reach out when you're in Boston."

"I could," she says slowly, lifting an eyebrow. Damn, I love how she even calls me out silently.

"I'll call you," I tell her, meaning it.

"We'll see," she says noncommittally.

"I mean it, Abbi. You're not walking out of here that easily," I half joke, wondering why the hell I'm complicating my life. Can't I just kiss her goodbye? No. I can't. Because I don't want her to leave.

"Are you for real right now?" she asks lightly, but her eyes search mine with a seriousness that causes the space between us to shift.

I shake my head. "You deserve a good man, Abbi. One who doesn't make you feel naive. One who keeps his word. Don't settle for less than that."

She draws in a sharp inhale, and I drop my head to kiss her lips.

I don't know why I say it like I could be that man. I'm not that guy and I know it the second the words are out of my mouth. But for her, I'd want to be.

The realization scares me because…Jesus, it's a lot. I don't do morning afters. I don't even do second-night stands. And everything that transpired between Abbi and me is a million times more than anything I've done in the past decade.

She leaves an hour later and for a bit, my condo feels empty without her presence. It's like she filled it up with energy, the kind Mom used to exude, and now that she's gone, the space plunged back into shades of gray.

I swear and force myself to go for a run. I need the workout and running helps clear my head. When I return, I strip my bed, suddenly desperate to wash the scent of Abbi—lilac and vanilla—off my sheets so it doesn't torture me.

My phone rings and I pick it up to talk to my sister. "Hey, Nikki."

"Luca?" Her voice is strangled and a cold fear drips down my spine.

"What's wrong?" I ask automatically.

"It's Pop."

"What happened?" I sink to the edge of my bed, the sheets pooling around my feet from where I tossed them to the floor.

"He had a heart attack."

I close my eyes, waiting for the words she hasn't said yet.

"The doctors think he's going to be okay but," Nikki sobs, "it's just so awful, Luca."

"Fuck." I swear, hanging my head. "How's Jenni?" I ask about our stepmother. Even before she married Pop, she was like a second mother to me.

"Not well."

"I'm getting on the next flight. Shit, Nik."

"I know. I know. Just, come home, okay? We need you."

"Of course," I say on autopilot. I'm already walking to my laptop, pulling up a search engine to find the first flight to Philly.

I leave the sheets on the floor, the condo a mess, as I throw together a bag and head to the airport. I spend the rest of the summer, until training camps start, in Philadelphia trying to get Pop on a new lifestyle routine. I take over his and Jenni's finances while he's out of work. I fill in as dad for my sisters' kids. I help my brother Robbie remodel his basement.

By the time I return full-time to Boston at the end of the summer, Abbi Walsh is a sweet memory. She's a reminder of a fun, exciting weekend I can never get back. She's a moment I savor on difficult nights. A woman who made me feel and want so much more than a weekend but ultimately, one who deserves more than I can give.

Abbi Walsh is a reminder that I don't do love. I only do heartbreak.

And I prove it because I never call her.

Keep reading *The Heart Chaser* !

HEY READER!

Hi Lovely Reader!

I hope you adored Bella and James's story. Their relationship holds a special place in my heart and while I often cried while writing their journey, I hope their HEA resonates loudly.

It would mean so much to me if you would please leave a review and share your thoughts. If you're loving Boston Hawks Hockey, make sure you read *The Heart Chaser*. Luca Pandatelli's story is a cocktail of sweet, heat, and second chance vibes!

If you're interested in learning more about my books, please sign up for my monthly newsletter. It's filled with humor, love, and your favorite hockey heartthrobs!

Or, come hang out in my Facebook Reader Group, Gina Azzi's Book Besties.

Thank you so much for all of your support!

XO,
  Gina

ALSO BY GINA AZZI

Knoxville Coyotes Football:

Faked and Fumbled

Surprised and Sacked

Trapped and Tackled

The Burnt Clovers Trilogy:

Rebellious Rockstar

Resentful Rockstar

Restless Rockstar

Tennessee Thunderbolts:

Hot Shot's Mistake

Brawler's Weakness

Rookie's Regret

Playboy's Reward

Hero's Risk

Bad Boy's Downfall

Lock 'Em Down

Boston Hawks Hockey:

The Sweet Talker

The Risk Taker

The Faker

The Rule Maker

The Defender

The Heart Chaser

The Trailblazer

The Hustler

The Score Keeper

Second Chance Chicago Series:

Broken Lies

Twisted Truths

Saving My Soul

Healing My Heart

The Kane Brothers Series:

Rescuing Broken (Jax's Story)

Recovering Beauty (Carter's Story)

Reclaiming Brave (Denver's Story)

My Christmas Wish

(A Kane Family Christmas

+ *One Last Chance* FREE prequel)

Finding Love in Scotland Series:

My Christmas Wish

(A Kane Family Christmas

+ *One Last Chance* FREE prequel)

One Last Chance (Daisy and Finn)

This Time Around (Aaron and Everly)

One Great Love

The College Pact Series:

The Last First Game (Lila's Story)

Kiss Me Goodnight in Rome (Mia's Story)

All the While (Maura's Story)

Me + You (Emma's Story)

Standalone

Corner of Ocean and Bay

ACKNOWLEDGMENTS

All of my sincere thanks and gratitude to the amazing women I've met through this writing journey!

This series wouldn't have come to fruition without the support, love, and encouragement from Amy Parsons, Melissa Panio-Peterson, Erica Russikoff, Dani Sanchez, Becca Mysoor, Virginia Carey and the phenomenal ladies of Give Me Books Promotions! I adore working with you all and am so thankful to know you!

Many thanks to Kate Farlow, Y'all. That Graphic. for designing an amazing series of covers!

All my heartfelt gratitude to the bloggers, reviewers, and readers for supporting my books. I am eternally grateful. I hope you love Bella and James!

And to my family. I love you all the world.

ABOUT THE AUTHOR

Gina Azzi writes Contemporary Romance with relatable, genuine characters experiencing real life love, friendships, and challenges. She is the author of *Boston Hawks Hockey* series, *Second Chance Chicago* series, *Finding Love in Scotland* series, *The Kane Brothers* series, *The College Pact* series, and *Corner of Ocean and Bay*.

A Jersey girl at heart, Gina spent her twenties traveling the world, living and working abroad, before settling down in Ontario, Canada with her husband and three children. She's a voracious reader, daydreamer, and coffee enthusiast who loves meeting new people. Say hey to her on social media or through www.ginaazzi.com.

For more information, connect with Gina at:

Email: ginaazziauthor@gmail.com
Twitter: @gina_azzi
Instagram: @gina_azzi
Facebook: https://www.facebook.com/ginaazziauthor
Website: www.ginaazzi.com

Or subscribe to her newsletter to receive book updates, bonus content, and more!